"I hope I haven't kept you waiting, William said, giving Emily Jane a hand up onto the wagon.

"Not at all. I needed to visit a little while with Beth anyway." She sat down and then turned and kissed each twin.

They giggled and tried to get her hat.

William pulled himself up beside her. As he took the reins he asked, "New hat?"

"Beth loaned it to me."

He smiled over at her. "It's very pretty on you."

A compliment? She felt a little uneasy.

A soft laugh drifted from his side of the wagon seat. "We're friends, Emily Jane. No need to get all nervous about a compliment."

How had he known? She cut her eyes under the hat to look at his profile. Was it possible that over the past few weeks they'd grown so close that they knew what each other was thinking? If so, that was dangerous. Maybe after today she should put some distance between herself and William. From her experience with people, those who could read each other's minds and expressions seemed to be in love. She wasn't ready for love.

Yes, distance after today would be the best solution for them both.

Rhonda Gibson lives in New Mexico with her husband, James. She has two children and three beautiful grandchildren. Reading is something she has enjoyed her whole life and writing stemmed from that love. When she isn't writing or reading, she enjoys gardening, beading and playing with her dog, Sheba. You can visit her at rhondagibson.net. Rhonda hopes her writing will entertain, encourage and bring others closer to God.

Books by Rhonda Gibson

Love Inspired Historical

Visit the Author Profile page at Harlequin.com.

RHONDA GIBSON

The Texan's Twin Blessings

HARLEQUIN® LOVE INSPIRED® HISTORICAL

Recycling programs
for this product may
not exist in your area.

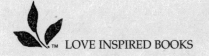 ™ LOVE INSPIRED BOOKS

ISBN-13: 978-0-373-28316-3

The Texan's Twin Blessings

Copyright © 2015 by Rhonda Gibson

www.Harlequin.com

Printed in U.S.A.

Forget the former things; do not dwell on the past.
See, I am doing a new thing!
—*Isaiah* 43:18–19

Tina James, thank you for always believing in my stories and trusting me to get them written on time. James Gibson, your love means more to me than you will ever know. Thank you for keeping the midnight oil burning so that I can find my way after a long night of writing. And as always, thank You, Heavenly Father, for giving me my heart's desires.

Chapter One

Granite, Texas
Late Spring 1887

Hot, aggravated and about at the end of his rope, William Barns stood on his grandmother's porch juggling his year-and-a-half-old nieces, Rose and Ruby. The little girls squalled louder.

"Eat!" Rose twisted sideways, her little voice pleading.

They were hungry, so was he, and as soon as his grandmother opened the door from the other side, she'd help feed them. Of that he had no doubt. He shifted the twins higher on his chest. Today they'd had milk and bread in their diets and little else.

The heat was getting to them and making the girls cranky; him, too, if he was honest about it. Colorado springtime and Texas springtime were very different in the way of weather, and the effects on him and the girls were going from poor to bad fast.

Why was his grandmother taking so long? If he remembered correctly, the house was not that big. He'd been a kid the last time he'd stood on this porch, and even then it had seemed small. William clinched his jaw in an effort not to get impatient with the girls and his grandmother. Surely she'd heard him knocking.

The trip from Denver, Colorado, had been exhausting. Rose and Ruby demanded his undivided attention. He'd had no idea how much was required of his late sister, until she'd been killed and he'd taken over the twins' care. What a load she had carried and carried well.

His heart ached at the loss of his sister, Mary. If only he'd gone to the bank that day, instead of her. The throbbing in his ankle reminded him why he'd stayed with the napping twins while his sister had gone to town and faced down two bank robbers. If only he hadn't slipped on the frozen snow and broken his ankle after the last ice storm they'd had, he would have been the one at the bank.

Rose, apparently tired of the juggling, chose that moment to throw up sour milk all over his shirtsleeve. Ruby, spying her sister's distress, let out a wail that pierced his eardrums.

As the curdled milk scent reached his nostrils, he briefly wondered how his delicate, prim sister had managed to take care of his darling nieces with the ease that she had. They burped putrid liquids, and the diapers, well, he'd almost taken to wearing a clothespin on his nose while changing them.

Exhausted, Rose laid her head upon his shoulder and shuddered her unhappiness. Mirroring her sister's actions, Ruby did the same. Regardless of their disgusting smells and loud crying, William loved his nieces with all his heart.

"I'm sorry, baby girls. I know you're hot and tired, and sick of me pouring liquid into you." He kept his voice soothing and calm. "Just hang on a few more seconds. Grandma's on the way, and she'll have something good for us to eat."

His chest ached with the sorrow weighing down upon him. He felt as if the responsibilities of the girls might be more than he could take. Why did everything have to change?

Memories flooded his tired mind. On the fateful morning he'd lost his sister, his brother-in-law and town sheriff, Josiah, had been out of town but was to return later in the day. William later learned that Josiah had been lured away by fake information that the robbers were in the town next to theirs. He'd hurried off to help the sheriff there, and while he'd been gone the criminals had robbed their bank.

Three rough-looking men had arrived in town shortly after the bank opened. They'd entered the bank, threatening those inside if the teller didn't turn over the money. When they'd escaped in a blaze of gunfire, they left Mary lifeless and the bank teller wounded.

Witnesses had whispered that it had all happened so suddenly. The bank robbers had taken Mary's money and left her for dead. She had stumbled out of the bank, clutching the morning's mail to her wounded chest. It was when she fell in a heap of petticoats that everyone realized she'd been hit by the gunfire. His sister had died on the dirty street, leaving behind an angry, grieving husband and two beautiful, motherless little girls. And him.

A piercing cry sounded within his left ear, pulling William from the painful memory. "Ruby, please don't scream." He looked to the dark window on his left. Where was his grandmother? Why hadn't she answered? He turned and pounded on the door with his elbow.

Aggravation at the delay crept up his spine and into his already pounding head. The longer he stood there, the worse he felt. William refused to give in to the irritation at having to wait for his grandmother; one angry man in the family was enough.

The memories he'd been shoving away flooded in once more. Josiah had allowed his rage and grief over the murder of his wife to run so deep he'd practically forgotten his daughters. William had been left with no choice but to take over the care of the girls. Once his sister had been put to rest, Josiah had gone after the murderers with the promise to come back for the girls, but William wasn't holding his breath.

Even though Josiah was a good lawman, William worried about his brother-in-law's state of mind. Josiah blamed himself for his wife's death. He'd even made the statement he wasn't sure he was a fit father and that if he couldn't protect Mary, what made him think he could protect his girls? William had tried to talk to him, offer comfort, but in the end, Josiah had left a bitter and angry man.

After three months of waiting, William couldn't stand living in the same town that his sister had died in. He'd left word with Josiah's neighbor that he was moving to Granite, Texas, and that Rose and Ruby would be waiting there for Josiah when he'd finished his business with the bank robbers. He worried Josiah might never come for his daughters—the man had been so resentful—and Josiah had probably taken risks that could end his life, leaving the girls orphans.

Rose trembled, and one look at her white face reminded William that he needed to focus on her and her sister instead of rehashing what had happened or worrying about what might have happened to their father. Until he heard from Josiah, he was responsible for the little girls, and right now they needed real food and a place to rest. He reached for the door handle and found it locked. William sighed. She wasn't home.

"Excuse me."

He turned to the soft voice that had managed to be heard over the little girls' cries. A young woman stood behind him in the yard. Her red hair blazed under the sun, and light freckles crossed her nose as if she'd too often forgotten to wear her bonnet. Green eyes filled with sadness looked up at him. The freckles across her nose and cheeks gave her the appearance of being very young, but the depth of emotion in her eyes made him think she might be older than she looked. Realizing he was staring, William responded. "Yes?"

"My name is Emily Jane Rodgers. I'm Mrs. Barns's neighbor." She pointed to the house across the street, then turned to face him once more. "Mrs. Barns no longer lives here." Her sweet voice seemed to drip with warmth and deep sorrow.

William shifted the girls, who had quieted down at the sound of the female voice. "Nice to meet you, Miss Rodgers. I'm William Barns. Where has my grandmother moved?"

Renewed sorrow seemed to fill her pretty green eyes. "I have a key to the house. Let's go inside, so that I can explain." She brushed past him, and scents of cinnamon and sugar filled his nostrils.

The girls stared at the redheaded woman. Ruby stretched out a chubby hand to grasp a strand of her hair as she worked the key into the lock. Thankfully, the little girl couldn't reach Miss Rodgers, but her failed attempt had her leaning farther, straining against his arm till he thought he might drop her. He tightened his hold on Ruby, turning aside from the temptation.

Finally the woman opened the door and stepped within the cooler interior. William followed as questions regarding his grandmother bombarded his tired mind. They stood in the sitting room, where all the furniture was covered with fabric of various colors. His hopes sank in his chest as he realized that if his grandmother had moved, she would have taken her things with her. He used his boot to shut the door.

Miss Rodgers dropped the key into the pocket of her apron that hung about her small waist and then moved to the window. She pulled back the heavy curtain to allow sunshine into the room before she turned to face him. Dust particles swirled in the air around them. "I'm sorry I have to be the one to tell you this, but Mabel passed away last month from a cold that had moved into her chest." Sorrow filled her voice.

He gasped. A new sharp pain pricked his heart. A stinging dryness scalded the backs of his eyes. William looked about for a place to set the squirming twins, who wanted to get down and explore this new place. William realized he didn't dare put them in the layer of dust that covered the floor. He shifted their weight and held them close to his aching chest.

He'd lost his sister and now his grandmother. Who was next? One of the twins? His brother-in-law? He'd also lost his fiancée, Charlotte, thankfully not by death, but she'd been clear that having children or taking care of someone else's was not a part of her future with him. They'd parted ways since he wanted children and intended to protect and keep his nieces until their father's return.

The questions returned once more. How much more could he take? And how was he going to care for the girls by himself until his brother-in-law returned? This was not how he had pictured his life. Doubt rose in multiples. Why was the Lord testing him? Had he offended Him in some way? He loved the fellowship with his Lord and tried to honor and please Him above all others. But his load seemed to get heavier every day. As if the Lord had heard his thoughts, William's troubled spirit quieted, and he forced his lips to part in a curved, stiff smile at the woman staring solemnly back at him.

Emily Jane watched the emotions cross the handsome face of the man in front of her. William Barns wore a dark brown cowboy hat. Wavy black hair peeked out from under the brim and curled about his collar. It was his sapphire-blue eyes that held her attention; they told a story of their own. From the depth of sorrow staring back at her, Emily Jane read that this wasn't the first time death had recently broken his heart.

Without giving her actions much thought, she reached for one of the babies, who had resumed kicking and crying. "Here, let me take one of them." Poor little mites needed their mother. Emily Jane felt sure that Mr. Barns mourned her death as well as his grandmother's; why else would he show up alone with the two little girls?

He placed the little child into her outstretched arms. "Shhhh, it will be all right." Emily Jane rocked from side to side as she held the small one against her shoulder.

The child settled down and sniffled but no longer cried as if she were being tortured. Emily Jane looked to Mr. Barns and saw that he copied her actions. She offered him what she hoped was an encouraging smile. "Do you have fresh diapers for these sweet girls?" Emily Jane asked, as she continued to rock and pat the small back in her arms.

"Out in the wagon." He spun on his booted heels and limped away. "I'll be right back," Mr. Barns called over his shoulder.

"Go!" The little girl in her arms tugged in the direction that Mr. Barns had left. She cried in earnest when he and her sister continued out the door.

Emily Jane pulled the darling close and patted her back some more. "He'll be right back." Emily Jane looked about the room during his absence. In the short time

Mabel Barns had been gone, the house had become quite dirty.

Would William Barns stay here now that he knew his grandmother had died? Or would he take his daughters and go to other family members for help with the children? She assumed the need for help with the girls had been what prompted him to visit his grandmother.

She refocused on the room as she jiggled the sobbing little girl in her arms. Dust covered every inch of the furniture, fireplace mantel and floors. If he stayed, it would take him a few hours to clean up the mess. Mabel had died a little over a month ago. Dusting was a daily job if you lived in Texas, especially Granite, a task Mabel had seemed to enjoy.

Emily Jane's throat closed. Fresh waves of sadness rolled over her as she mourned the loss of her friend. The child in her arms began to twitch and quiet down as if she sensed Emily Jane's sorrow.

"Let's get this wet diaper off of you, little one." Emily Jane walked to the sofa and pulled the dust-covered protective sheet off of it. To keep the sofa from getting wet, she took off her apron and laid it on the cushion. Then Emily Jane sat down and began to unpin the soiled cloth diaper.

She guessed that the child was about a year old, maybe a little older. Twins were often smaller than other children. Her black wavy hair matched the color of her father's, and brilliant blue eyes shone from her face. A frayed yellow ribbon had been tied in her hair. "You sure are a pretty little girl," Emily Jane said in a soft voice, happy the child was no longer screaming and crying. The tot looked like her handsome father.

Emily Jane shook her head to erase the memory of melancholy within his eyes. She didn't want to focus on William Barns's good looks, either. No, she wasn't interested in handsome men. She had a new life ahead of her. One of independence with no controlling husband or demanding children to steal her joy of baking.

The little girl looked up at Emily Jane and sucked her thumb while Emily Jane pulled the wet cloth from under her. As soon as she was free of the sodden diaper, she pulled her thumb from between her lips and said, "Shew wee."

Boot steps clacked against the wood floor. Then Mr. Barns handed her a leather pouch that resembled a saddlebag. "Shew wee is right." His warm voice brought a grin to the child's face. Emily experienced an unusual feeling in the pit of her stomach. What would it feel like to have someone's happiness within your power? She'd probably never know since she had chosen another direction for her life. One where she decided which path to take instead of a man doing it for her.

Emily Jane took the bag and found the clean diapers. As soon as she got the cloth pinned into place, she handed the first little girl over to Mr. Barns and took the second child.

"Thank you, miss, but you really don't have to do that." He moved as if to change places with her.

"I don't mind," Emily Jane answered as she proceeded to change the second child. The big man hobbled about the room. He touched the fireplace mantel and sighed. She wondered what had happened to his ankle but didn't think it was her place to ask. As soon as the second child was diapered, Emily Jane stood.

"Did Grandmother sell this house to you?" he asked. His voice broke, and he turned his face away.

Emily Jane shook her head. "No, a few days before her passing, she gave me a key and told me that if any of her kin should show up to let them in. I suppose she was worried you'd arrive after bank hours and wouldn't be able to get the extra key from the bank and so therefore wouldn't be able to get into the house."

Confusion furrowed the skin of his brow. "Does the bank own the house?"

"I'm not sure. All I know is what she told me. That Doc had done all he could for her and to give you the house key. Oh, and she also instructed me to tell you that you need to go to Mr. Fergus at the bank and tell him you are her kin. He has further information as to what is to become of this place." Emily Jane knew her words were rushed, but she hadn't expected a handsome man with two small children to be the "kin" that Mrs. Barns had predicted would come.

Mr. Barns frowned and voiced his thoughts. "How did Grandmother figure I was coming? There was no way she could have known. I didn't even know myself until a short time ago."

Emily Jane shrugged. "I'm not sure if she knew which of her grandchildren would arrive. She sent a letter off, but I don't know to whom. I assumed, since you are here, it was you."

He shook his head. "Maybe her letter was one of

the letters that Mary dropped on the day she died. The wind blew several letters away, but in all the ruckus no one heeded them."

The soft words were spoken as if he were talking to himself. Emily Jane was pretty sure he wasn't speaking to her. His blue eyes were focused in the past as if he'd forgotten she and the little girls were in the room. But now she knew the little girls' mother's name and that she'd recently died.

Not willing to be ignored, both of the children began to whine and fret once more.

He seemed to snap out of the memories and return to them. His voice sounded tired and hopeless as he said, "They are hungry. I was hoping Grandmother would be able to feed them and help me get them ready for bed."

Emily Jane looked about the house. It wasn't fit for children, at least not without a good cleaning. She sighed as her motherly instincts took over. Being the oldest of twelve, Emily Jane was used to helping her mother by taking matters into her own hands, while her father took care of business. "Let's go over to my house, and I'll find them something to eat." She didn't wait for his answer, simply scooped the child off the couch and headed to the door.

She heard him follow and decided to have a quiet talk with herself regarding the Barns family. It was her Christian duty to help him get settled into their house. After that, William Barns and his girls were on their own. She didn't have time for children, and no matter how much he might need a wife, she did not need a husband. Emily Jane glanced back at him. William Barns was a handsome man; he'd find a woman to marry soon and it wouldn't be her.

The last thing Emily Jane wanted was to get married, especially to a man who already had two children. She didn't want children. After helping her parents with eleven brothers and sisters, Emily Jane had had enough of kids to last her a lifetime. Plus, she also didn't want a controlling man in her life. She'd had twenty-three years of her father controlling her and her mother. No, sir, Emily Jane Rodgers wasn't going to allow a man to control her again. She had bigger plans for her life. Someday she'd open her own bakery and be able to support herself. She'd own her home and be able to buy new things instead of having to wear hand-me-downs, supplied by the local church ladies.

Emily Jane opened the door to the house that she shared with Anna Mae Leland. Anna Mae was the local schoolteacher. They'd met when they'd both answered Levi Westland's mail-order-bride advertisement. Well, Anna Mae had willingly answered it; she, on the other hand, had been forced to answer it by her father. He'd decided twelve children were too many to feed, and Emily Jane was the oldest and the one he could get rid of the easiest. It hurt that her father and mother had so easily sent her away, to a man she'd never met in a place she'd never been. How could a parent do that to a child, especially their firstborn? Emily Jane didn't plan to have children, but if she did, they would be loved unconditionally; that much she knew for sure.

The screen door shut behind him as Mr. Barns followed her inside the house. Emily Jane led him to the kitchen. She set the child she held on the braided rug beside the table, walked over to the cabinet and scooped up two empty pans and two large metal spoons. "Please, have a seat, Mr. Barns, and I'll have dinner ready in just a few moments." Emily Jane handed the little girl on the floor a spoon and placed one of the pans down in front of her. That would keep the child busy for a few minutes. She motioned for Mr. Barns to set his bundle of joy down beside her sister.

He did so with a sigh and a smile that said *thank you*.

Emily Jane nodded and then handed the second little girl the other spoon and pan. She'd have to stop thinking of them as little girls and ask what their names were. While he pulled out a kitchen chair, she turned to the stove.

Again, she had something to be thankful for. Emily Jane had already fried up chicken, made mashed potatoes and warmed up a jar of green beans just before she'd seen him and the girls arrive. She expected Anna Mae to arrive home from school any minute now.

And then what? He couldn't stay in the dusty house tonight, and he couldn't stay here.

She glanced at him over her shoulder. His deep blue gaze met hers. Emily Jane could get lost in the depths of his needs. She could…but she would not. She simply couldn't allow that to happen.

The girls banged happily on the pans. The noise filled the room and prevented the need for polite conversation. Emily Jane didn't want to enjoy the sound of children playing, but deep down she did. She also didn't want to be aware of the man sitting at her kitchen table. But she was. They reminded her of home and all that she'd lost when she'd answered Levi Westland's mail-order-bride ad all those months ago.

Would she be able to ignore the man and children in her kitchen? Had things just changed in her life? If so, how was she going to distance herself from the handsome man and his beautiful girls?

Chapter Two

"Thank you for the offer of supper. I'll be happy to pay you for what we eat." William laid his hat on the table and ran weary fingers through his hair.

The young woman, Miss Rodgers, turned from the stove with a platter of fried chicken. She set it down on the table. "That won't be necessary. I always make more than we can eat."

"We?" It hadn't dawned on him that Emily Jane Rodgers would have a husband and her own children to take care of. He'd been so absorbed in the loss of his grandmother and the dilemma of what to do with the girls that he'd not even considered the marital status of the woman before him.

She nodded. "Anna Mae and I."

Was Anna Mae her sister? His gaze moved to the sisters, who banged happily on the pans with the spoons she'd supplied. They were very close and affectionate with each other. He had heard that was the way with twins. Would they someday live together? He sighed tiredly. Right now, their future was as unclear as his own.

Miss Rodgers walked back to the stove for more food. She turned with a bowl of green beans and a plate of biscuits. His stomach rumbled with hunger. It had been a while since he'd had a good home-cooked meal. During the trip, he'd made sure the girls had food and milk but hadn't worried about his own stomach.

She gave him a knowing smile. He had no doubt in his mind that Miss Rodgers had heard his belly rumble. "Anna Mae Leland is the schoolteacher here. She should be home any moment." She placed the rest of the food on the table. Her gaze swept over the girls before she moved to the sideboard and pulled out plates and silverware.

"Are you sure she won't mind having company?"

"I'm sure. Anna Mae loves children, so these two will be a welcome sight to her." Miss Rodgers smiled at him again as she placed the plates on the table.

Her pearly white teeth flashed, but her eyes didn't hold the smile. Did she feel obligated to help him? Miss Rodgers seemed nice, but her gaze seemed dubious at best. Was it because they were alone in the house together?

He cleared his throat. "I need to go take care of the horse and wagon." He looked to where the girls played contentedly. Should he ask her to watch them while he unloaded the wagon and found housing for the horse? Or just assume she knew he needed her to do so.

They looked up at him with their mother's trusting eyes. Rose and Ruby were his responsibility. He'd take them. William stood and stepped toward the girls. Weariness rested upon him like the shroud of death that seemed to haunt his family at the moment.

"If you'd like, you can leave the girls with me."

Her soft voice held no regret at the suggestion, so William nodded. "Thank you. I won't be gone any longer than it takes to get the horse and supplies settled."

"Your grandmother kept her little mare in the lean-to in the back. It's small, only two stalls, but you are welcome to put your horse there also," she offered as she poured milk into two cups.

He nodded. "I'll look into putting him up at the livery tomorrow."

Just as William got to the door, Miss Rodgers called after him. "What are the girls' names?"

He turned to face her. "The one with the yellow ribbon is Rose and the other is Ruby. Those ribbons are the only way I can tell them apart, so please don't take them out of their hair." Shame filled William. What uncle, who had taken care of his nieces for as long as he had, couldn't recognize them without their silly bows? He hurried out the door before Emily Jane could ask him the question he'd just asked himself.

What must she think of him? Showing up with two little girls, dirty little ones at that, and not knowing that his grandmother had passed away? William crossed the dirt road. He moved to the back of the wagon and began pulling out the few belongings he'd brought. He told himself it really didn't matter what she thought. Emily Jane Rodgers had no say in what he did. Other than being their neighbor, she held no place in his or the girls' lives. And to be honest, he had too much on his plate to worry what some silly woman thought of him.

He had to admit, though, that she was very pretty and had been helpful. And so far silliness had not been part of her character, more a cautious, no-nonsense attitude toward his circumstances. She had known just what to do for the girls and had been willing to feed them. Was she just being neighborly? Or had she seen him as a single man with two children and a possible husband?

William shook his head. No matter how pretty or helpful Miss Rodgers was, he had no intention of becoming her husband. Or anybody's husband, for that matter. He picked up the closest box and realized being tired put very wayward thoughts into one's mind. Miss Rodgers was simply a nice woman. Very pretty and very nice. Nothing more. He hoped he was wrong that she might see him as a possible husband; he definitely wasn't looking for a wife.

He limped up the porch and entered the house. It was time to focus on himself and the girls. They needed a place to sleep tonight. William walked straight through the sitting room and into his grandmother's bedroom. Her bed rested against the center of the back wall. Other than the dust that covered everything, it looked much like it had five years ago when he'd last visited her. She had a small cabinet for clothes, a washbasin by the window and a small writing desk against the opposite wall. A side table sat on the other side of the bed and held a kerosene lantern and her Bible. He set the box of clothes down inside the doorway and then went to explore the rest of the house.

He followed a short hallway to the other side of the building where the kitchen and another bedroom rested. His grandmother had used the other bedroom for a sewing room as well as her guest room. Would the girls be too far away from him if he put them in this space?

William sighed as he went back out to the wagon. He lifted an oblong box from the bed that had served as Rose's cradle during their trip and carried it into the house and his grandmother's room. Then he went back for Ruby's. The girls would sleep in the room with him until they were old enough to be put in their own room. Plus, he'd need to clean only one room tonight.

On the way back outside, William noticed the bag that held the girls' diapers and drinking cups beside the sofa where Emily Jane had left it. He scooped it up and continued on to the horse and wagon.

It didn't take long to find the lean-to behind Emily Jane's house and take care of the animal. What had happened to his grandmother's horse? Miss Rodgers had said that she kept her here. William made a mental note to ask her about the little mare.

Taking a deep, unsteady breath, he hurried around the house, only to stop disconcerted at the door. Was he supposed to knock or go on in? He knocked.

Footsteps hurried across the floor. So far he hadn't heard the girls crying; that was a good sign, right? A rush of fragrances, sugar and cinnamon, hit him when she opened the door. He breathed deeply, enjoying the calming smells, making another mental note to cook something spicy at his grandmother's so the stale smell would leave.

"Mr. Barns, please, come on inside. You didn't need to knock. I expected you to return." She spun around on her heels and hurried back to the kitchen.

The slight bite in her voice had him hurrying after her. Had the girls misbehaved while he was gone? The diaper bag slapped against his side as he went to check on his nieces.

The scene that met him almost had him laughing out loud. Each girl sat in a chair by the table. Miss Rodgers had tied them to the chairs with what looked like aprons. Their faces were clean and their eyes sparkled as they gnawed on chunks of bread. They smiled up at him.

He eased into a chair beside Ruby. "I hope they weren't too much trouble."

Miss Rodgers sat across from him. "Oh, no, they were just hungry. Now that they're eating, they seem content and happy."

The front door opened and closed in the sitting room. A voice called out, "Emily Jane, I'm home."

This must be the Anna Mae that Miss Rodgers had mentioned.

"I'm in the kitchen," Miss Rodgers called back. She offered him a smile. "I'm sorry for the yelling, but if I don't answer she will think it strange."

He grinned back. "So the yelling back and forth is normal?"

"It's become a part of our routine." A slight blush filled her cheeks, and he wondered why.

"You would not believe my day." The woman called Anna Mae stopped abruptly, her gaze taking in the scene at the table.

Light brown hair, piled on the top of her head in a bun, and big brown eyes made Anna Mae Leland look plain next to Emily Jane. At least, that was William's first impression of her. She wore a simple gray dress, dusty brown shoes and a beige apron. He wondered if she dressed like that as a way to hide or become invisible to those around her.

"Oh, I'm sorry. I didn't realize we had company." Her brow crinkled, and then she looked at the two girls. A smile replaced the scowl. "Who are these darling ladies?" she cooed.

The little children smiled happily in return and kicked their legs back and forth. Who wouldn't smile at someone whose tone of voice had gone from normal to doting?

Miss Rodgers introduced them. "Anna Mae Leland, this is William Barns, Mabel's grandson, and his daughters, Rose and Ruby."

William stood and shook the hand Anna Mae extended toward him. His hand engulfed her smaller one.

"It's nice to meet you, Miss Leland, but I have to correct Miss Rodgers. Rose and Ruby are my nieces, not my daughters."

"Oh, I'm sorry. I assumed they were yours." Her voice drifted off as if caught in a high wind.

"Nothing to be sorry about, Miss Rodgers. It was an understandable mistake," William assured her, returning to his seat.

Both ladies were seated and, after a short grace, began filling the girls' plates with soft food. Mixed emotions threatened to overwhelm him. He didn't know whether to be relieved or offended at this liberty. He'd been the only caretaker of the girls since their mother had been killed. To suddenly relinquish that duty left him floundering, a bit as if he'd lost something precious. He shook his head. What on earth was wrong with him? This was what he'd needed his grandmother's help with. It was as simple as that.

William then filled his plate. As he sank his teeth into the first bite, he closed his eyes in pure pleasure. "Ummmmm," he all but groaned. He hadn't tasted fried chicken this good in… He didn't know how long. "You are a wonderful cook, Miss Rodgers," he praised.

"Thank you."

Miss Leland wiped Ruby's mouth and then said, "Wait until you taste dessert. Emily Jane is the best baker in these parts."

William watched Emily Jane finger a loose tendril of hair on her cheek as if embarrassed at her friend's praise.

"Thanks, Anna Mae." Her voice was smooth but insistent. "But we both know that isn't true. Violet is the real baker. I still have lots to learn from her before I can ever open my own bakery."

So she wanted to open her own bakery. Which to his way of thinking meant she wasn't lazy. Good for her. His sister had been a hard worker with dreams of her own, also. Too bad her life had ended before she'd had a chance to realize them.

William listened to the women talk. His gaze moved to his nieces, who were making a mess of their dinners but were so happy he didn't have the heart to make them stop. He was surprised that neither Miss Rodgers nor Miss Leland asked him questions regarding the girls and the lack of their mother and father.

In the short time since he'd arrived in Granite, Texas, he'd learned that Anna Mae Leland was the schoolteacher who loved children and that Emily Jane Rodgers was a friend of his grandmother's and an aspiring baker. Yet, neither knew much about him, which to his way of thinking wasn't all bad.

The last thing he needed was for either of them to start looking at him as an eligible bachelor. Since Charlotte's rejection, he had no interest in women. His focus would be on the girls until their father returned. They were his sole concern now.

"Will you be staying long in Granite, Mr. Barns?" Miss Leland asked.

William rubbed his chin. "I guess that depends on what the banker says about the house and if I can find a job."

Miss Leland nodded as if she understood. "Well, you might talk to Mr. Moore over at the general store. His wife just had their first child, and I hear he's looking to hire someone."

Working at the general store wouldn't be so bad, at least until his money arrived at the bank. Selling the mercantile in Denver had made him a wealthy man, but until the money arrived he'd need to work. Not that he wouldn't work after the money came in. It wasn't in his nature to be lazy and watch others labor. "Thank you, Miss Leland. If all goes well at the bank tomorrow, I'll stop by the general store."

Rose and Ruby chose that moment to let everyone know they were done eating and ready to move to another activity. Their cries filled the house and had both women jumping to pick them up.

"I need to get these two down for the night." William reached for Rose.

Miss Rodgers caught his attention. "Where?"

"I'll take them to my grandmother's house. Her bedroom isn't that bad." He hoped she didn't think he was yelling at her. The girls' cries were so loud that he had to raise his voice to be heard.

She shook her head. "It's too dusty for them there."

Before he could respond, both women handed him a little girl.

"Try to comfort them. We'll be back in a little while. Between the two of us, we'll have the house livable in no time," Miss Leland instructed him as the two ladies walked out of the kitchen.

William hurried after them. The screaming children seemed unaware of the noise they were making. "I can't let you do that," he protested.

"It's no trouble at all," Miss Rodgers called over her shoulder as they left the house.

He continued after them, aware of several older women looking out their windows or standing on their porches. Instead of protesting further, William hurried across the road to his grandmother's house. *I'll be glad when I get control of my life once more,* he thought as the children howled and the women charged onward, on a mission to clean his grandmother's home. He hurried into the house behind them, then stopped abruptly and sneezed;

not once, not twice, but three times in a row. Dust particles swirled so thick he could hardly see the ladies jerk-
ing covers off the furniture. Then the twins sneezed. "I
think we'll just sit out on the porch awhile," he muttered to
himself, since the ladies paid him absolutely no attention.

Emily Jane loved working at the bakery, but on mornings like this, she wished her hours weren't so early. Her
new neighbors had kept her up most of the night with
their cries for attention, and getting up at three in the
morning had her even more tired than normal. A yawn
filled her chest as she placed plates of pancakes in front
of Mrs. Green and Miss Cornwell, two of her neighbors.
She turned her head to release the yawn.

"Thank you," Mrs. Green said tiredly between huge
yawns. "I didn't get a lick of sleep last night."

"I know," Miss Cornwell said, pouring honey over
her pancakes. "Those babies cried almost the whole
night. Disgraceful."

Emily Jane should have walked away, but instead
she turned to face the women and said, "They weren't
that bad."

"No? Didn't you hear them?" Mrs. Green asked, as
her blue eyes searched Emily Jane's.

"Yes, I heard them, but they were in a strange new
place and were overtired. I'm sure they'll settle down
once they get used to their new home," she answered,
wiping down the table beside them.

"So he's staying, then?" Miss Cornwell lifted the
fork to her lips but waited for Emily Jane to answer.

"I don't know." Emily Jane didn't want the women

assuming she knew more about William Barns's business than she should. Although she did wonder what he'd found out at the bank this morning.

The bell over the door jingled as three more ladies from her neighborhood entered the bakery, Mrs. Wells, Mrs. Harvey and Mrs. Orson. They hurried to where Mrs. Green and Miss Cornwell sat. Mrs. Harvey slipped into a chair at the table next to the other two women.

Mrs. Wells covered her mouth as a yawn overtook her. "Excuse me. I didn't get a wink of sleep last night with all that crying."

"We were just talking about that," Mrs. Green said, leaning forward in her seat.

Mrs. Orson shook her head. "I don't think anyone got any sleep last night. Mr. Orson paced the floor all night. It was very annoying. I'll be glad when that man takes his children and moves on."

Emily Jane decided to change the subject. "Ladies, what can I get you this morning?" she asked with a forced smile.

"Just coffee for me," Mrs. Orson answered.

Mrs. Harvey smiled up at her. "Do you have any of those fruit-filled pastries?"

Emily Jane returned her smile. Fruit-filled pastry was one of the new items she'd suggested that the bakery start serving. "Yes, ma'am, we have apple and peach this morning."

"I'd like to try the peach and a cup of your coffee."

"I'll have the same." Mrs. Wells dropped into the chair opposite her friends. Her bulky figure pressed against the table as she leaned forward to continue the conversation Emily Jane had interrupted. "Has anyone learned if they are staying? Mabel was a friend of mine, but even she would have understood our reluctance to having crying children in our quiet neighborhood."

Seldom did they ever agree upon anything, but it seemed lack of sleep had all five graying heads nodding in unison.

Emily Jane left them to their gossiping. Why did they have to be so mean? Rose and Ruby were children who had simply been overtired the night before. She placed the fruit pies on two small plates and poured two cups of coffee, then returned to the women's table.

"What are we going to do, if he stays here?" Mrs. Orson demanded.

She set the plates and steaming cups in front of the women. "I really don't think the girls will be that much trouble once they are settled." Emily Jane straightened her spine and resisted the urge to yawn again. "You know, talking about Mr. Barns and his children like this isn't very Christian-like, ladies."

Mrs. Green huffed. "Well, if you like Mr. Barns and his screaming children so much, why don't you marry the man and keep those kids quiet?"

Emily Jane stood there with her mouth hanging open. Were they serious? She…marry a man to keep his children quiet? She glanced about the table. The other four women nodded their heads in agreement.

"I am not the marrying kind, ladies. I have dreams of opening my own bakery someday, and those dreams do not include a man with two children." She offered each of them a smile, before hurrying to the kitchen and away from their speculative looks.

A little while later, Emily Jane entered the front door of her home. She carried the box of baking supplies to the kitchen table. After talking to her neighbors, her thoughts had clung to what they'd said. She admitted to herself that they were right in that Rose and Ruby had cried most of the night. It amazed her that the girls' voices had carried so clearly upon the still night air, keeping most everyone in the neighborhood awake. But the plain and simple fact of the matter was that she could do nothing about their unhappiness. She wondered briefly why that bothered her so much.

She emptied the box, placing each item on the kitchen table. Today she was going to try her hand at adding a new ingredient to her oatmeal raisin cookie recipe. One of the joys of her job was that Violet, the manager of the bakery, supplied the ingredients for her to bake up new recipes. In return, once the recipe was perfected, Emily Jane fixed it at the bakery. Customers seemed to love her new creations.

As she mixed the flour with the rest of the ingredients, Emily Jane's thoughts drifted to the women. She'd been surprised at their suggestion that she marry William Barns. Did they really think that if she married him, then the girls would settle down? How rude of them.

Emily Jane stirred the mixture hard and fast. There was no way she'd marry William Barns. She had no intention of marrying anyone and definitely not a man with children. The girls did remind Emily Jane of her own sisters, but that was no reason to get married to a complete stranger, not that he'd asked her. She shook her head. No, she wasn't getting married now or anytime soon; she had a dream of opening her own bakery someday, and that dream didn't include a family or a man who might be like her father and think he could control everything she did.

Chapter Three

William stood holding a niece on each hip. He stared at the group of five women, wondering if they had lost their minds. He could see one or even two of them being a little addled due to age, but all five?

"We're not asking you to move away, at least not right now. All we're asking is that you consider Miss Rodgers as a future bride. She could help you with the girls, and she really is a sweet little thing," Mrs. Harvey said as the others nodded their agreement.

When the women had stopped him on the sidewalk in front of the bank and introduced themselves as his neighbors, he'd been happy to meet them; but now they were butting in where they didn't belong, and he planned to put a stop to their meddling. "Look, ladies, I know you mean well, but I have no intentions of marrying Miss Rodgers or anyone else. Now if you will excuse me, I'm going home." William thought they'd move to the side and let him pass.

He thought wrong.

Mrs. Orson put both hands on her chubby hips and demanded, "Why not? Those girls need a mama. If they had a mama, she'd know how to keep them quiet so a body could rest at night like God intended. Miss Rodgers comes from a large family. She's perfect and knows how to take care of small children."

So that was it; they didn't care about Miss Rodgers. They just wanted him to keep the girls quiet. Rose sucked her thumb with her head on his shoulder. Ruby's chubby little hand played with the hair on the back of his neck. He returned his attention to the ladies. "You're right, but I'm not the man to get one for them. I'm sorry we disturbed your sleep last night. I'll try to keep them quieter."

"If you are going to stick around here, won't you need a wife to take care of the children while you work?" Miss Cornwell asked in a quiet voice.

The elderly woman did have a point. He'd need someone to help him take care of the girls but didn't think the woman had to be his wife. Surely he could pay someone to watch Ruby and Rose.

Thanks to his visit to the bank, William now knew that his grandmother's house belonged to him and his sister, Mary. A lump formed in his throat as he thought of Mary. Now that she was gone, William would make sure that the girls would own the other half of the house. He'd made arrangements for his money from the sale of the mercantile to be transferred from the bank in Denver to the Granite bank. Then he'd walked over to the general store and asked about the job Miss Leland had mentioned the night before.

Mr. Moore had eyed the girls and then agreed to give

William the job. He'd asked William if he could work
from ten in the morning until four in the afternoon, and
William had agreed.

"You ladies wouldn't happen to know of any young
ladies who would be willing to watch the girls while I
work, would you?" He hoped the change of subject would
sidetrack them enough to drop the idea of him marrying Miss Rodgers.

Mrs. Orson sighed. "You got a job?"

"Why, yes, ma'am, I did." He looked directly at the
sour-faced woman.

She shook her head. "I see. The only lady I know of
who is home during the day and able to keep up with
two small children would be Miss Rodgers." Mrs. Orson
looked to the other women for agreement. "Emily Jane
gets home around eight thirty every morning. Isn't that
right, ladies?"

The group nodded. He could see the spark of joy and
scheming in their eyes. William couldn't believe he'd
walked right into their plans for him and Emily Jane.
Well, hiring the woman to watch the girls and marrying
her to watch the girls were two very different things.

Rose began to fuss at standing in place too long. Ruby
decided it was time to join her sister in the protest, and
she too began whining and trying to push out of his
arms.

"If you will excuse me, ladies, I need to get these
wiggle worms home."

William took a step but stopped when Mrs. Green
called to him.

"Mr. Barns, you will check with Emily Jane about watching the girls, won't you?" she inquired.

"She is really good with young children. After all, she has had lots of practice," Mrs. Harvey prompted.

They were an insistent bunch, he'd give them that. He grinned at Mrs. Harvey. "I'll ask her, and thank you for the recommendation." William hurried down the sidewalk toward home but could still hear them as he walked away.

"He really seems like a nice young man."

"I think he and Emily Jane would make a nice couple, don't you, Lois?"

"I do hope those girls settle down soon. I need my sleep," another grumbled.

"Well, after a woman gets her hands on them, I'm sure they will become little darlings, and Emily Jane is just the woman for the job," Mrs. Orson said in a no-nonsense tone.

Their voices faded as William hurried toward the house. As soon as he started walking again, the girls quieted down. They were already little darlings. He really didn't see that having a woman in their lives would change them that much.

Each girl laid her little head on his shoulder. It was a short walk to his grandmother's house, now his and the girls' new home. He reached for the doorknob and found a small cloth bag hanging on it.

William ignored it; even though his curiosity was stirred, his hands were full. He carried the girls inside for a morning nap. After changing their diapers, he put them in their cradles. Thankfully, they curled up and went to sleep almost immediately.

Tiptoeing from the bedroom, William sighed and closed the door. His gaze moved about the sitting room. Thanks to Miss Leland and Miss Rodgers, the house now looked and smelled fresh. Once they'd started cleaning the night before, they hadn't stopped until the whole house shone.

He remembered the bag on the front doorknob and went to retrieve it. The sweet scent of sugar and spice filled his nostrils. William pulled it open and saw two cookies inside. Had Emily Jane brought them over? Or perhaps another neighbor. Until he found out, William decided not to give them to the girls.

After the racket the girls had made last night, it wouldn't surprise him if one of the neighbors put a sleeping draft in the cookies. He grinned at the silliness of his thoughts. Still, he'd wait on giving them to the girls until he was sure they were safe.

He walked over to a big chair and sank into its cushions, laying the cookie-filled bag on the side table. A yawn stretched his mouth wide. Nap time for the girls was one of his favorite times of the day. Often at night, one or both of them would wake up fussy. When was the last time he'd gotten a full night's sleep? As his eyes drifted shut, William's thoughts went to Emily Jane Rodgers. Would she watch the children? If so, he silently prayed she could get the girls into a regular sleeping routine.

Emily Jane pulled a fresh batch of oatmeal raisin cookies from the oven. She never tired of the baking smells that filled the kitchen. This recipe was no exception. She'd played with the ingredients a bit and liked the results. *A pinch of this and a pinch of that* had been her mother's motto, but Emily Jane liked the results of being precise with her measurements. She wrote everything down as she went, and if the dessert turned out well, she could fix it over and over again without adjusting anything.

She put the cookies on a cooling rack and sat at the table to sip her coffee. All morning she'd been thinking about the neighbor ladies. How could they be so mean? Yes, children were noisy, yes, they cried, and, yes, the twins' voices did carry on the night breezes, but that was still no reason to wish them gone. A smile teased her lips as she thought about how they would have reacted if they'd lived near her family. Her five brothers and six sisters were far from quiet.

Living out in the middle of nowhere pretty much explained why she and her sisters Sarah and Elsie had never married. There were no boys nearby to marry. Anxiety spurted through her. Had twenty-two-year-old Sarah and twenty-one-year-old Elsie been forced to answer mail-order-bride ads, too? Emily Jane hoped not, but then again, if it worked out as well for them as it had for her, maybe it would be the best thing for her sisters.

She thought over her own experience as a mail-order bride. Thanks to her father's decision to lessen the mouths he had to feed, Emily Jane had answered an ad. She'd arrived in Granite, Texas, expecting to be courted by Levi Westland. His mother had written to Emily Jane and two other women telling them to come to Granite. She'd promised Emily Jane that if Levi didn't choose her as his bride, then she'd help her find a husband.

Emily Jane shook her head as memories flooded her mind. She hadn't wanted a husband then but wanted to be obedient to her father's wishes and had come to Granite. It had been a relief when Levi had chosen Millie Hamilton as his new wife.

After Levi and Millie's wedding, Bonnie Westland had offered to make good on her promise of a husband, but Emily Jane had assured her she was happy without one right now. Thankfully, Bonnie had understood but still assured Emily Jane that, should she change her mind, she'd be willing to help her find the perfect man. As if there were such a thing as a perfect man.

Emily Jane walked to the sink and placed her coffee cup in the hot soapy water. She hadn't written her family since she'd arrived in Granite. The last thing she wanted was for Pa to tell her to come home and start the husband hunt all over again.

Still, she often thought about her siblings. Her sense of loss was beyond tears. She missed their laughter; she missed her sisters whispering in bed at night so as not to wake their parents. She found herself listening sometimes for their voices. And the little ones—tears welled within her eyes—how she missed cuddling their bodies close, burying her nose in their necks and smelling the powdery softness. Her lips pressed shut, so no sound would burst out. It had been a long time since she'd felt such a strong urge to cry. She straightened her shoulders and dared the tears to fall. Yes, Ruby and Rose made her homesick to see her family again, but her time of grieving the loss of her siblings was over. She'd proved adept at handling herself without any help from others and couldn't afford to be distracted by homesickness.

Emily Jane placed the cooled cookies into the metal cookie bin and decided to work on a new batch. Cookies that were different, plus a new recipe would take her mind off family. She'd wanted to try her hand at making lemon cookies and had gotten the ingredients to try them.

A knock at the front door pulled her away from the bowl of flour. Emily Jane wiped her hands on her apron. She'd had more company in the past two days than she'd had in a month. A chuckle escaped her as she realized that that really wasn't much company, just Mr. Barns and his nieces. Very seldom did anyone come calling during the day.

She pulled the door open and found them standing on the porch as if just by thinking their names they'd appeared. "Hello, Mr. Barns. Please come in."

He stepped inside and inhaled. "Something sure smells good in here."

Emily Jane grinned at the two girls looking over their uncle's shoulder. "I just baked a batch of oatmeal raisin cookies. Would you like to try them?" Heat filled the room, making it warmer than it had been a few moments earlier, so Emily Jane left the front door open.

"If it wouldn't be too much trouble, we'd love to try them. Wouldn't we, girls?" He followed Emily Jane into the kitchen.

"No trouble at all. I've been experimenting, so you'll be the first to taste my new creation." She took Rose from him and set her on the floor.

He set Ruby down beside her sister and frowned. "Experimenting?" William placed the girls' bag on the floor at his feet.

Emily Jane saw the worry on his face and laughed. "Yes, experimenting. I do it all the time with cookies, cakes, bread and different kinds of pastries." She picked up a cookie and handed it to him.

She scooped two sugar cookies from a plate on the sideboard and handed one to each of the girls. "Here you go," Emily Jane said as their chubby little hands wrapped around the sweet treats.

Emily Jane watched William take a big bite and then close his eyes. "Well, what do you think?" The lines of concentration deepened along his brows. She waited for his reply, surprised at her feelings of uncertainty.

He swallowed and then opened eyes that brimmed with appreciation. "I think you can test your cookies out on me anytime. These are delicious." William popped the rest of the cookie into his mouth and looked to the sideboard, where more cookies rested on various plates.

"How about some coffee to go with a small plate of cookies?" Emily Jane moved to the coffeepot and poured him a generous cup.

"Both sound wonderful." He sat down at the table.

Emily Jane's gaze moved to the girls, who happily nibbled at their sugar cookies. She should have set them at the table but no matter; the crumbs could be swept up after they left.

"Did you leave a couple of cookies on my door this morning for the girls?" William asked.

She nodded. "I hope you don't mind."

"Not at all. I just wanted to make sure it was you before I let them have them." His grin brightened his face.

Emily Jane decided not to focus on his good looks and placed several cookies onto a dessert plate. She carried them to the table and set them in front of William. "So, what brings you over? Surely it wasn't the cookies I left for the girls." She sat down across from him.

"Straight to the point. I like that in a woman." He set his coffee cup down. "This morning I had a chat with the neighbor ladies."

She looked down at the angelic faces covered in cookie crumbs. *Oh, please, Lord, don't let him be here to ask me to marry him and take care of the girls.*

"And they suggested you might be interested in watching the girls while I work." He searched her face, his eyes curiously observing. She wondered briefly what he expected her face to reveal. Emily Jane had no idea. His voice was calm and steady and gave nothing away. "This morning Mr. Moore offered me a job working in his store from ten to four every day. He suggested I find someone to watch the girls and start work this afternoon. I sort of hoped you'd be able to watch them today."

She wanted to help him, she really did, but the thought of growing attached to the girls worried her. And how much time would they take from her experimental cooking?

"What hours did you say you would have to work?" Something in his eyes beseeched her to help.

"From ten to four."

She found herself nodding. "I'll help, but only until you can find someone else."

A sweet grin split his lips, revealing straight white teeth.

"That's all I'm asking. Thank you. I'll be back a few minutes after four to pick them up. Thank you again."

William hurried from the house as if he suspected she might change her mind at any moment.

As the door closed behind him, Emily Jane asked herself the hard questions. Had she done the right thing by agreeing to help him? Emily Jane knew it was the right thing to do, but was it the right thing for her? Was it possible she'd lose her heart to these darling little girls and William?

Chapter Four

Emily Jane didn't have time to think any more about the choice she'd made in watching the girls. Rose began to cry almost as soon as the door closed behind William. She scooped down and picked up the little girl. "Now what are you fussing about? He'll be back soon." She patted the little girl's back.

Thankfully, even with a wet diaper, Rose stopped her complaining and nestled close to Emily Jane. She looked down at Ruby and saw the little girl crawling toward the sitting room.

First thing she'd need to do was find a way to confine the twins to one area. Unlike their uncle, Emily Jane couldn't hold them both at once, at least not all the time, and strapping them to a chair all afternoon wasn't an option. "You two are lucky I have little brothers and sisters and know how to build a fun pen for you to play in."

She set Rose down and snatched up Ruby before she could crawl from the room. Someone knocked at the front door. "Now, who do you suppose that is?" Emily

Jane asked Ruby, who wiggled in her arms, trying to get down.

"Who is it?" Emily Jane called.

"Elsie Matthews, dear."

Mrs. Matthews was a sweet woman who lived two houses down. In her late sixties, she was the least of the busybodies who lived in the neighborhood. "Come in, Mrs. Matthews. We're in the kitchen."

The door opened, and the older woman stepped inside. "I hope I'm not disturbing you."

Emily Jane motioned her in. "Not at all. I was just figuring out how I would manage these two this afternoon. Can you stay long?"

"Long enough. What can I help you with?" She pulled her shawl from around her slight shoulders and hung it on the nearest kitchen chair.

Rose crawled over to the older woman and pulled on her skirt. "Up," said the little girl, smiling.

Emily Jane watched as Mrs. Matthews scooped the child into her arms and tickled her belly. "So you were one of the wee folk making all that noise last night, weren't you?"

In reply, Rose giggled.

Emily Jane carried Ruby to the center of the kitchen and set her down again. "They both need baths. Would you mind keeping an eye on them for just a second while I step out back and get the washtub?"

"Be happy to, but are you going to drag in that big tub just to give these two a bath? Wouldn't it be easier to just wash them one at a time in the washbasin?" Mrs. Matthews placed Rose beside her sister.

Emily Jane laughed. "Yes, but the washtub will hold them both. I'm going to use it as a pen so that I can get some work done."

"That's an excellent idea." Mrs. Matthews's light auburn hair streaked with gray bobbed on the top of her head as she nodded her approval.

Emily Jane hurried to where their washtub sat by the back door. Normally they did their laundry on Saturday, so the tub would be available for the girls to play in for a couple of days yet. William should have someone else lined up to watch the girls by then.

Rose and Ruby giggled and crawled after Emily Jane. Mrs. Matthews laughed. "Oh, no, you don't. You two have to stay and play with me for a few minutes." She knelt down, offering her apron strings for them to pull on.

Emily Jane lugged the big tub inside. It was wooden with metal rings around the top, middle and bottom of it, the perfect size to hold two little girls. Normally Anna Mae helped her carry it inside, but since she wasn't available and Mrs. Matthews had her hands full with the girls, Emily Jane tugged on it until she got it into the kitchen.

Mrs. Matthews hurried over. "Here, let me help you with that."

Together they set it against the wall by the back door. "I think you might need something soft inside for them to sit and play on."

"I'll go get a blanket, be right back." She hurried to her bedroom and grabbed a small nine-patch quilt from the foot of her bed. It was her reading quilt. She enjoyed curling up in it and reading her Bible before going to sleep each night.

When she returned to the kitchen, she saw that Mrs. Matthews stood holding Rose with Ruby sitting at her feet pulling at the buttons on her black shoes. "This should do it." Emily Jane spread the quilt out in the bottom of the tub and then reached for Ruby. Mrs. Matthews added Rose.

The girls grinned up at them. They really were sweet little things. Emily Jane went to the cupboard and pulled out spoons and pans for the girls to play with.

"Would you like a cup of tea?" Emily Jane asked.

Mrs. Matthews sat down in a chair at the table. "I'd love one. And while you are making it, I'll keep an eye on the girls. Maybe you could tell me how you ended up with these two this afternoon?"

Emily Jane nodded. "Mr. Barns, Mabel's grandson, started work this afternoon at the general store. Some of our neighbors suggested I'd be a good person to watch them." She poured water into a large pail for the girls' bath and also filled the teapot.

"Oh, I'm sure they did." Mrs. Matthews laughed. "They came over to the house this morning, complaining about the girls crying last night. You'd think they were all a hundred years old the way they gripe."

Trying to hide a smile, Emily Jane nodded. "Yes, they came by the bakery this morning, too."

"Meddling old hens." Mrs. Matthews's hazel eyes met hers. "I'm sure they had a lot to say."

Warmth filled Emily Jane's cheeks as she remembered them suggesting she marry William Barns and give the girls a mother. She shook her head at the memory. "Can you believe they suggested I marry him?"

"Why?" Mrs. Matthews tilted her head to the side and scrunched up her brow. "I mean, for goodness' sake, you just met the man."

Her expression was comical, and Emily Jane giggled. "To give his nieces a mother. They seem to think a mother would be able to stop them from crying at night."

"That's preposterous." Mrs. Matthews cooed down at the twins. Emily Jane gazed at the girls, who looked so much like William. *Where are their parents?* she wondered. *And why aren't they taking care of the girls?*

A few minutes after four that afternoon, William knocked on Emily Jane's front door. Weariness seeped through his bones like honey from a leaky jug. Working with Mr. Moore hadn't been hard. It was the sleepless night up with the girls. His energy level was zero and his nerves stretched tight.

She opened the door with a smile and stepped back to allow him inside. The aroma of fried ham drifted to William, reminding him he still needed to feed the girls. His stomach growled, so to cover his embarrassment, William said, "Something sure smells good in here."

"I'm glad you think so. We saved a plate for you." Emily Jane motioned for him to follow her.

He didn't need to be asked twice. William shut the door and did as she bade. His gaze took in the clean kitchen and the girls.

Surrounded by blankets, they were playing in a large washtub. Their hair and faces looked freshly washed, only neither wore their ribbons. Shock filled him. How was he going to tell them apart? "Miss Rodgers, what happened to the girls' hair ribbons?" He knew the question came out tight and sounding angry, but he couldn't stop the feelings of confusion and fear coursing through him.

Ruby and Rose squealed with happiness at the sound of his voice. They scrambled to pull themselves up on the side of the tub. He knelt and gave them both hugs. They smelled of soft, clean powder.

"Oh, they were horrible, so I threw them out." She pulled a covered plate from the back of the stove and turned to face him.

"I remember specifically telling you that those ribbons were the only way I could identify them. Did you forget?" As he looked into the identical faces, he felt robbed. Something important had been taken from him. How was he going to know which girl was Rose and which one was Ruby?

She set the plate down on the table. "No, I remember. But since Rose has a birthmark behind her right knee, I didn't think you'd mind me throwing out the ribbons. They were pretty ragged, and I plan to replace them. I just haven't had time yet."

William picked up the little girl closest to him and looked at her leg. How had he missed the small brown mark that looked like an ant behind her knee? He should have seen it. Maybe the girls did need a woman's care. He kissed Rose on the cheek and then put her back into the tub. "No, that won't be necessary."

Ruby extended her arms, reaching for William to

give her a cuddle and kiss, too. He obliged by picking her up and kissing her soft cheek. She giggled.

When William set her back down, he noticed two colorful cloth balls in the tub with them. Picking one up, he said, "These are pretty."

Emily Jane poured a glass of water and set it beside his plate. "Mrs. Matthews, another one of our neighbors, brought those by earlier for the girls. You should come eat this before it gets cold."

William gave the ball to Rose and stood. "I appreciate all you've done for the girls today."

"It wasn't much."

He laughed. "You gave them a bath. That's huge. I put off doing that until I can't stand the smell anymore. They are a handful at bath time." William sat down and lifted the cover from his plate of fried ham, mashed potatoes and green beans.

Her gentle laugh had his gaze moving to her face. "Well, that explains a lot."

William laughed with her and then offered a quick grace before forking a chunk of ham and chomping into it. "You know, if you keep feeding us, I'm going to have to pay for my meals here, too."

Rose chose that moment to fuss. She was tired of being in the tub. Emily Jane walked over and picked her up. "Shhhh, little one, Anna Mae has a headache. We don't want to wake her, do we?" She leaned the little girl against her shoulder and rubbed her back.

"I'm awake," Anna Mae said as she entered the room. She smiled at William and the girls on her way to the coffeepot. "I think my headache has about run its course." She poured a cup of the fragrant liquid.

Emily Jane smiled. "I'm glad."

Anna Mae returned to the table and sat down. "How was your first day at work, Mr. Barns?" She took a sip and studied him over the rim of her cup.

William sat up a little straighter in his chair. He cleared his throat before saying, "I believe it went well. Wilson says I'm a natural."

Anna Mae nodded. "I'm sure you are. Isn't today the day that supplies arrive from Austin?" she asked, still keeping her gaze locked on him.

"Yes, ma'am. It is."

Anna Mae grinned across at him. "Please, there are no ma'ams here. Call me Miss Anna Mae, and you may address Emily Jane as Miss Emily Jane. I believe that is formal enough for around town and here at home. Don't you, Emily Jane?"

"That will be fine."

William nodded his agreement. He could tell by the stiffness in her voice that Emily Jane wasn't pleased with him calling her by her given name but that she'd complied out of politeness.

"Now that that is settled, would you mind telling us what arrived from Austin today?" Anna Mae asked, setting her cup down.

Ruby had been left out of the conversation long enough. She squealed, letting them know she too wanted out of the tub.

William rose to get her.

Anna Mae waved him back into his seat. "I'll get her. Please, continue eating and tell us all about your day."

William did as Anna Mae requested. He found the schoolteacher to be a delight. She seemed truly interested in his everyday goings-on, and Ruby cuddled close to her as if they were meant to be together. Of the two ladies, Anna Mae might be a better choice for the girls as a new mother. Even so, he didn't feel the same attraction toward her as he did with Emily Jane. That line of thinking was dangerous. William focused on his food.

He finished his meal as quickly as possible and then stood to leave. "Thank you for dinner and taking care of the girls today, Miss Emily Jane." William picked up the girls' bag. "Tomorrow Mr. Moore and I are going to put up a poster announcing that I need someone to watch the girls. Do you mind taking care of them one more day?" While he talked, William dug around the blankets in the tub.

Emily Jane handed Rose to Anna Mae and then picked up his dirty dishes. "That will be fine." She stopped and watched him for a moment. "What are you looking for?"

He straightened and said, "The girls' stuffed animals."

She carried the plate, silverware and cup to the dish tub. "They are still in your bag." Emily Jane poured more hot water over the dishes.

William turned with a frown on his face. "Then how did you get them to take their afternoon nap? They can't sleep without their toys."

Emily Jane turned with a sweet smile. "They didn't take an afternoon nap."

As if to confirm her words, Rose yawned. Ruby followed suit. The little girl snuggled closer to Anna Mae.

"No nap?" William couldn't believe it. Over the past few weeks, he'd taken to putting the girls down for an hour or more every morning and again in the afternoon so that he could get some much-needed rest, too.

She shook her head. "No nap."

"Why not?" William asked.

Anna Mae answered. "So that they will sleep tonight." She stood and handed a very sleepy Ruby to William and Rose over to Emily Jane.

"And they didn't fuss?" he asked as Ruby cuddled up against his shoulder.

Emily Jane wiped her free hand off on her apron. "No, they were too busy playing with Mrs. Matthews and sampling cookies. Tomorrow we'll start with a short nap in the afternoon and then see how well they sleep. But for tonight you should have no trouble whatsoever getting them to sleep the night through." She smiled at Rose, who stared back at her with big blue eyes.

Baffled at how easily Emily Jane seemed to have taken care of his nieces, William patted Ruby on the back. He did like the idea of them sleeping all night.

Anna Mae shook her head. "My head is beginning to ache again. Emily Jane will help you get home."

"That isn't necessary." William walked to Emily Jane with the idea of taking Rose into his free arm.

Rose curled up against Emily Jane's chest. "Nonsense. It won't take me a minute to walk over and lay her down." Emily Jane's face softened as the little girl closed her eyes and stuck her thumb into her mouth.

He nodded. "All right." William followed her as she led the way across the kitchen, through the sitting room and outside. Her light blue skirt swished against the wooden porch steps as she descended.

"It's a lovely evening." Her soft voice floated back to him much like the fireflies that buzzed about the yard.

A cool breeze brushed across his cheeks, bringing with it the ever-present scents of cinnamon and sugar. He inhaled. "It sure is."

They walked side by side to his house. *His house.* Six months ago, William wouldn't have thought he'd be in Granite, Texas. Sorrow hit him full in the chest. If he'd known six months ago that both his sister and his grandmother would be gone, he'd have spent more time with them and less time trying to build a business.

"So far, spring is my favorite season in Texas." Emily Jane pulled him from his sad thoughts.

He slipped around her and opened the door. "I take it you aren't from around here?" William stepped back so that she could slip past him.

"No, I grew up in Kansas." She walked back to the bedroom and laid Rose down in one of the cradles.

William placed Ruby into the other. Both girls curled up and closed their eyes. He was amazed at how quickly they went down.

William asked, "When was the last time they were changed?" William hated asking such a delicate question, but the thought of them, their bedding and their toys being wet in the morning didn't appeal to him.

He'd rather change them now and not have to deal with the mess later.

A dimple in her right cheek winked up at him as she grinned. "Right before you arrived. They should stay dry for the rest of the night. I doubled their diapers just in case they fell asleep before you got them home." She walked toward the bedroom door.

Why hadn't he thought of doing that at night? Emily Jane truly was a woman who knew how to take care of children. He followed her from the room and then gently shut the door behind them.

Emily Jane continued toward the front door. She stepped out on the porch. "I'll see you tomorrow."

"Thank you again." William leaned against the doorjamb and watched her hurry back to her house. She really was a pretty little thing, red hair, green eyes and that cute dimple that had made its appearance tonight. Given enough time, would Miss Emily Jane change her mind and be interested in taking on a more permanent position watching his nieces?

Chapter Five

The next morning as he entered The Bakery, William marveled at the fact that both girls had slept through the night. He carried them to the nearest table and sat down. Aware of several sets of eyes upon them, he sighed. People were forever staring at him and the twins. He wasn't sure if it was because it was uncommon to see a man with two little girls alone or if it was because the girls were twins.

"Good morning. You must be William Barns." William looked up into the face of a smiling woman. "My name is Violet Atwood. What can I get for you and these two darlings this morning?" Violet's hazel eyes studied him with a curious intensity.

Had Emily Jane mentioned him and the girls? Was that how Violet Atwood knew of them? Or had others been talking about him? His thoughts went to the group of ladies who'd spoken to him the day before. Now there definitely was the possibility that they had mentioned them.

He realized that Miss Atwood was waiting to take his order. William cleared his throat before saying, "Good morning. I'd like a cup of coffee for myself and a slice of bread for the girls. Nothing too sweet." William didn't mention that the cookies he'd given them for breakfast already had them squirmier than two playful puppies. He looked down at his nieces.

Rose was attempting to grab Ruby. Ruby pulled against his arm to get at the salt and pepper shakers on the table. It was all he could do to hold on to the two wiggling girls. He sighed.

"Be right back with your order."

He nodded and tightened his grip on the children. His gaze followed Violet Atwood about the room. Her graying brown hair had been piled up onto the top of her head. Miss Atwood wore a brown day dress with a white apron that covered her ample stomach. William wasn't sure about her age but was impressed with the way she zipped about the tables, refilling coffee cups and then hurrying back to the front of the bakery, where he could see her laying out slices of bread on a plate and pouring his cup of coffee.

She seemed to be the only one working in the small establishment. Had Emily Jane already finished for the day? He'd hoped to see her this morning.

Ruby knocked the salt over, and Rose kicked her feet with joy at the sight. The two girls giggled, bringing more attention from the other diners. William righted the saltshaker and pushed a little farther away from the table.

"I imagine those two keep you pretty busy." Violet

set the plate of bread and coffee on the opposite side of the table out of Rose and Ruby's reach. "I have just what you need to be able to eat and drink in comfort. Be right back."

William didn't have time to comment as she whirled around and headed through a small side door that he'd assumed earlier led to the kitchen. Both Rose and Ruby were pulling against his arm to get to the plate of bread. He wished he had some form of harness to put on the little girls. William both dreaded and welcomed the day they'd be able to walk and sit in a chair on their own.

The sound of wood bumping against wood drew his attention back to the side door. He could see Violet wrestling with something and then heard Emily Jane's soft voice. "Here, let me help you with that, Violet." Emily Jane came through the door and held it open for the older woman.

"Oh, thank you, Emily Jane. I don't know what I'd do without you."

Emily Jane's teasing laughter and words floated to him. "Learn to prop the door open before trying to force a high chair through it?"

Violet giggled like a schoolgirl. "I suppose so. Now, get out of my way so that I can get this to our customers."

Emily Jane turned around. Her big green eyes settled on William and the little girls. He wondered if she'd be upset that he'd brought them to her place of work; after all, she'd seen quite a bit of them since they'd arrived.

A smile brought the dimple in her cheek out of hiding as she followed Violet to their table. "Good morning, Mr. Barns." Emily Jane reached for Rose, who at the moment was pulling on the tablecloth, inching the bread and coffee closer with each tug.

He handed his niece over. "Good morning to you, too." William turned his attention to the high chair. It stood about thirty-five inches tall with a dark varnish over red with stenciled white flowers on the wide headrest. "I wish I had brought one of those from Mary's house. It sure would have made things easier at home."

Violet finished making sure it was secure and motioned for Emily Jane to place the little girl inside. "You can always stop by Levi Westland's furniture store and see if he has any more available. He made this one special for the bakery." She ran her hand over the pinewood.

"That's a splendid idea." William grinned up at her. Rose banged her small hands against the wooden tray in front of her. Ruby tried to do the same to the table but William moved her to his other side, farther away from her target.

"Emily Jane, are you going over to the general store on your way home today?" Violet asked as she placed a bit of bread into Rose's hand. She handed the other half to Ruby.

Emily Jane nodded. "Want me to pick up something for you?"

While Ruby's hands were full of bread, William reached for his coffee. Maybe now was the time to go to the general store, too. He needed to replenish his grandmother's cupboards, and if Emily Jane was going and had any suggestions on what he'd need, he'd welcome them.

"Well, if it's not too much trouble. We could use more coffee." Violet patted Rose on the head.

"No trouble at all." Emily Jane smiled at her boss.

William jumped into the conversation. "Well, speaking of trouble, I'm not sure what to pick up to replenish Grams's cupboards. Would you mind if the girls and I tagged along with you?" He sipped his coffee and watched her over the rim of his cup.

For a brief moment, Emily Jane looked as if she were going to refuse his request. Her gaze moved from him to the girls. He suspected it was the way the girls were gobbling their bread, as if they'd not eaten all morning, that persuaded her to agree. "I'll be happy to help you find what you need." She turned toward the kitchen, untying her apron strings as she left the table. "Let me finish up in the kitchen. I'll only be a few minutes."

"Take your time." William smiled into his cup. So far the day was turning out quite nicely. The girls had slept in; he'd managed to have a cup of coffee, and now Miss Emily Jane was going with them to the general store. She'd know what he'd need for the house and the girls. His mood turned a bit somber as the familiar feelings of insecurity attacked him. There was so much he didn't know about the care and future of little girls. Which, if he were truthful, was why he'd ended up at The Bakery today anyway. He'd forgotten to replenish the cupboards. Anyone else would have remembered that babies needed to be fed as soon as they arose in the mornings, but, no, he hadn't even thought of it.

And their clothes. He continued the self-incriminating examination. Who would change a baby's diaper without getting the needed items first? He'd changed Ruby this morning and forgotten the clean diaper. He shifted nervously in his seat, assailed by a terrible sense of helplessness. He ate a slice of the bread and finished his coffee.

"I'm sorry. That took a little longer than I'd anticipated." Emily Jane breezed back in as swiftly as she had left. Her gaze moved to the girls. "Are we ready to go?" she asked, smiling at the girls.

"We're ready." William stood. The soft scent of cinnamon teased his nose as Emily Jane bent over and lifted Rose from the chair. "I thought you had escaped out the back door so you wouldn't have to be troubled by us today," he teased.

"I'm sorry," she said, her voice soft and clear. "I couldn't leave till I cleaned up the mess I made. Violet works the crowd alone when I'm gone, and the added work would not have been fair."

Her face was full of strength, shining with a steadfast and serene peace. He realized that he felt hope when he was around her. Things didn't look so bleak. She laughed softly at Rose's gaze of happiness when she kissed her on the neck, eliciting soft giggles from the child. Suddenly the morning seemed to be going splendidly.

William turned toward the door without waiting for her to follow. He felt totally bewildered by his behavior. First he was sad at the loss of his family, then happy at having Emily Jane enter his life, then uncertain how to deal with the girls and his slight attraction to Emily Jane. What on earth had caused this tumble of confused thoughts and feelings?

Not since he was a kid had a woman caused so many conflicting emotions. And he'd just met this one. Maybe he was turning into a ninny. A setting hen. It had to be because he'd been taking care of babies. That had to be it. Everyone turned to mush around them. He clenched his jaw and imposed an iron control over his thoughts. Enough. He needed a little time away from Emily Jane to remind himself that she had no power to change him. She did not hold the key to his happiness, nor his thought process. And contrary to what the little old ladies in this town thought, he was not going to marry her only to have his heart broken when she decided that taking care of Rose and Ruby was too much work.

Chapter Six

Emily Jane enjoyed the walk to the store. Rose giggled as they strolled. The twin pointed at a little boy and his dog as they ran across the street. Ruby giggled along with her while William strode in silence. She couldn't help but wonder if he regretted inviting her along. His brows were pulled into an affronted frown, and a muscle flicked in his jaw. She didn't know him well enough, so she couldn't decide if he was angry or contemplating some deep subject.

The bell jingled overhead as he held the door open for her. She stepped inside the store and waited for a few seconds to give her eyes a moment to adjust. The wonderful scents of spices and leather filled her senses.

Carolyn Moore stood behind the counter. "Emily Jane, how good to see you." She walked over to where they stood. "Who is this cute little girl?" Carolyn asked, touching Rose's arm.

Rose tucked her thumb in her mouth and laid her head on Emily Jane's shoulder. She pressed her body as close to Emily Jane's as she could. For a brief moment, protectiveness rose in Emily Jane. She realized how foolish that was, considering the store owner was a good friend and would never hurt the child.

"This is Miss Rose." Emily Jane smiled at them both.

Carolyn laughed. "It's nice to meet you, Miss Rose." She turned her attention to William and the child he carried. "And who might this be?"

When William didn't answer but stood with his mouth twisted in a wry smile at Carolyn's teasing, Emily Jane answered. "That is Miss Ruby." Carolyn knew who both girls were, of course, but knew the method of pretend surprise would make the girls feel more comfortable. She was an old hand at winning children over.

"Well, hello, Miss Ruby." Carolyn laughed. "My, aren't we all being so formal today?" She waved her hand in front of her face much like Emily Jane assumed a woman of wealth would wave a fan.

Carolyn's laughter was contagious, and soon Emily Jane's, Ruby's and Rose's giggles joined in. William stared at them all as if they'd lost their minds. Emily Jane couldn't help but laugh harder, looking into his bemused face.

Mr. Carlson, Carolyn's elderly father, called from the back of the store. "Women sure are a funny breed. William, come on back here and let the women get their cackling done." He busily set up a checkerboard that was his constant companion.

"I'd love to, Phillip, but I need to get some shopping done before I return to work here in a bit," William called back to him.

Emily Jane enjoyed the way his voice rose to answer the other man. It was loud enough to be heard but not booming like her father's. So far there wasn't much she'd found dislikable about the man. From his beautiful blue eyes to his full lips. He carried himself with a commanding air of self-confidence, and yet there were times when he appeared so vulnerable.

Reining in her wayward thoughts, Emily Jane pulled her gaze from his handsome face and looked to Carolyn. Being caught staring at William caused heat to travel into Emily Jane's cheeks. She quickly blurted out, "Violet asked me to pick up some coffee for her, too."

The other woman grinned and nodded. "I'll have Amos run it over. He's been pestering us for a job this morning. We use him as needed to run deliveries for us, so he'll be happy for the work. I told him to come back in a bit, so he should return soon."

Emily Jane dug into her purse and pulled out a coin. "Would you make sure he gets this for helping me out?" She handed the money over with a smile and prayer that Carolyn would forget whatever thoughts she had about her and Mr. Barns. Amos and his mother could use the extra coinage, and Emily Jane was always happy to find a way to assist them. "Also, tell him to stop by the house when he gets done."

Carolyn looked at her with a quizzical expression. "We're paying him, Emily Jane."

Relief washed over Emily Jane that Carolyn seemed to be distracted now. "I know, but I want to make sure he knows he's appreciated." And that was the truth. Amos worked hard to help his ma out, and he was growing into a fine young man. For that Emily Jane was grateful.

An understanding glance passed between them before Carolyn tucked the money into her apron pocket and turned her attention to William. "Now, do you need any help with your shopping, Mr. Barns? I know you know where everything is, but with these two sweeties, I'm not sure you will be able to gather up what you came for. If you'd like, I could take your list and gather your supplies for you."

William shook his head. "No, thank you. I'm sure there are more things I'll need that I forgot to put on the list. Luckily, Miss Emily Jane has agreed to help me with the girls, so I should be able to manage for now."

Emily Jane nodded. "I'm going to pick up a few spices, too." She noticed a small wagon sitting beside the door. It had tall railings on each side and the back. Emily Jane pointed at it. "Carolyn, may we use that wagon?"

"Oh, yes. Of course."

She carried Rose to the wagon and set her inside. "Look, Rose. Want to ride?"

The little girl giggled and kicked her small legs. Emily Jane picked up the long handle and pulled Rose to William and Ruby.

"What a great idea." He put Ruby down beside her sister. The two girls laughed and banged against the wagon's sides. He dug inside the bag he had flung over his shoulder and gave both the girls their stuffed animals.

"Those should keep them busy while we get our shopping done." William made his way to the sugar and flour barrels. He pulled a sack from the pile and began filling it with sugar.

She heard him humming as he scooped the white granules into the bag. Emily Jane looked back at the girls, who seemed content to slap at each other with their toys and giggle. Experience with her siblings told her the girls wouldn't be content long. She hurried to help William complete his shopping so that she could get on with her own.

For the next thirty minutes, Emily Jane and William piled merchandise on the front counter while the children played in the wagon. She helped him pick out canned goods that the girls could eat, as well as breakfast foods such as eggs and salt pork.

Emily Jane looked at the mountain of supplies and decided that his basic shopping was complete. William had moved to the men's department, which consisted of ready-made shirts, pants and boots.

Happy to have his shopping done, she turned her attention to the fabric and ribbons. Emily Jane chose yellow and green ribbons to replace the girls' bows. Impulsively, she added matching yellow and green fabric. The girls needed new dresses, and since she was good friends with Susanna Marsh, the local dressmaker, Emily Jane decided to add those to William's pile.

Next, Emily Jane walked to the wall of spices. She needed baking soda, baking powder, cinnamon and ginger to resupply her baking cabinet at home. Thankfully, Levi Westland, the owner of The Bakery, had agreed to let her have a running tab at the general store so that she could practice making various sweet breads, tarts, pies, cakes and cookies for the eatery or she would not have been able to afford all the wonderful seasonings.

Someday she'd have her own bakery. It would be as big as The Bakery and would have round tables with blue-checkered tablecloths. She'd pay extra for a large glass window so that people passing by could see inside. And she'd also find a way for the smell of her freshly baked goods to vent outside and entice passersby to come inside.

The recipes she created each day and passed on to The Bakery were hers, and someday she'd be making them in her own store. She'd need to move from Granite, so that she wouldn't be in competition with Mr. Westland and Violet. Moving was not something she looked forward to doing. Emily Jane frowned, as she wondered once again where she would go.

A loud crash and the sound of splashing liquid snatched her from her daydreams. Twin cries erupted, and a strong vinegar odor permeated the small store, alerting everyone that the children were loose and wreaking havoc on their surroundings. Emily Jane followed her nose and reached the scene of the accident first. Pickle juice spread slowly across the floor. Candy and glass also splayed around the scene. The expressions on the twins' faces made Emily Jane want to double over in laughter, but the seriousness and cost of pulling the pickle barrel over and knocking it against the counter, causing the candy jar to break, could be more of a reason to join the crying girls. She rushed to their side.

Where was everyone else? Her gaze flashed to the front counter. Carolyn hurried through the door that led to their quarters behind the store. Mr. Carlson looked as if he'd just been startled from a nap, and William stood beside the boots, his mouth opened in a quick intake of breath. Surprise and dread had siphoned the blood from his face, and he appeared frozen in his steps.

Rose and Ruby screamed louder as their dresses and undergarments absorbed the liquid. Rose kept lifting one foot as if offended that the sticky juice covered it. Emily Jane lifted Ruby from the mess but held her out from her body, which infuriated the little one, and she curled her legs up trying to wrap them around Emily Jane's waist. Finally she could hold it no longer. Undiluted laughter floated up from her throat and burst from her lips in a great peal.

For a brief moment he'd allowed himself to relax. William had thought the girls were secure in the wagon, and he'd be able to shop without having to worry about them. He'd been wrong. What a nightmare. He should have known better.

He righted the pickle barrel, struggling to maintain an even, conciliatory tone to comfort the girls. "Shhhh." The noise did not cease. He looked Rose over to make sure she wasn't cut or hurt. The candy jar had broken into four pieces, none of which were close to the girls. He sighed as he picked up Rose and held her out in front of him like a sack of onions. He and Emily Jane looked like twin statues; but laughter danced in her eyes, and her lips curled into an irresistible grin. She looked quite lovely, and he found the thought vaguely disturbing.

More disturbing, though, was the racket the babies made; then Emily Jane surprised them all. Her nose crinkled, her lips puckered, and she blew through her lips, making a whistling sound that caused both Ruby and Rose to stop crying. Twin sets of blue eyes lifted to study her face. Their expressions stilled in wonder.

Carolyn ran to them. "Are they all right?" she asked.

"They are fine. Just wet," Emily Jane answered with a grin. "Aren't you, darling?" She wiggled the girl as if gently shaking the moisture from her dress.

"Mrs. Moore, I am so sorry," William began.

She stopped him by laying her hand on his arm. "It's not your fault or the girls'. It's mine. I knew I should have moved that barrel and placed it closer to the wall this morning." She laughed and dropped her hand. "But instead I was going to wait and have you do it this afternoon." Carolyn motioned for him to hand her Rose.

William did as she indicated and handed the wiggly girl over. He picked up the barrel. "Where would you like me to put it?" If the barrel had been full, the girls could never have tipped it over. His job was to fill it every evening; only yesterday they hadn't received new pickles to fill it with. When full, it would have been hard for even him to move.

"Over by the counter." She placed Rose into the wagon. "Bring the other baby over here, too, Emily Jane." Carolyn pointed to the wagon, and Emily Jane waddled to it, the baby extended awkwardly in front of her. Mr. Carlson came from the back room carrying a mop and a handful of rags. "Here, William, take these and wipe the bottom of the barrel before putting it down." He handed William the rags, then went to where the pickle juice covered the floor.

"Thank you, Phillip. I'm so sorry for the mess. Just give me a minute, and I'll come mop up the juice." William wiped the bottom of the barrel and then hurried to where Phillip sloshed the pickle juice around with the mop.

Emily Jane stood beside the wagon. She held their stuffed animals and danced a pretend waltz with them, entertaining Rose and Ruby and keeping the peace. Every time one of the twins reached for the stuffed animals, Emily Jane exaggerated a dip or swayed even faster. Rose began to sway with her, apparently hearing the same silent music. William stared at the scene and admired Emily Jane's intuition. She was a natural. Then why did he sometimes get the feeling she didn't like children?

Carolyn brought him a bucket to wring the juice from the mop. "It's amazing how fast little ones can make a mess." She gently removed the mop from his hands. "Here, I'll clean this up. Why don't you take the girls home and get them out of those wet dresses? I'll have Amos deliver your supplies when he comes in."

Emily Jane reached to take one of the girls from the wagon.

"I really am sorry," William apologized again.

"Emily Jane, leave those babies where they are. You can use the wagon to take them home and not have to soil your own clothes." She turned to William. "Don't give it another thought. Accidents happen. I'm just glad the little ones weren't hurt."

He nodded. "Thank you. I'll be back in a couple of

hours." William took the wagon handle and pulled it through the door Emily Jane held open.

"I need to go pay for my things," she said when he had passed the threshold.

William nodded. Her voice sounded tight. He hesitated, blinking with bafflement. Hadn't she just appeared happy, dancing around the girls? But if he could garner a guess, he'd say she wasn't happy now. "I'm sorry we ruined your morning."

"Nonsense. Let me go pay for my things, and I'll help you get the girls cleaned up." Emily Jane shut the door behind her as she reentered the store.

He pulled the girls toward home. The older they got, the harder it was to take care of them. Emily Jane had tried to sound cheerful when she'd offered to help clean up the girls, but he could tell the incident had upset her.

Maybe she felt he'd taken advantage of her kindness. Maybe he had.

William's thoughts were full and troubled as he looked back at the little girls. They were happy to be riding in the wagon, and their big eyes darted from left to right, taking in their surroundings, completely unaware of the trouble they'd just caused. He sighed.

As soon as he could find someone else to watch them, he'd put some distance between himself and Miss Rodgers. He wanted to remain friends with her but feared the girls' antics would only make her feel used, and William didn't want that.

He had only a little over an hour, and the girls needed a bath and fresh clothes. Thankfully, he'd rinsed out their other two dresses the day before and they were cleaner than what they wore now. There was no time to warm up bathwater for them, so the girls would have to do with a quick wipe down with a wet cloth.

"Mr. Barns! Wait!" Emily Jane called.

William pulled the wagon to a stop and paused for her.

When she caught up to him, Emily Jane said, "I thought you would wait for me."

"Oh, I figured you'd had enough of us by now. And I have to get these two pickles home and cleaned up before I bring them over to your house." He offered her a smile.

Emily Jane looked at the two girls. "That's why I stopped you. I always have hot water on the back of the stove."

Her sweet smile gave him hope that with her help, he'd learn how to take better care of the girls. A hope that died almost as swiftly as it had arrived. He should have been watching the girls at the store. What if Emily Jane helped him clean the girls now and then decided they were more work than she'd anticipated? What would he do then? Who would watch them?

The wheels of the wagon crunched on the dirt and rocks as he fell into step beside her. "Well, thank you. I know we've taken up most of your day, and I hadn't meant for that to happen."

His voice washed over her like a soothing balm. What was it about this man that made her want to help him? Was it his warm, caring voice, his brilliant blue eyes or the fact that he held an injured air about him? Emily Jane transferred her gaze to him. "You're welcome." She held the door open to the house and watched as he lifted the wagon onto the front porch. The muscles in his arms bulged, revealing the outward strength he possessed.

"I'm going to have to get me one of these," he said, stepping onto the porch and then pulling the wagon past her into the sitting room.

Emily Jane laughed. "I'm sure Mr. Westland will have one or maybe can make you one." She brushed around him and the girls and walked to the kitchen.

The wagon squeaked along behind her. "I hope so, but it looks like it will be this afternoon before I can get by there."

"I'll go get fresh towels and soap. Go ahead and take the girls to the kitchen." She hurried to her bedroom to gather what she'd need to get the girls clean again.

When she entered the kitchen once more, William and the girls waited patiently. Emily Jane knew the tots were getting sleepy and hoped the bath would revive them enough to eat lunch. She'd put them down for a nap later. She set the soap and towels down beside the sink, pulled an oversize tub from under the cabinet and began filling it with hot and cold water. Thankfully, the bucket of water she'd had heating on the stove wasn't too hot.

As she lathered the washcloth with the bar of soap, William pulled the little girls' dresses off. Emily Jane straightened and reached for the first child. "Let's give whoever you have ready a good scrubbing."

William handed over a smelly little girl. She kicked

her legs, revealing the birthmark behind her right knee. "Here you go. She's all yours."

"Come along, Rose. Let's get this pickle smell off you." Emily Jane set the little girl into the water. The sweet smell of lavender-scented water filled the air.

Rose giggled and splashed.

"Where should I put these?" William asked, holding up Rose's and Ruby's dresses and diapers. He crinkled his nose at the strong vinegar scent that floated from the garments.

"There is a washbasin just outside the back door. Drop them in it." While William took care of the soiled clothes, Emily Jane quickly began cleaning the little girl's face, arms and legs. She washed Rose's hair and then wrapped her up in a fluffy towel.

William reentered the room, and Emily Jane handed him Rose and picked up Ruby. She quickly dunked her into the warm water and proceeded to bathe her.

"You are very fast. I figured this would take a while." He held Rose close to his chest and inhaled the lavender fragrance of the soap.

Rose tittered and kicked her little feet within the soft towel.

"I've had lots of practice," Emily Jane answered as she poured water over Ruby's head, rinsing the soap from her hair. "Normally, I'd let them play in the water for a few minutes, but this tub is very small and the water will cool fast. I don't want them catching a cold." She picked up another towel and scooped Ruby from the water.

"Mrs. Orson mentioned you come from a large family."

So the neighbors had been talking about her. Emily Jane wasn't surprised. She was curious about what they'd said. "What else did Mrs. Orson have to say?" With the used washcloth, Emily Jane wiped pickle juice off the boards in the wagon, then gently lowered Ruby into it, still wrapped in the towel. She flinched at the sharpness in her voice.

Emily Jane motioned for him to do the same with Rose but kept her eyes trained questioningly on his face. He shrugged. "Not much, just that they thought you would make a good mother for the girls." William took the wagon handle and pulled it toward the door.

Shocked that Mrs. Orson and her friends would be so bold, Emily Jane shook her head. "I am not getting married."

The events of the entire day taunted her and reinforced her feelings on the matter. She didn't want to get married, did not want children. Today she'd forgotten the girls for just five minutes and look what had happened. Children needed constant supervision and care. What if they'd fallen and hit their heads? Or found something more dangerous to get into. The way she figured it, he needed to know that she didn't plan on marriage to anyone. What must he think? Then a shocking notion hit her full force. Had he heard the rumors about her and the other mail-order brides?

Chapter Seven

William heard the conviction in her voice and wondered what had ruined her thoughts of marriage. Wasn't it every little girl's dream to get married? He listened to her footsteps follow him across the house and out the front door. He could be mistaken, but it seemed they dragged a little, as if she were being coerced to come along.

His fiancée, Charlotte, had wanted marriage but not children. William realized now in hindsight that he should have asked Charlotte why she didn't want children. Instead he'd been hurt that she'd broken off the engagement so easily. Of course, Charlotte hadn't loved him; she'd just liked the idea of having an easy life as the wife of a businessman.

He'd been lucky to find out Charlotte's true feelings about raising a family before they'd gotten married. He wanted children, but now wasn't the time to dwell on it. His focus at the moment was the raising and care of his nieces, not on getting a wife and having more children.

He lifted the wagon from the porch and set it on the ground, then drearily headed for home. The girls needed fresh diapers and dresses before he could go to work. His brain was in tumult. He needed to be alone to settle his thoughts. A man couldn't work with things all muddled up in his head.

"You don't have to come with us, Miss Emily Jane. I'm able to dress the girls on my own. I've been doing it for months now." William wished he hadn't added the last sentence. It sounded cold and bitter, most likely due to the stresses of the past few months and this morning's pickle disaster.

He noticed that she walked a few more steps before stopping. He looked back at where she stood and saw that she clenched her hands in front of her. "I'm sorry, Mr. Barns."

He paused, blank, for a moment too startled by her words to comment. Was he destined to be in a permanently confused state of mind when dealing with women?

"What are you sorry for?"

He noticed a faint blush steal into her cheeks. Her shoulders lifted as she drew a deep breath. "I snapped at you a few moments ago, and I shouldn't have." She unclenched her fingers, then twisted them in the folds of her apron.

Before he could speak, she held up her hand.

"Please, let me finish. I am not going to get married. Yes, I came here as a mail-order bride. That is true. But now that I don't have to fulfill that promise of marriage, I have other dreams. Dreams that don't include a husband

and children at this time." She took a deep breath, and her eyes searched his. "Dreams that a husband would never allow."

A window curtain fluttered in the house next door. William caught a glimpse of Mrs. Green peeking out at them. He motioned for Emily Jane to follow him back to his house. "Come inside and we can discuss it further." He walked toward his house and hoped she'd follow. Emily Jane Rodgers wasn't the only one who didn't want to get married, and he needed to tell her so.

He pulled the wagon to his front porch and lifted it up. He scooped a girl under each arm, carrying them like sacks of potatoes. They giggled, and he regretted the action immediately. For serious conversation, he needed them sleepy and pliable; not wide-awake and playful. He entered the house and, with his foot against the door, held it open for Emily Jane. Mrs. Green's curtain fluttered again. William sighed and left the door open, praying it would prevent further gossip and save Emily Jane's reputation.

She walked forward, running her hand over Rose's damp hair as she passed. He smelled cinnamon and apples. She took Rose from his arms and tickled her belly. Rose buried her face against Emily Jane's shoulder and wrapped her little arms around her neck. Emily Jane hugged her close, kissing the side of her head.

"I hope you get someone to watch them soon. Doing so will help the neighbors forget about you and me marrying." She sat in the rocking chair and unwrapped Rose, using the towel to further dry her hair. She motioned for him to stand Ruby in front of her.

Their baby chatter filled William's ears as he hurried to the bedroom to gather fresh diapers and dresses. There was absolutely no doubt in his mind now that, like Charlotte, Emily Jane did not want to take care of his nieces. And just what kind of dreams could a woman have that didn't include a husband and children?

He returned to the living room and scooped Ruby into his arms. While he dressed her, William talked. "I'm not ready to stand up in front of a preacher with you, either." He offered what he hoped was a friendly smile, but it felt more like a grimace to him. "Like you, marriage isn't something I can consider until these little girls' daddy returns for them." He ran his fingers through Ruby's dark curls. He looked over her head to find a probing query in Emily Jane's eyes. He quirked an eyebrow questioningly.

She looked away. "Doesn't it bother you that the neighbors want us to get married?"

William shook his head. He placed a freshly dressed Ruby onto the sofa beside him, then took a wiggly Rose from her. "No. They mean well." He paused. "Well, they mean well for themselves. All they want is for these girls to sleep all night so they can sleep. Can't blame them for that. I'd like for them to do that, too." He pulled a little blue dress with white flowers on it over Rose's head. Maybe if he kept his hands busy, he wouldn't want to kiss the pretty lady who looked so confused and vulnerable right now.

Emily Jane's expression stilled and grew serious. "And after their pa returns, will you be racing to the altar with some lucky woman?"

He felt his jaw tense. She didn't want him for herself, didn't want the twins, but felt she had the right to question his plans? The funny thing was, he found himself eager to answer.

"No. I think I'll take my time in choosing a bride." He raised his head and looked her in the eyes. "I was engaged a few months ago, but when my fiancée learned that I was taking on the girls, she canceled the wedding. Seems she didn't want or need children in her life." William's eyes searched her face, probing, trying to read her thoughts. For reasons he couldn't quite yet fathom, he needed to know if Emily Jane felt the same way as Charlotte.

Compassion filled her features. She sat forward and looked at him intently. "I'm sorry to hear that, Mr. Barns." She seemed to consider the situation thoughtfully. Her head bent, and she studied her hands. Nervously, she stroked the arms of the chair, finally offering a little shrug. "But I guess it was better you found out before you got married."

He nodded. She was right, but it didn't take away the sting of rejection that still lingered close to his heart. "What about you? What is this dream you mentioned?" William shifted sideways and handed each girl their stuffed animals. Both girls rocked, bouncing themselves off the back of the couch.

Folding her hands in a pose of tranquillity, Emily Jane answered, her posture defying her appearance of calmness. Her eyes danced with excitement, and her body movements held a restless energy. "I want to open my own bakery," she blurted out.

He exhaled a long sigh of relief. So that was all it was.

"And you can't do that with a husband and kids?"

Emily Jane answered in a firm voice. "No."

"Why not? Carolyn Moore helps her husband run the general store, and they have a child. Couldn't your husband help you?"

She laughed cynically. She looked at him as if he were out of his mind. "I can't imagine a man willing to help a woman out with her business. Carolyn helps Wilson Moore with his business, not the other way around. And she's still expected to take care of the baby, the house and Mr. Moore."

Rose threw her stuffed animal in his direction. William caught it and handed it back to her. "I see your point, but if the right man comes along, he might be willing to work alongside his wife."

"*Might* is a big word, Mr. Barns. Taking care of children always falls to the wife. No, I'm happy with the idea of not getting married and not having children." Emily Jane stood. "We should probably get these girls over to my house, so you can get to work." She picked up the stuffed animals and the scattered blocks he'd left on the floor earlier that morning and put them in the bag that William had brought into the sitting room.

William loaded the girls back in the wagon. As he pulled them across the street, he considered all that Emily Jane had said. She seemed very sure of her decisions, and that bothered William. She had tarred all men with the same brush. He wondered why. It had been his experience that people responded certain ways because of things that happened to them. Either in the distant past or present. He looked down at her as she walked beside him on the dirt street. She carried herself confidently, her hair ruffled slightly by the breeze. Had someone in her past made her think that a husband wouldn't share her dreams? Wouldn't desire to be a helpmate?

If he were to marry her, William knew that he'd support her in the pursuit of her dream. But he wasn't going to marry her. He wasn't going to marry anyone. Emily had said herself that she didn't want children. Were all women more concerned with becoming independent? If so, did they all want to give up motherhood? Or had he tarred all women with the same brush?

Later that day Emily Jane told Anna Mae about her discussion with William. She shook her head in disbelief at Anna Mae's reaction. Disappointment rang from her friend's voice like a church bell over the valley.

"Please, say you didn't tell him you weren't interested in marriage or having children," Anna Mae moaned. "That isn't something you tell a man, Emily Jane." Anna Mae was starting to sound like her mother.

"Why not?"

"It just isn't done."

Emily Jane placed both hands on her hips. "Why? Because he's a man?"

"That's part of it." Anna Mae stood and handed Ruby the stuffed toy the little girl had thrown over the edge of the pen Emily Jane had created for the twins moments earlier.

"What's the other part?" Emily Jane turned back to

the stove and poured fried potatoes from the skillet onto a platter. Then she prepared to turn the steaks one last time, waiting for Anna Mae's answer.

"Well, men talk to each other. What if Mr. Barns goes around telling everyone that you aren't the marrying kind? Where will you be when you are ready to get married?" Anna Mae walked to the door and took a deep breath.

"He's not going to go telling all the single men that I don't want to get married. Not that there are that many single men here. And even if he does, I don't care. It will save me from having to tell them." She flipped the meat over. "Besides, I don't see you trying to find a man to get married to."

Anna Mae turned from the doorway. "You know good and well that I can't even think about getting married until I'm finished teaching. It's in my contract with the school-board members. Besides, right now teaching is all that I'm interested in. Not men." She picked up Ruby and cuddled her close.

Emily Jane focused on putting the meat onto a platter. Having the children and William around had been fun, but now she wanted to focus on her baked goods. Tonight, after supper and after William and the girls went home, she intended to try a new crepe recipe.

It did not escape her notice that if she were married, her intentions would be out of the question. She'd have children to put to bed and darning to do on their clothes once they were asleep. Not to mention taking care of her husband. How many evenings had she sat and sewn

Father's and her siblings' clothes? Too many. And the worst part was, it was expected.

Anna Mae put Ruby back inside the pen and picked up Rose. She lavished on Rose the same love she'd shared with her twin moments before. Emily Jane wondered what thoughts swirled around in her friend's head. Did Anna Mae regret signing a two-year contract to teach in Granite? She didn't really know that much about her friend other than she had also answered Levi's advertisement for a mail-order bride. She knew, too, without a doubt, that Anna Mae loved to teach and that for the most part she kept to herself when she wasn't at the school.

"I'll go gather the girls' dresses and diapers off the line. I'm sure they are dry by now." Anna Mae set Rose beside her sister, who promptly hit her with a stuffed animal. The two girls giggled and chattered away as if they understood one another, yet neither spoke more than one or two words clearly.

"Thank you." She knew from experience that Anna Mae would be outside for a while. Anna Mae enjoyed walking under the shade trees in the backyard and did so quite often. "Dinner will be ready as soon as Mr. Barns arrives," Emily Jane called after her friend.

"I won't be long." The back door shut with a soft bang.

Ruby pulled up and looked over the side of the pen. Her blue eyes searched the back of the room. Emily Jane assumed the little girl was looking for Anna Mae. Anna Mae had a way with children that Emily Jane envied.

Both Rose and Ruby seemed fascinated with Emily Jane's red hair, but neither acted as attached to her as

Ruby did to Anna Mae. Over the past couple of days, the little girl had bonded with the schoolteacher.

Emily Jane wondered if Anna Mae reminded Ruby of her mother. She couldn't help but be curious about the girls' father. What was he like? And why wasn't he here taking care of the girls instead of William? And what had happened to their mother? But more important, why did she care? Emily Jane couldn't answer the last question. She just knew that she did care, and that in itself was dangerous.

On his way home from work, William couldn't shake his thoughts of Emily Jane. Her pretty green eyes had clouded over with hurt when she'd talked about not getting married or having children. Did she secretly want both worlds? The one where she'd have her own business and the one where she'd be married and have beautiful redheaded babies?

He started up the front porch steps, then paused. He tilted his head, intently listening for what had caught his attention. He heard it again. "Mr. Barns." Anna Mae stepped around the side of the porch, a finger to her lips. She motioned for him to follow her.

She'd caught him off guard, and that made him irritable. Didn't she or Emily Jane worry about their reputations? He walked to where she stood but refused to go around to the side of the house. He looked over his shoulder and saw Miss Cornwell on her front porch watching them intently. William returned his attention to Anna Mae. "What can I do for you, Miss Anna Mae?"

"Shhh," she whispered loudly. He barely refrained from laughing. "For starters, you can keep your voice down. I don't want Emily Jane to hear us." She tucked a strand of brown hair behind a shell-shaped ear.

He decided to enjoy this secret meeting and whispered back, "Okay, what can I do for you?"

She must have seen the humor in his expression because she chuckled softly and then answered, "Nothing. I just wanted to talk to you about Emily Jane, and I don't want her to hear us."

Not sure what to say to that, William waited for her to continue.

"She told me about your conversation."

William cocked an eyebrow at her. He didn't know which conversation Anna Mae referred to but couldn't imagine it was the one about marriage. Still, if it wasn't that one, then why be so secretive?

"Emily Jane told me she explained to you that she didn't want to get married and didn't want children. I think you should know why she said that." Anna Mae looked up at him with big brown eyes. "Emily Jane comes from a very large family and she's the oldest. All her life she's taken care of younger brothers and sisters. I'm sure that Emily Jane is afraid she will become attached to you and the girls, and she's trying to force you away. Please, bear with her. She's just trying to find her way right now. Her father was hard, even to the extent of making her come here as a mail-order bride, so marriage isn't something she's seeking right now. But, please, Mr. Barns, don't tell anyone else of your conversation. I feel sure she'll want a husband and children someday."

William didn't know what to say. What did she think? That he was going to run out and let all the eligible bachelors in Granite, Texas, know that Miss Emily Jane Rodgers didn't want to get married? Seriously, what kind of men had these two women been dealing with? He shook his head. "Of course not."

She visibly relaxed and sighed at the same time. "You have no idea what this means to Emily Jane."

Why did he get the feeling Anna Mae was the one afraid of losing out on marriage and children? Was she trying to protect her friend from what she feared would happen to her? So many questions had troubled his mind today that William's head began to pound.

She stood before him with her hands clasped over her apron. "Thank you."

"Miss Anna Mae, I think you should know that I'm not looking for a wife or a mother for the girls." William watched her face. Anna Mae seemed to have that same look that the neighbor women had presented. She didn't believe a word he'd just said.

When she didn't reply to his statement, William pressed on. "If that is all you needed, I should go inside and get the girls."

Anna Mae smiled. "Emily Jane fixed steak and potatoes. You are in for a real treat tonight. She really is an excellent cook." She turned to go back around the house.

"Miss Anna Mae," he whispered after her.

She stopped and looked back at him. "Yes?"

"Aren't you coming inside?" He motioned to the front door.

Anna Mae hurried back to him. "Oh, no, not that way. I'm going to grab the girls' clothes off the line and come through the back door. Remember, don't mention our conversation to Emily Jane." She turned and walked away again before he could respond.

William retraced his steps to the front door. He waved to Miss Cornwell to let her know he was aware of her curiosity. She lifted her hand in return, then stomped into her house.

Women, at least the women in Granite, struck him as an odd bunch. They were nosy, secretive and stubborn. He started to knock on the door, then paused as something Anna Mae had said struck him as odd.

So, Emily Jane's father had forced her to answer the mail-order-bride ad. Why would a man do that to his daughter? Was he the reason she was against marriage? The throbbing in his head grew. William raised his hand once more and knocked on the door.

He fought the feeling of protection that welled up in him thinking that Emily Jane had been forced to answer an ad to marry a man she'd never met. Who did that to their daughter? Did her father realize the emotional damage he'd inflicted on her? William couldn't wrap his mind around any possible reasoning the man might have had. He shook his head. Why was he wasting time on something that was none of his business and he couldn't fix even if it were? He reminded himself that his sole responsibility was to Rose and Ruby. He couldn't allow himself to dwell on Emily Jane and her feelings.

Chapter Eight

Emily Jane met William at the door with a child on each hip. "I hate to rush you away, Mr. Barns, but I have extra baking to do tonight, so I've packed your dinner and the girls' dinner for you to take home." Her stomach muscles tightened at the startled look on his face. Would he be angry that she was sending them away?

Guilt hit Emily Jane like a baker kneading dough. After Anna Mae had left to get the clothes, Emily Jane had decided she couldn't stand the idea of having another meal with William and the girls. She needed to put distance between them. She couldn't change her feelings this far into realizing her dreams, and she didn't plan to do anything that might make her have feelings for William or the twins. Being in repeated close proximity might cause that to happen. At least, her heart seemed to warn her it could be a possibility.

"Uh, thank you." William reached for Ruby.

Once the child was on his hip, Emily Jane handed

him the girls' bag. "I'll carry Rose and the food basket over for you."

William nodded. As they crossed the street, he said, "Look, Miss Emily Jane, if fixing dinner for us is too much, you don't have to do it. I'm sure I can take care of the girls' meals." He opened the door to his house and set Ruby and the bag inside the door before reaching for Rose.

Emily Jane sighed. "Fixing the meal is no trouble, Mr. Barns. I just need to work and thought this would be easier on both of us." She backed away, unable to break some invisible bond his warm blue eyes seemed to hold over her.

"Well, thank you for taking care of the girls today. I..."

Emily Jane didn't let him finish. She turned to leave before he could ask her to help with the children tomorrow. Closing that door of opportunity firmly, she waved goodbye over her shoulder and hurried across the street, calling out, "You're welcome. Good night."

She burst into her house with the finesse of a raging bull. Her heart beat loudly in her chest. She panted like an overheated puppy. What was wrong with her? She placed an unsteady hand against her heart to calm its wild pounding. Since when did she run from men and little children?

"Well, that was interesting." Anna Mae stood observing from the kitchen doorway.

"What?" Emily Jane knew she failed miserably at acting casual. She pushed her hair out of her eyes and walked toward her roommate and friend.

Anna Mae moved aside and allowed her to pass. "Watching you rush him out of here like the house was on fire." She paused, giving her next question more weight. "Why did you do that?"

Should she give Anna Mae the same excuse she'd given William? It wasn't a lie. She did have work to do. Emily Jane hurried to set the table, avoiding Anna Mae's gaze. "I don't want to get attached to them, Anna Mae. And you know why?"

"Because you are afraid to fall in love and have a family? Afraid it will mess up your plans of owning your own bakery?" Anna Mae set two glasses on the table and filled them with cold milk she'd pulled from the root cellar.

"No, I'm not afraid to fall in love and have a family. I'm choosing not to fall in love and have a family. There is a difference. And if I don't fall in love and have a family, then I don't have to be afraid of never owning my bakery." Emily Jane slid into her chair and waited while Anna Mae said a quick prayer over their evening meal.

Anna Mae began to eat in silence. Her quietness made Emily Jane pick at her food and wiggle about in her seat. She hated when Anna Mae used her schoolteacher approach against her.

It wasn't just about falling in love and having a family. It was also about having a man like her father in her life who took away all possibilities of being independent. Emily Jane pressed on, explaining further. "Really, Anna Mae, I don't need a man in my life right now." She'd begun to sound like a little girl again; Emily Jane hated that sound.

"I didn't say you did. What I am saying is that that man needs help with those little girls, and for some reason the good Lord has put you in his path." She gave Emily Jane the "don't interrupt" look before continuing. "Mr. Barns told me himself that he is not looking for a wife. So, relax." She laid her fork down. "All he's asking from you is that you help with the girls."

Emily Jane wondered how much the good Lord had to do with it and how much the neighbors had to do with it. She sighed and took a sip of milk. If Mr. Barns had told Anna Mae he wasn't interested in marriage, well, then, maybe he wasn't. She sure hoped that was the case. Either way, it was time to change the subject. "How was school today?"

"All right, I guess. Mr. Sorrow came by and said that Matt wouldn't be attending any longer. He has a field to help take care of." She picked up her plate and carried it to the slop bucket. "You would think he'd be more interested in Matt's education. The boy doesn't want to be a dirt farmer like his father."

Anna Mae continued to discuss her students. Emily Jane listened, thankful that the schoolteacher's mind had been diverted from her and the Barns family. While Anna Mae talked, they worked together to straighten the kitchen.

Once the kitchen was clean, Emily Jane changed her mind about making the crepes and gathered ingredients to bake a batch of sticky buns. Making the buns always made her feel better, and right now she needed to feel better. About herself. Regret troubled her mightily for sending William and the girls away.

"I think I'll go read for a while," Anna Mae said.

Emily Jane nodded as she mixed the ingredients for the batter. It would take about an hour and a half for the dough to rise. Her mind, already on the prospect of making a fresh batch of yum yum cookies, wandered back to her reaction to William and the girls. Was she being silly? All he'd ever asked her to do was watch the girls. Why, he'd never even flirted with her. Why on earth did she keep thinking he wanted to marry her?

Emily Jane covered the top of the dough with a cloth and then mixed ingredients for the yum yum cookies. She beat the whites of two eggs to a stiff froth, then gradually added a cup of sugar, a heaping cupful of desiccated coconut and two heaping teaspoons of arrowroot. As she worked, Emily Jane knew she'd need to apologize to William for her rude behavior. She buttered a large baking pan and dropped teaspoons of dough about an inch apart onto the pan. When the pan was full she dusted her hands together and slid the cookies into the oven.

While they baked, she vigorously cleaned the kitchen again, driven by some need to work out her problems with manual labor. She tried to reason out why she'd behaved the way she had. Why did she feel threatened every time she thought of marriage and having a family?

Emily Jane sighed. She didn't want to marry a man who would dictate her every move. Her father was that sort of man. When he'd overheard her and her mother talking one evening over a plate of sticky buns about Emily Jane's dream of owning a bakery, he'd laughed and told her that no self-respecting husband would allow his woman to work outside the home. Shortly after that, Pa had tossed a newspaper in front of her and told her it was time she found a husband. It had hurt when he'd continued to tell her that he had enough mouths to feed and she'd need to make her own way now.

Emily Jane wiped down the table. It had hurt so much more when her sweet mother had stood beside her husband and pointed at Levi Westland's mail-order-bride ad, telling her Mr. Westland would probably make her a fine husband. Her parents had more or less abandoned her after that. In the days that had followed, they'd spoken very little to her; had even given her chores to her younger sisters, making Emily Jane feel unwanted and unnecessary. Just thinking of that time shattered her insides and jabbed at her confidence. At the end of two weeks she'd known it would not improve if she stayed. She'd answered the ad and received a letter from Mrs. Westland. Levi's mother had promised if Emily Jane would come to Granite, Texas, she'd make sure Emily Jane found a good husband. She'd left the day after the letter arrived, and her family had not contacted her since.

Thankfully, though, Levi Westland had chosen Millie Hamilton for his bride, leaving Emily Jane free to pursue her dream of owning her own business and giving her freedom from marriage. She glanced at the kitchen clock and then checked on her cookies. Pulling them from the oven, Emily Jane wished her mother were there to share them. The old saying must be true. A child never stopped desiring the love of a mother, even when that mother cut your heart to shreds.

She sought to erect a wall between herself and the emotions rioting through her. She quickly put the cookies on a cooling rack and placed more on the pan to bake. Well, she'd chosen the wrong recipe tonight. Yum yum cookies were her mother's favorite. How could she help but think of her? Had her mother taken over the cooking at home?

At a young age her mother had given the three oldest daughters permanent chores. Emily Jane cooked and baked, Sarah did the laundry and Elsie taught the little ones to read and write. The two oldest boys worked the fields with their pa. Ma probably took care of the cooking now, if she wasn't expecting again. The baby, Nellie, was two, so it was about time for Ma to have another child. The last two pregnancies had left Ma so weak she couldn't do much of anything but sit in her chair and sew.

Tears pricked the backs of Emily Jane's eyes and slipped from the corners. She'd suffered a great loss. She missed her family. She dashed tears away with the back of her hand and grabbed a plate. There was no time for weeping over her lost family. She plucked warm cookies from the cooling rack and put them on the plate. It wasn't William and the girls' fault that her family had abandoned her, and it was time she apologized for her rude behavior to them. She headed to the door, silently praying that William wasn't a man who would make her beg for his forgiveness.

* * *

William sat on his porch relaxing. The squeak, squeak of the rocker lulled him to a peacefulness that had been lacking the past couple of months. After dinner, Rose and Ruby had gone to bed with no muss or fuss, the house was fairly clean, and the evening breeze felt cool on his smooth, freshly shaven face. This was the good life, as far as he was concerned. What more could a man want than a full stomach, a happy family and a rocking chair for evenings just like this one? His gaze moved to the house across the street. He sighed.

A woman moved about the kitchen, the lamplight casting long, eerie shadows. A few minutes later he watched a light come on in one of the back rooms. William assumed Anna Mae lit the lamp in the back of the house since he could still see movement in the kitchen, and he'd learned already that the kitchen was Emily Jane's domain.

His full stomach proved she was a fine cook. He'd really overdone his share of eating tonight. The steak had been done to perfection, the potatoes were tender, and she'd added a pudding that had teased his sweet tooth to distraction.

William's thoughts returned to the red-haired, freckled woman across the street. What would she be like if she ever lowered her guard around him? He yawned. He'd probably never know, especially if someone else stepped forward to take care of the girls.

Right before he'd left work, he and Wilson had hung two posters outside the general store. William thought back to the words on the paper. *Help Wanted: Some-*

one to watch twin girls, age one. Contact Mr. William Barns inside.

Would anyone answer his ad? And if they did, would he be able to trust them with Rose and Ruby? He ran a palm over his tired eyes. The girls were a handful. William worried an older woman would quit as soon as she started. He hoped a young woman would answer his cry for help.

He looked up and was surprised to see Emily Jane crossing the dark road. What was she doing out this late in the evening? Had she come for her basket? William thought about standing when she arrived at the bottom of the steps but was too weary to do so. "Good evening, Miss Emily Jane."

Emily Jane jumped but managed to catch the plate she carried before it hit the ground. William realized that his chair sat back in the shadows and she probably hadn't seen him. "I'm sorry I startled you."

"No, it's all right. I'm the one who came to say I'm sorry." She stepped up on the porch and leaned against one of the railings.

William used his boot and set the rocking chair into motion. "What do you have to be sorry about? Dinner was excellent and the girls were happy when I picked them up. A man can't ask for much more than that."

Emily Jane stood with her back to the moonlight. A halo of silver encircled her head. William couldn't see her face very well in the shadows and wondered if the moonlight would bring out the freckles across her nose.

She cleared her throat as if nervous or preparing to say something difficult. "I shouldn't have rushed you and the girls away this evening. That was very rude of me, and I apologize." Emily Jane bowed her head and fiddled with her apron.

William noted the sound of submission in Emily Jane's voice and for reasons unknown to him didn't like it one bit, nor the slumped stance she'd taken. He preferred the woman who looked him in the eyes and spoke her mind. The little redhead should be expressing herself in a confident way, not like a whooped puppy cowing behind her master.

He stood and walked over to her. Placing a hand under her chin, William raised her head so that he could see into the depths of her eyes. Just as he expected, defiance and shame warred for dominance. They were there in her eyes for him to see.

In a soft voice he offered, "You do not owe me an apology, Emily Jane." For a brief moment, he wondered if Anna Mae had made her feel bad about her treatment of him and the girls this evening. He shook off the thought. Still holding her head up so that he could look her in the face, William continued. "You said you had work to do. That was good enough for me." He caressed her cheek with his thumb, then gently released her chin.

Surprise and relief crossed her face. She opened her mouth to say something and just as swiftly snapped it shut. She seemed confused that he'd given her permission to be herself.

William sank back down in the rocking chair. "Would you like to sit for a spell?" he invited, pointing to a second rocker.

Emily Jane held out the plate for him to take before

sitting down. "I hope you like yum yum cookies," she said when he took the plate, "because that's all I have for a peace offering." Emily Jane tucked her skirt under her legs and then set the chair to rocking.

"I like all cookies." William lifted the towel that covered the confections and pulled one out. He balanced the plate on his knee and then took a big bite from the sweet treat. The rich flavors teased his taste buds, and he closed his eyes and made a noise in the back of his throat. "Ummm, ummmm."

Emily Jane smiled. "Sounds like you enjoy eating my cookies."

"It is a very good yum yum. I'm not sure there will be any left to share with the girls in the morning." He popped the last of his cookie in his mouth and reached for another.

She shook her head, causing him a moment's pause in praising her more for her cooking. Why did women tell you with their eyes that they loved the attention you gave them but with their mouth and actions say something entirely different?

"You really should start making them eggs and bread for breakfast. They are eating way too many sweets."

"Can I help it if they are like their uncle William and love your cookies?" He finished off the second treat with a flourish.

"Yes. You are the adult." Emily Jane realized what she'd said and slapped a hand over her mouth.

He took one look at her face and burst out laughing. "There is the woman I like to see. You're right. I need to fix them healthier meals."

"Oh, Mr. Barns, I am so sorry. I spoke out of turn."
Emily Jane stood.

William reached out and grabbed her hand. "Please,
don't leave." Her wrist felt warm in his hand. He could
feel her pulse as her heart pumped.

Emily Jane turned and looked back at him. In the
shadowy darkness his blue eyes beseeched her to stay.
She realized it was time that they had a talk. For as
long as she watched the girls, they would, of necessity,
be spending time together. Emily Jane wanted to make
sure he understood her reasons for not wanting marriage and children. She sat back down.

"I put up an advertisement today." He set his rocker
into motion once more. "As soon as a suitable person
applies, you will be free from taking care of the girls."

His voice sounded dejected, almost hurt that she didn't
want to keep the girls. Emily Jane wanted to reach out
to him, to explain, but where did she start? She'd never
even sat on a porch with a man, much less spoken inti-
mately with one. And to her way of thinking, speaking
about marriage to a man, either for or against it, was
certainly intimate. Her head was puzzled by the new
thoughts. Why had it worried her so much that he might
be upset at her rudeness earlier in rushing him from the
house? She'd used a firm tone many times with men to
get them out of The Bakery or to spur her dad or uncles
into gathering wood for the stove. Pensively, she looked
into the darkness. She had to admit, though, it had bothered her greatly.

A firefly blinked in the front yard, interrupting her

musings. She watched several others join it. The insects always brought her comfort. She sighed. "Mr. Barns, it's not that I want to be free of the girls. They are actually very sweet."

"Is it because you have work to do that you don't want to continue watching them?" he asked.

"No, it's more like I grew up with lots of little brothers and sisters and, for the past few months, have enjoyed not having to take care of them. I know the neighbor ladies suggested you marry me, and just today they suggested again that I should offer to marry you, too. But I am not ready for marriage or having children. For the first time in my life, I feel free." Emily Jane looked in his direction.

William stared out across the yard, watching the fireflies, too. Did he ever think about the days before he took over the care of the twins? Was he missing his freedom now?

"Will you ever want to get married and have children of your own?" he asked, his head turned to look at her, and his eyes held Emily Jane's.

The deep sea-blue pulled her in, leaving her feeling breathless and warm at the same time. "I don't know. I've been taking care of children since I was five years old. Surely God has other plans for my life besides being a mother and a wife."

A soft chuckle drifted toward her. "Some women believe that being a mother and wife is what God plans for them to do."

Emily Jane nodded, her eyes searching his face, trying to probe into his thoughts. "Yes, but God has different plans for different people. Wouldn't you say so?"

"I would. Marriage isn't for everyone." He released her gaze and looked out over the yard again.

She detected a hint of sadness in his voice and something stirred within her. She knew about his fiancée but couldn't help wondering if the right woman came along, would William offer his heart to her.

He tucked his hand under the cloth and pulled out another cookie.

Was he eating for comfort? Or simply giving his hands something to do? He'd said Charlotte, his fiancée, had left because of the girls. To make him feel better, Emily Jane said, "You know, you aren't going to have the girls forever. Surely their father will come get them, and then you'll be free to find a woman who wants children and can get married."

"True, but like you, Charlotte had other plans for her life and they didn't include having my children. Who's to say that the next woman I want to marry doesn't feel the same way? No, I think I'll just keep my heart to myself for the time being." He looked at her and winked. "Less chance of it getting broken that way."

William tried to make light of the conversation, but she saw in his eyes that he felt rejected and unloved. Emily Jane said the first thing that came to her mind. "She must not have loved you." Immediately she realized she'd spoken aloud. "I'm sorry. That was rude."

William turned and looked at her again. "No, you spoke the truth. I didn't love her as much as I thought I did, either."

"No?"

He shook his head. "If I had loved her as much as I should have, I'd have asked her to reconsider and convinced her I didn't need to have my own children. Instead, I let her go. But I still dream of a wife who loves me and wants to have my children. A dream that I fear is hopeless."

Hadn't he said moments earlier that he didn't want to get married? "But I thought you weren't in any hurry to get married."

William laughed. "I'm not. After my sister died, I promised myself I'd take care of her daughters, so first, I have to make sure that Rose and Ruby lack for nothing and are kept safe until their father comes for them. Secondly, before I offer marriage again, I will make sure that I love the woman enough to give up everything for her."

Would he ever find a woman that he loved that much? Emily Jane stared into his handsome face. Was there really that type of love in the world?

Emily Jane admired William. He knew what he wanted and was willing to wait for just the right person. And now she knew he wasn't interested in marrying her—how could he be? She'd just told him she didn't want children. Emily Jane relaxed.

"You know, the girls really aren't that much trouble. If you'd like, I could continue watching them for you while you are at work. I'm sure their father will be along soon to get them." She leaned back in her chair and gave it a gentle push with her feet.

He did the same. The sound of the rockers creaking

on the porch filled the cool evening air. "I don't know, Miss Emily Jane. You have work to do."

Did he want her to beg to watch the girls? If so, it wasn't going to happen. She tucked a wayward strand of hair behind her ear. "Well, it's your choice. Hiring someone new means the girls will have to get used to someone else, and you will have to take extra time carrying them over to whoever watches them. Plus, I'm sure that the one that answers your ad will want payment, where I am happy just to watch them. Like I said, though, the choice is yours." She tried to hide her playful grin.

"Well, since you put it that way, I'll give in and let you take care of them." William couldn't control the laughter that sprang from his throat.

It came out clear, strong and warm. Emily Jane rested a hand against her stomach that fluttered like the fireflies' wings in the yard. There was no doubt in her mind that all the ladies in Granite would be contending for his attentions soon.

Why did that thought leave a bitter taste in her mouth?

Chapter Nine

"Does this mean we can be friends as well as neighbors?" William asked, hoping that the playful, sweet Emily Jane would stick around awhile. Now that she knew he wasn't interested in marriage, maybe she would become friendlier and less stiff around him.

She stood. "Yes, I'd like that. And from now on, you and the girls will eat dinner at our house." Emily Jane smiled at him, then walked to the steps.

William followed her. He stood on the top step. "Thanks for the cookies. I think we should call them peace-offering cookies, don't you?"

Her sweet laughter floated on the breeze to him. "I like that. I think that's the name I'll give Violet tomorrow for the menu. Good night."

"Good night." He watched her until she stepped inside her house with a final wave.

As he turned to go inside, William wished Emily Jane wanted marriage and children. She'd make some man a perfect wife.

But not him.

What he hadn't told Emily Jane was that he couldn't see marriage in his future. Unlike Emily Jane, most women hid the fact that they didn't want a family. He wanted children, and now that Charlotte had proved how easy it was to deceive him about their true feelings of having children, William didn't trust himself to find a woman who was honest and open like Emily Jane had been tonight.

He took the cookies to the kitchen and looked about. It didn't feel homey like Emily Jane and Anna Mae's. His grandmother hadn't been a woman to put up lacy curtains or keep frilly towels lying about. William sighed. He missed his grandmother and sister. Loneliness crept into his chest as he realized he would never have the homeyness of a woman's touch in his house again. He rubbed his chest in an effort to ease the dull ache that seemed to have taken up residence there.

After a restless night, William rose the next morning with a headache and two little girls crying for dry diapers and full tummies. He wondered how mothers did all that they did in a day. When was he going to have time to do laundry, fix meals and make sure the girls were happy?

The rest of his morning was hectic, and by the time he knocked on Emily Jane's door, his nerves were shot. Rose and Ruby seemed happy, but William wasn't sure how much longer he could continue at this pace.

Emily Jane answered the door. Her smile turned

into a frown when she saw his haggard looks. "Rough night?" she asked.

He offered her what he hoped was a charming smile. "More like a rough morning." William kissed Rose on the cheek before handing her to Emily Jane.

"Do you have time for a cup of coffee?" she asked, stepping back so that he could enter with Ruby.

William sighed. A cup of coffee sounded wonderful. Between changing the girls' diapers, fixing breakfast for them and cleaning them up after eating, he hadn't had time to make coffee, too. He rubbed the stubble on his chin. "A cup of coffee would be nice, but it will have to be a fast one."

"Fast cups of coffee are my specialty." The sweet smile sent a fresh appreciation through him for the woman standing beside him. "Come on, girls. Let's fix Uncle William a cup of coffee before he keels over."

His name on her lips sounded like music to William's ears. It was the first time she'd used it, and he wanted to hear it again and again. William shoved the silly thought aside. Lack of sleep made a man loopy in the brain.

Emily Jane hadn't expected him to show up unshaven and rumpled. Were two little girls just too much for him? If so, how had he managed before he'd gotten to Granite? Of course, now that she thought about it, he'd been out of sorts that day, too.

She placed Rose in the pen she'd created, handed her one of the cloth balls and then hurried to get a coffee mug and pour William a cup. "This should perk you up," she said, handing him the coffee.

"Thank you." He continued to hold Ruby as he took a drink.

Emily Jane reached for the little girl. Ruby came into her arms and snuggled against her neck. She hugged the little girl close before placing her in the pen with her sister.

Of the two girls, Rose seemed the most affectionate. She smiled the easiest and laughed more often than her twin. Emily Jane patted Ruby on the head. Later she'd get the little girl out and give her an extra cuddle, too.

William sat down at the table and sighed. "This is really good coffee, Miss Emily Jane. One of these days you'll have to show me how you make it. Mine never turns out this smooth."

She laughed. If you weren't careful when making coffee, you could end up with coffee grounds in your cup; she had a feeling William drank a lot of grounds. "Are you hungry? I'm sure I can put together a plate of bacon and biscuits."

"No, thanks. I took your advice and made the girls a pan of scrambled eggs and buttered bread. They don't eat as much as I thought, so I had lots of eggs for breakfast this morning." He drank from his cup as if he was still washing down the eggs and bread.

Emily Jane turned to pick up Ruby from the pen. Ruby squirmed in her arms, pushing against her shoulder. Emily Jane hid her smile. The poor man had stuffed himself with eggs and bread this morning. No wonder he was tired. "I see."

He drank the rest of the liquid in his cup. "Thanks for the coffee. I better get to the general store." William stood to leave. "I hope you don't mind we are a little early. I wanted to run by the furniture store and see if Mr. Westland has any more wagons for sale."

Emily Jane held Ruby's hands as she tried to walk across the kitchen. Unlike Rose, who liked to cuddle, Ruby wanted down to explore. If Emily Jane guessed correctly, Ruby would be the first to walk. She wasn't as timid about falling, and she didn't cry as quickly as her sister. She laughed. "I don't mind at all. I hope he has an extra wagon." She swung Ruby up into her arms. "We're going to have a good day today, aren't we, Ruby?"

Ruby pushed against her shoulder in protest, wanting back down, but Emily Jane's back couldn't take the bending over any longer. She returned her to the pen. William grinned at the two girls. "They really are sweet little things, aren't they?"

Emily Jane looked at them. "Yes, they are. But, like all children, they have minds of their own and often their thoughts do not align with ours." She offered him a smile. "I wish I could tell you the older they get, the easier it will be, but that's not entirely the truth."

He laughed. "Good to know." William bent down and kissed each of the girls on the head. "Be good for Miss Emily Jane. I'll be back after work, hopefully with a bright new wagon. Bye-bye." He stood and wiggled his fingers at them.

"Bye-bye," the girls echoed, but it sounded more like *bite, bite*. They tried wiggling their fingers like him and ended up poking them in their mouths in cute embarrassment.

William chuckled aloud. "Thank you for watching them. They seem very happy to be here."

Emily Jane hated to admit it but said, "I enjoy having them." And it was the truth. She missed her little sisters, and taking care of Rose and Ruby seemed to ease the loss a bit.

Once he was out the door, Emily Jane went into her bedroom and quickly sorted her dirty clothes. Then she moved into Anna Mae's room and did the same. If she hurried, she'd be able to get them washed and on the line to dry before she'd need to start supper.

"Hey, girls, want to help Emily Jane wash today?" she asked, dropping the laundry beside the front door.

"Go!" Both Rose and Ruby called out at the same time.

Emily Jane walked back to them. "Yes, you get to go. We need to visit Mrs. Matthews for a few minutes." She scooped up the girls, one in each arm, and then carried them out the door and across the street to the other lady's house.

She knocked with her elbow.

A few moments later, Mrs. Matthews answered. "Come in, child, and bring those little darlings with you."

"I really don't have the time to stay but was wondering if maybe you could help me with the girls for a few minutes."

"Sure, Emily Jane. What do you need me to do?" She stepped out onto the porch and took Rose from Emily Jane's arms.

"Do you mind if I leave them with you for just a few

moments while I run over to Mr. Barns's house and borrow Mabel's washtub? The girls are using mine for a pen, and I'd really like to get some laundry done today." Emily Jane blew a stray lock of hair off her forehead.

Mrs. Matthews closed the door and started down the porch steps. "Of course I don't mind. But I'd rather just go to your place to watch them, if you don't mind. I can put them back in their pen and watch them play with those balls I made them." She continued on across the street, not waiting for Emily Jane to answer.

As she followed the older woman, Emily Jane felt a laugh building in her tummy. Mrs. Matthews didn't want the twins to destroy her perfectly cleaned home. Who could blame her?

Emily Jane trotted after the older woman. "Thank you. I promise I'll get the tub and be back as fast as I can." She hurried up the steps ahead of her neighbor and held the door open.

"Don't give it a second thought and don't rush." She passed Emily Jane as she walked inside. "This is what friends do. We help each other." Mrs. Matthews headed for the kitchen, where she deposited Rose into the pen.

Ruby wasn't going to be left behind and called, "Down!" She pushed against Emily Jane's shoulder.

"Hold on, you little darling." Emily Jane eased Ruby into the washtub with her sister. "There, now. You two can play for a few minutes."

Mrs. Matthews made her way to the coffeepot and clear jar full of cookies. "Do you mind if I make myself a snack?" she asked, pouring a cup of the coffee and reaching for the cookies at the same time.

"Help yourself. I'll be right back."

"Thanks. I can't ever resist your cookies."

Emily Jane laughed. "Have as many as you want. I'm off to get the other washtub." As she left the kitchen, she heard the girls yell, "Eat!"

Mrs. Matthews's laughter followed Emily Jane out the door. Emily Jane welcomed the soft breeze that brushed the hair off her forehead as she made her way to William's house. She circled around to the back, where Mabel had always left her washtub on the back porch.

She didn't think William would mind her using it. She hurried to the washtub. Just as she reached for it, she heard a high-pitched whimpering that sent a shiver down her back.

Chapter Ten

Emily Jane crept cautiously toward the washtub sitting on the back porch of William's house. The cries grew louder as she approached. She peered behind the tub, and twin blue-black eyes stared back at her. Emily Jane recognized the little pups as baby foxes. They huddled behind the tub shivering. "Oh, you precious babies." Matted tearstains marred their beautiful dark faces. Their fur had splotches of red within the facial mask and along their bodies. How long had they been crying? And where was their mother? "Where's your mommy?" She cooed and rubbed the tops of their heads. They tried to lick her hands, their tails wagging up a frenzy, feet scratching the sides of the bucket as they tried to climb out.

She searched about for their mother, not seeing her. She looked down upon them and realized they were too young to be on their own. Their fur still had the markings of a five- or six-week-old puppy, but soon everyone would recognize they were fox pups. Her father, and probably most of the men in town, would say to drown them, but that wasn't Emily Jane's way. She gently picked them up and set them inside the tub.

The fox pups whimpered as Emily Jane dragged the washtub across the street. She continued on around to the back of the house, where the well stood. Thankfully, it was sheltered under a large elm tree. Summer was quickly coming upon them, if the heat from the sun today was any indication.

Emily Jane wiped a few beads of sweat from her brow. She reached in and stroked the little foxes' soft heads. A light breeze blew, cooling her brow and reminding her that she had work to do. She stood. The fox pups and the girls shouldn't be too hot while she scrubbed the bedclothes.

The tub wasn't as heavy as hers, but, still, tugging it about had winded her. Emily Jane placed her hands on her hips as she stared down at the babies. What was she going to do with the fox pups while she did the wash? Her gaze moved about the yard. Then to the small lean-to that housed William's horse.

A soft snicker greeted her as she entered the shed. "Hello, little lady." Emily Jane reached out her hand, palm forward, toward the mare.

The horse bumped Emily Jane's hand with her velvety nose. She blew gently on Emily Jane's palm.

Emily Jane rubbed her nose and laughed. "You sure are a friendly girl. Are you lonesome out here by yourself?"

Head bobbing was Emily Jane's answer. "I'll try to come out more often, then," she promised, looking about the lean-to.

Her gaze landed on a small wooden crate against the far wall. "That might work." Emily Jane walked the short distance and picked it up. She turned it over to make sure the bottom was secure. "Yes, this will do nicely." As she got ready to leave, Emily Jane stopped long enough to pat the horse once more before returning to the well.

Mrs. Matthews stood on the back porch. "What do you have there?" she asked, wiping her hands on her apron.

"A crate to put pups in."

"Pups? What kind of pups?" Mrs. Matthews stepped off the porch.

"The kind that need care. They are too young to be on their own," Emily Jane answered, scooping the first fox cub from the washtub and placing it into the wooden crate.

Mrs. Matthews gasped. "Emily Jane, that is not a puppy! That's a fox cub." She placed her hand over her heart as if she'd just had the shock of her life.

Emily Jane would have laughed, but knew instinctively she was about to fight her first battle to keep the baby foxes. "I know, but they are still babies and have no mama to take care of them."

"You mean to keep them?" the older woman asked as Emily Jane picked up the second fox pup and put it with the first. She hurriedly used her apron to wipe out the bottom of the washtub.

Emily Jane noted that both fox pups were girls. "Yes." Feeling mischievous, she added, "Unless you want them."

"Oh, no. Once the men find out you're keeping fox

cubs, there's going to be a town meeting. Take my word for it."

"Town meeting? You're kidding, right?"

Mrs. Matthews shook her head, her eyes saddened as she looked down on the little fox pups. "No, the farmers around here don't take kindly to foxes." She made a tsking noise with her tongue and teeth before turning to reenter the house. "I'll go check on the girls."

Emily Jane hurried after her. "I don't see what the big deal is over a couple of fox pups." She understood the men feared the foxes would get into their henhouses, but they were in town, not out on the farm.

Rose and Ruby stood, holding the side of their washtub. They squealed with joy as the women entered the kitchen. "Up!" the little girls chorused.

"In a minute," Emily Jane answered. She hurried to the clothes that were by the front door and carried them to the back door. Then she returned to pick up Ruby.

"What are you doing now?" Mrs. Matthews asked.

Seeing the perplexed look on the older woman's face, Emily Jane answered, "I'm going to put the girls in the lighter washtub and do the wash in ours. That way when I'm all done, I'll be able to get the girls back into the house without having to disturb you." She smiled so that Mrs. Matthews wouldn't think she was ungrateful for her aid.

"Here, let me help." She scooped up Rose and the toys.

Emily Jane grabbed the quilt that cushioned the bottom of the metal tub. She followed Mrs. Matthews back outside. The older woman stopped beside the tub and waited for her. Rose looked like a kitten trying to crawl over Mrs. Matthews's shoulder.

As fast as she could, Emily Jane spread the blanket over the bottom of William's washtub and set Ruby inside. "There you go. You girls have a new place to play."

Mrs. Matthews set Rose down beside her sister. "Are these two ever still?" she asked, placing both hands on her hips and watching as the girls tried to pull up to the side of the tub.

"They must be when they sleep." She laughed.

"Come on. I'll help you carry that other tub out here and then I think I'm going to go get a bite to eat and take a nap." She didn't give Emily Jane time to react, simply headed back to the house.

"You two be good. We'll be right back." Emily Jane hurried up the back porch and followed her friend inside.

Together they managed to get the tub outside and in the shade of the tree. The sound of fox pups whining could be heard on the soft breeze. Rose and Ruby stood on tiptoe, trying to see over the edge of the tub. They had curious looks on their tiny faces, eager to learn what made the noise. Mrs. Matthews frowned in the direction of the wooden box.

Emily Jane sighed. "I'm not going to keep them forever, Mrs. Matthews, just until they are old enough to fend for themselves." The fur babies were hungry. She didn't want to take time out of her afternoon to feed them, but what else could she do?

"That's good to know, dear." She looked at the girls. "I suppose I'll head home now, unless there is something else I can do for you, Emily Jane?" The expression on her face said she was tired and hopeful that Emily Jane was finished with her.

Emily Jane smiled at her friend. "No, you have been more than a help to me today. Thank you."

Mrs. Matthews nodded. "If you need me, I'm just down the road."

Emily Jane waved goodbye and then turned to her wards. How had she, a woman who didn't want to keep children, ended up with four? Two real children and two furry ones? She guessed she should count her blessings. Only one pair had to be diapered. She chuckled out loud. What would William think of the fox cubs? Would he too expect her to get rid of them?

William liked Levi Westland. The man was fair in his prices and seemed to have a big heart for the local business. Thankfully, he still had a wagon for sale, which William was more than happy to buy. He dug deep in his pocket and paid for the wagon and two high chairs.

"If Amos comes by, I'll have him take the chairs over to your place," Levi said, pocketing the money.

"Don't go to any trouble. I'll go by the house and hitch up the wagon." William looked about the store. If he was going to hitch up the wagon anyway, he might as well see if there was anything else he needed.

The store held lots of rocking chairs, kitchen chairs, tables of all shapes and sizes and several chests. His gaze moved to the wall where several wooden pictures hung. They resembled puzzles, only stained and framed.

"If it's all the same to you, I'd like to offer Amos the job." Levi began to sweep at the clean floor.

William remembered that the young boy also helped out at the store, running errands. Wilson Moore had explained that what money the boy made he gave to his mama to buy supplies and food. Amos had brothers and sisters, and the family needed his money. To William's way of thinking, that spoke highly of the boy. He nodded. "Sounds just fine to me."

"Thank you. I'm sure his ma will appreciate the extra money."

He couldn't pull his gaze from one of the pictures. It drew him back time and again. It was a big elk with different shades of colored wood accenting the muscles along its neck and legs. "What's the story behind the pictures?" William walked closer to the wall and reached up to touch the smooth wood. "Do you special-order them?"

"No, they are created right here in Granite." Pride filled Levi's voice. "My wife is the artist behind each one. I simply take her drawings and cut the wood into the pieces she's drawn. Once they are glued into place, she puts the finishing touches to them."

William moved from one to the other. There was a cat, dog, raccoon, hummingbird and mountain lion. The mountain lion's eyes seemed to bore into William's. "They seem so real."

"Yeah." Levi walked up beside him and looked at the mountain lion. "That one is a little too real for my taste, but it is one of our bestsellers." Levi returned to his sweeping.

The dark mountain eyes pulled at William. He had to agree with Levi; it was a little too real for his taste, also. "Well, I guess I should be going. I'm sure Miss Emily Jane has had enough of the girls to last her for a while."

Levi nodded. "I heard she was taking care of your kids while you worked." He leaned the broom back against the wall.

William laughed. "Well, you heard it partially right."

Levi raised an eyebrow and crossed his arms over his chest. "How so?"

"They aren't my girls. I'm their uncle." William walked toward the door. He was sure Levi had further questions but was too polite to ask.

Just as he started to leave, Levi asked, "Has anyone invited you to Sunday services?"

William shook his head. It would be nice to attend. He hadn't heard a good preaching since his sister's death. Taking the girls alone had been too big of a job. As soon as one settled down, the other would raise a ruckus. Since he spent more time outside the service than inside, he'd just stayed at home. But he missed the fellowship. Would Emily Jane be willing to attend with him?

"We meet at nine on Sunday mornings. This Sunday we're having a picnic to welcome summer. You're welcome to sit with my wife, Millie, and me." Levi uncrossed his arms and picked up a dust rag.

"I just might take you up on the offer. Thank you."

He reached for the doorknob.

"Good."

William opened the door, picturing himself, Emily

Jane and the girls walking up to the church on the hill. It felt good to consider going to services again. But he didn't even know if Emily Jane attended church, and if she did, would she want to spend the day with him?

Levi called after him, "Tell Emily Jane Millie and I said hello."

William nodded and then closed the door behind him. How long would it be before Millie decided to visit Emily Jane? How long before the whole town wanted to know his story? Would Emily Jane tell them? Or steer them in his direction?

He realized she didn't have a lot that she could tell. All Emily Jane knew was that his sister had died and his brother-in-law would be coming for the girls. At least, he hoped Josiah would be coming for them.

For the first time since his arrival, William focused on his future plans. If Josiah didn't return for the girls— and the only way his brother-in-law would abandon Ruby and Rose was if he were killed—then they were his responsibility for life.

Did he want to stay here in Granite? His gaze moved about the town. Levi's furniture store was on a side street; if he looked to his right, he could see Beckett's hardware store, the stables and, a little farther up the hill, the school. When he turned to the right, he could see several open lots.

William walked toward Main Street. He passed the bank on his left and a doctor's office on his right. To the left of the bank stood the saloon and once again open town lots. Granite, Texas, had the potential to grow into a much larger town.

He crossed the street and passed the eatery before coming to the general store. William had a few minutes before he had to be at work, so he decided to continue looking over the town. The sweet scent of feed and fertilizer drifted from the feed store as he passed it.

Circling to his right, William looked up the hill and saw the whitewashed church with a tall steeple and bell on the top. What would it be like to attend that church every Sunday? If he stayed, he'd soon find out. A small house sat next to it; he assumed it was the preacher's home. Half a mile from the church sat the sawmill.

He continued on, admiring the other businesses as he went. His thoughts went back to Levi Westland. According to Wilson, Levi owned three of the businesses in town, including the furniture store, Beth's Boardinghouse and The Bakery, where Emily Jane worked.

Levi had made sure to give jobs to the widows in town so they would be taken care of. Didn't the Bible plainly say that we should take care of them? William silently said the prayer. *Lord, if it be Your will for me to remain an unmarried man and help others, I'm willing to follow where You lead.*

He circled back to Main Street once more. As he passed the blacksmith shop, the livery, the jail and finally the eatery, William felt a peace overcome him. God hadn't confirmed that he'd remain unmarried, but He hadn't tossed a scripture back at him that man was not meant to be alone.

William heard the sound of laughter when he arrived at Emily Jane's house. It was coming from the backyard, so he circled around to see what was going on. Emily Jane, the girls and two puppies were playing under the big elm tree beside the well. The pups leaped about the girls, and Emily Jane laughed as the girls squealed their joy.

"Can I join in? This looks like fun."

Emily Jane turned to him with a big smile on her face and dancing in her eyes. The girls stopped their playing and looked to him. Both little girls flashed big smiles at him, also, revealing two tiny teeth in each of their mouths.

The puppies continued to frolic about the little girls, which immediately took the girls' focus off of him. Rose fell sideways with laughter. Ruby grabbed at the nearest puppy's tail.

"The more the merrier," Emily Jane said, turning her attention back to the playing children.

William continued toward them. Where had the puppies come from? He started to ask and then realized that these were no ordinary pups but fox pups. "Emily Jane, where did you get these fox pups?"

She grinned at him. "At the fox-pup store?" she teased.

Didn't she realize the seriousness of the situation? What if their mother showed up? "I'm serious."

Emily Jane squared her shoulders. "I found them behind your house. They were alone, frightened and hungry. So I brought them back here."

Something in her eyes put him on the defensive. "What about their mother? Did you consider her when you brought the pups over here to play with my girls?" He didn't wait for her answer. William scooped up Rose and then Ruby. He carried them like a sack of potatoes into the house.

The smell of beef stew teased his hungry stomach. Rose and Ruby wiggled and began to cry. It was obvious that they were not happy at having to leave their new furry friends. William set them down on the floor and ran his fingers through his hair. The little girls immediately took off crawling toward the back door.

Once more he scooped them up and then sat down at the kitchen table. His heart pounded in his chest at the thought that the mother fox could have returned at any time and attacked Rose, Ruby or even Emily Jane. What had she been thinking?

Emily Jane followed a few minutes later, tugging on the washtub that she'd used for the girls' pen. Her eyes dared him to say something. She took Rose from him and put the girl into the tub. Then she did the same with Ruby.

Planting both hands on her hips, Emily Jane turned to him and answered his earlier question. Fire flashed from her eyes. "Yes, I did think about the fox pups' mother. I don't think she is alive, or she would have been with her pups. They were hungry and ate as if they hadn't eaten in a day. They were also very thirsty. I've kept an eye out for their mother all day, and she never came." She took a deep breath and then continued. "If you think for one minute that I would put these girls in harm's way, you have another think coming, William Barns."

Chapter Eleven

Emily Jane stared down at the man sitting at her kitchen table. Calm blue eyes looked up at her. There was no anger in their depths, only understanding. What did he have to be understanding about? Hadn't he just accused her of not caring about the girls' welfare with his actions? Or had she misread his motivation for picking up the girls and taking them into the house?

"I don't think you meant to harm the girls, Emily Jane. But I also don't think you thought your actions through. A mother fox isn't something to trifle with." He folded his hands in his lap and looked back at her.

She sat down in the chair opposite him. "Look, I know that the mother fox isn't around. I would never have let the girls play with the fox pups if I thought she was."

"I know that. I simply reacted. I'm sorry." He continued to hold her gaze.

"I'm sorry, too."

The girls stood holding on to the rim of the tub looking at the adults. Emily Jane would never hurt Rose or Ruby. William was right; if the mother fox had returned, the little girls might have been injured.

Emily Jane turned her attention back to him. "I won't let them play together anymore."

William's smile warmed her heart. "I didn't say they couldn't play together, but I would like to wait a few days and make sure their mother isn't going to return before they do."

"Aren't you going to tell me to put them back where I got them from?"

He laughed. "Would you do it?"

A smile tugged at her lips. "Nope."

The front door opened, and Anna Mae called out that she was home. Emily Jane answered her call and then stood up. "I best get supper on the table." She walked to the basin and washed her hands.

"What do you think Anna Mae will say about your fox pups?" William whispered across the room.

Emily Jane did her best Anna Mae schoolteacher imitation. She put one hand on her hip and shook the other one at him. "If you think those nasty fox cubs are coming in this house, you better think again." Then she giggled.

"What fox cubs?" Anna Mae demanded from the doorway.

William's rich laughter washed over Emily Jane like warm summer rain over the tulips. She wanted to bask in the sound of it. By not telling her she'd have to get rid of the fox pups, William Barns had endeared himself to her just a little bit.

* * *

The next morning, the bell jingled over William's head as he entered the general store. His boots sounded loud on the wood floor. It wasn't a large store, but it did have most of what the town needed. Unlike his store in Denver. His store had grown as his business had grown.

Carolyn looked up from where she stood behind the counter. Dark circles under her eyes told the tale of a sleepless night. "Good morning." She stifled a yawn.

"Good morning. Little Wilson having trouble sleeping?" William asked as he walked behind the counter and pulled a green apron from a hook underneath it.

She offered him a weak smile. "Afraid so. My little fella had a tummy ache last night."

William tied his apron on. "Is he sleeping now?"

Carolyn nodded and yawned again.

"Why don't you try to take a nap, too? The store is quiet, and I can always call up the stairs if I need to." He picked up a dust rag and headed to the canned-goods shelf.

"You don't mind?" she asked, pulling her own apron off and stuffing it under the counter.

William smiled at her. In the past few months he'd had his share of sleepless nights due to babies wanting to doze in the day and be up at night. "Not at all."

"All right, then. Wilson and Pa are over at the Crawford ranch. They should be back shortly. Thanks, William." She yawned again, gave a weak wave and opened the door behind the counter that led to their living quarters.

The store seemed quiet once she'd gone. William walked about studying the shelves. They didn't seem very full. Was it because people had made a lot of purchases? Or were the Moores having financial problems that prevented them from restocking the shelves? How could he find out without hurting their pride? A man didn't meddle in another man's affairs. He'd make it a matter of prayer, and the Lord would work it out. He had no doubt of that.

He dusted the cans and shelves while his mind worked. He had his own life to figure out. He needed direction. A plan. He liked knowing a bit about his future, and he wasn't afraid of hard work. In fact, he welcomed it. There was nothing more satisfying than accomplishing something and seeing a job well done. So, what was he going to do? That was the question uppermost in his mind at the moment. If the Moores were in financial trouble, would they allow him to help them out? His mercantile had sold for a nice sum of money. Maybe Wilson would be interested in a partnership. If not, should he consider starting another business here in Granite?

Excitement coursed through him. It felt good to consider his options. For months now, he'd lived from moment to moment, without time or strength to think or plan ahead. The twins took every minute of his time, and he fell into bed exhausted each night. But now, with Emily Jane's help, he had time to think on things, and that was important to him.

For the first time in a while, William found himself totally alone in his thoughts. He had needed this time for himself. A broom rested next to the end of the shelf he was dusting. William picked it up and headed to the front with it. He'd sweep the boardwalk and think there.

He opened the door and stepped out into the warm sunshine. The posters he'd put up a couple of days before hung in the breeze. William reached up and pulled one down. Emily Jane had agreed to watch the girls until Josiah returned, so he no longer needed the posters.

Crumpling the papers, William stuck both into his apron pocket. The broom swished the dirt about as he continued to sweep. The sun warmed his neck and shoulders.

"Good morning, Mr. Barns," a young voice called as Amos ran up the sidewalk.

"Good morning, Amos. What's the rush?"

"I was stopping by to see if you all had any deliveries for me."

"Not this morning," William answered, resting on his broom.

"All right. Thanks." Amos stuck his hands in his pockets and continued down the boardwalk. His shoulders drooped, and his boots kicked at small pebbles as he left.

The first thing William decided to do was give Amos a more permanent job, once he decided on a business to open in Granite. He looked to the broom in his hand. "Hey, Amos!" he called after the boy.

Amos turned and returned to him. "What can I do for you, Mr. Barns?"

"Well, I was hoping you would finish sweeping up here for me. I just remembered I do have an order in the store that will need to be delivered." William handed his broom to the nodding boy.

"Be glad to. Thank you, sir." Amos grinned as he swept at the boards.

William reentered the store. The bell jingled over his head. He began gathering up cleaning supplies. His place needed a good cleaning. He'd send the stuff to Emily Jane with a note asking her to keep them at her place until he got off work. The smile grew on his face as he wrote out the order. Amos would earn a little money this morning, and he'd have a cleaner home tomorrow morning.

Emily Jane sat on her front porch with a bowl of dried beans in her lap. She brushed the hair from her forehead and smiled. The laundry was done. The babies were all fed, clean and napping. The warm scent of bread baking coming through the open window gave her a sense of great accomplishment.

She picked a rock from the beans and tossed it into the yard. Her gaze moved to the little wooden box at her feet where the two fox cubs slept. Would the men in town truly be upset if they discovered she kept baby foxes? If they were anything like her pa, they would be.

Mrs. Green's dog barked. Emily Jane looked up to see Amos coming down the street carrying a large box. He seemed to be heading to her house. She frowned. She hadn't bought anything from the general store that needed to be delivered.

"Good morning, Miss Rodgers. Mr. Barns asked me to drop this box off at your house and said he'd pick it up when he comes to get the girls." Amos set the box on the porch.

"Oh, I see. Well, thank you, Amos, for bringing it over. Would you like a cookie or two?" She gave him a smile, knowing he'd jump at the chance to have fresh cookies.

He nodded. "Thank you."

"Good. I'll be right out with the cookies." Picking up the bowl of beans, she continued on inside. First, she checked on the girls. They were curled together like a couple of sleeping puppies. Each had thrust a thumb into her mouth. The desire to reach down and wipe the soft curls from their foreheads overwhelmed her. Resting the bowl of beans on her hip, Emily Jane gave in to the urge and did just that.

Rose smiled in her sleep; Ruby scowled. So much alike and yet, so different. She ran a finger across Ruby's soft brow, easing the frown away.

Careful not to wake them, Emily Jane went to check on her bread. She set the beans down on the table beside the cooling loaves. She'd made two extra for William and the girls, knowing he wasn't much of a cook. Or at least, he didn't seem to be.

Taking a dipper of cold water from the bucket, Emily Jane made a glass for herself and one for Amos. She sipped at the cool liquid, then put several cookies into a cloth for Amos and his family to eat later. Then she chose two more for Amos to munch on now. Emily Jane put everything onto a tray and carried it all back outside.

"Here, let me help you with that." Amos hurried up the steps and took the tray from her.

Emily Jane turned and shut the door behind her so as not to wake the girls with their conversation. "I decided your family might like a few cookies, too. I hope you don't mind taking them home to your mother." She smiled at Amos and returned to her chair.

"Oh, thank you. I'm sure the kids will love them." He sat down on the porch step. "I can't stay long. I'm hoping Mr. Westland has a delivery or two for me to do today." He handed her her glass of water and stuffed a whole cookie into his mouth.

Emily Jane hid her grin behind her glass. Amos was a good boy, and she liked his mother, too. When he'd finished his snack and ambled back down the road, she glanced into the box that he'd set down earlier. A turkey feather duster, sponges, sulfur soap, borax and a washboard rested inside.

It was obvious that William had plans of deep cleaning his new house.

Emily Jane rose and returned to the kitchen. She rinsed the beans several times. She could always tell when cooked beans hadn't been washed really well. They had a dirt taste to them. Tonight she'd set them to soak and tomorrow they'd be ready to cook. A small hunk of salt pork added to them and a cake of corn bread would make a great meal. She couldn't wait till the people with gardens started bringing in fresh vegetables to sell. Sliced cucumber, tomatoes and baby onions would taste so good.

With the beans setting on the table, she headed back to the sitting room to check on the girls. They still slept peacefully, but it would soon be time to wake them. Until then, Emily Jane tiptoed past them and hurried out the back door. She checked the ends of the sheets for dryness, then pulled them from the clothesline.

She carried them to each bedroom and dumped the correct set on the beds. First she made up Anna Mae's, then her own.

Straightening from smoothing the bedsheet, she smiled intentionally. Perhaps tomorrow she'd check on the little girls' beds and wash their sheets, as well. In fact, it wouldn't hurt to check on them now.

Emily Jane tiptoed back through the sitting room, out the front door. She picked up William's box and crossed the street. Would he be upset if she used the products he'd ordered to clean his house?

Chapter Twelve

The house looked amazing. William had noticed the child's wagon on his front porch when he'd arrived home. Now he saw the two high chairs and the box with cleaning supplies in the kitchen. Both indicators that Amos had visited, but who had cleaned his house? Maybe Emily Jane would know.

A few minutes later, he knocked on Emily Jane's door before entering. William wiped his feet on the rug as he waited for her response.

"Come on in. We're in the kitchen," Emily Jane called from the back of the house.

As soon as he entered the kitchen, she asked, "How was your day?"

"Pretty good. Levi had the chairs and wagon I wanted. I was wondering if you'd like a set of high chairs over here, too." He walked over to the girls and kissed each of them on their soft curls.

Rose smiled up at him. Joy radiated from her little face. Ruby studied him with a slight grin. He could tell she was happy to see him, too, but as always, she seemed more guarded in her expression of happiness. He'd be glad when the twins could talk more. It would be interesting to see what each of them was thinking.

"That depends. How long do you think it will be before their father comes for them?" She placed a platter of pork on the table.

William sat down and sighed. "I have no idea."

"I'd hate for you to spend money on extra chairs and then he returns and not need them." She set a bowl of green beans and a plate of biscuits on the table and then turned to get cups and the coffeepot.

"If he comes and decides to stay, he will want them, too. Do you need help with anything?" William asked as she brought the coffee to the table.

Emily Jane stopped and looked at him as if he'd grown horns on his head. Slowly a smile spread across her face, and the dimple in her cheek winked at him. "No, but thank you for offering."

When she smiled and that dimple presented itself, William felt his heart's rhythm pick up a beat. *Get ahold of yourself,* he silently ordered. *A woman's smile shouldn't have this effect on you.* "Do you know if anyone besides Amos went into my house today?" he asked to take his mind off her cute smile.

A guilty expression crossed her face. "I went over for a little while this afternoon."

He fought to keep from grinning at her. "And cleaned my house?"

She nodded, wringing her hands in her apron. "I hope you don't mind."

He couldn't contain his enjoyment at her guilty expression a moment longer and laughed. Once he'd gotten control of himself, William answered, "No, I don't mind, but if you keep doing things for us I'm going to have to pay you."

A slow grin spread across her face. "You three keep making messes like that, and you won't be able to afford me."

This time he didn't try to get control of his laughter. Her sense of humor pleased him to no end. After several long moments, he gasped. "Then I guess we'll have to learn how to clean up after ourselves, won't we, girls?"

The twins grinned happily. Feelings of warmth spread through William. Being with Emily Jane and the twins felt homey and right. He pushed the thought away and welcomed the sound of Anna Mae's voice when she came in and called, "I'm home!"

"We're in the kitchen, Anna Mae," Emily Jane answered.

The schoolteacher entered the room with a smile. Like William, she went straight to the girls and gave them each a kiss on the cheek. "How are my pretty girls tonight?"

Ruby immediately started reaching for the young teacher. "Up!" she said with a big smile on her face. Her black curls bounced in time with her jumps.

William shook his head in wonder. "You know, Miss Anna Mae, I think you are the only person that Ruby is ever that happy to see." It did his heart good to see his niece respond to Anna Mae like that. He'd begun to worry about her. After her mother's death, Ruby had become quieter than normal and seldom smiled. But her happiness at seeing the young schoolteacher gave him hope that she'd revert to her old self soon.

Anna Mae laughed and untied the little girl from her chair. "I'm happy to see her, too." She hugged Ruby close, then turned to Emily Jane. "What can I do to help?"

Emily Jane grinned. "Just wash up. Everything is ready and on the table now."

Anna Mae gave Ruby one last squeeze and then returned her to the chair. It took a moment to get her tied back in, but as soon as Ruby was secure she said, "I'll be right back," then headed to the washbasin on the back porch.

"Go!" Ruby called after her.

William reached over and patted Ruby on the head. "She'll be right back."

Ruby frowned at him. Ruby babbled something to her sister that was gibberish but that Rose must have understood because she mimicked the sound. Both girls smiled and looked toward the door that Anna Mae had just left through.

"She really loves Anna Mae," Emily Jane said, setting glasses of milk onto the table.

Before William could answer, Anna Mae returned and slid into her seat beside Ruby. "See, that didn't take long," she said to the little girls.

Emily Jane pushed Ruby's plate to Anna Mae and Rose's to William. He accepted the plate, knowing the twins would make a mess with the food before prayer time if she'd put them in front of the girls.

"Eat!" Rose yelled, banging her hands on the table.

A wide grin broke out over Ruby's face, and she did the same.

William shook his head at the girls. He kept his features firm as he said, "No, you know we say prayers first."

Both girls bowed their heads and waited. Thinking it was cute the way they responded, he looked to the two women to see their reactions. Emily Jane and Anna Mae had mimicked the girls and bowed their heads, as well.

He lowered his head and quickly said grace, all while fighting the chuckle that wanted to burst forth. What was it about having dinner with Emily Jane, Anna Mae and the girls that filled him with joy? Were they starting to feel like his family?

Before he said the final "amen," William reminded himself not to get too close to either of the young women. He wasn't ready for a wife or love. His only concern was for the two babies sitting at the table. They were his responsibility. There was no time for love or thoughts of love.

"Amen." All four of the females at the table echoed his final word.

William and Anna Mae pushed the girls' plates before them. Anna Mae reached for the potatoes and William the pork. As they filled their plates, Anna Mae said, "Emily Jane, I see you still have the fox puppies." Caution filled Anna Mae's voice as she said, "Emily Jane, you know you can't keep them, right?"

"Wrong. I can and will keep them." Emily Jane reached for the pork as if what she'd just said wasn't a big deal.

"They are so little. How are you going to feed them?" Anna Mae pressed.

Emily Jane finished chewing and laid her fork down. "Just like I did this afternoon. I'll feed them broth and finely chopped meat until they are old enough to eat more."

"The men are going to have a fit." Anna Mae sighed loudly.

"Maybe, but I really don't see where it's any of their business what I do in my own home." Emily Jane straightened in her chair and looked at William.

If she thought for one minute he was going to cross horns with her, then Emily Jane had another think coming. There was no way he was going to argue over two fox cubs. He spooned potatoes into his mouth and turned his attention to Rose, avoiding eye contact with Emily Jane.

"Well, they are still young," Anna Mae commented.

Emily Jane's voice softened. "Yes, and even if I wanted to return them to the woods, they wouldn't be able to fend for themselves. So I've decided to keep them, at least until they are old enough to take care of themselves."

William wiped at the potatoes in Rose's hair. "Don't handle them too much. You want them to be able to adjust to the wild when you release them."

"I won't. Only enough to feed them. I'll also keep them out of sight of the men in town. Hopefully, they won't find out about them, and there won't be any trouble over the little mites."

Her voice sounded sad. William didn't know if it was because she'd have to give up the fox pups or if it was because she had wanted to cuddle them. Something told him that Emily Jane would try not to handle the fox pups too much but would fail.

Anna Mae changed the subject by telling them about her day. It seemed the schoolboys were up to more mischief than usual. They'd locked one of the girls in the outhouse the entire lunch period. Then later in the afternoon, they'd also thought to dunk one of the girls' pigtails in the inkwell only to end up with ink all over their faces. The little girl they'd chosen was quicker and had thrown the contents of the inkwell at them. She had both Emily Jane and William laughing.

Life here in Granite was interesting, to say the least. During his short time here, he'd met Emily Jane and Anna Mae, who were both turning out to be fun friends.

What more could a man ask for? The unbidden answer came to him swiftly. *A warm home and a wife to share it with.* Would he ever have that? Could he ever trust a woman enough to share his home? His life? Even his heart?

Emily Jane walked down to Levi's store. The smell of wood and oil greeted her nose as she entered. Since William and the girls had arrived, she hadn't done any shopping other than grocery shopping at the general store.

"Well, hello, Miss Rodgers. What brings you in here this fine day?" Levi stood off to the side, oiling down what looked like hinges.

"Hello, Mr. Westland. Anna Mae's birthday is coming up, and I wanted to see if you have a wooden box or something else that I can get her." She walked over to a small table that held several boxes.

"Feel free to look around."

"Thanks." Emily Jane picked up each box and admired the artwork on them. They were pretty; she wanted something special for her best friend, but what?

She continued around the room. The animal pictures on the wall fascinated her. Emily Jane stopped in front of an elk. He looked so lifelike that she couldn't help but stare at him. One glance at the price tag told her she couldn't afford it without putting a big dent in her savings.

"Millie outdid herself on him," Levi said, coming to stand beside her.

Emily Jane nodded. "I'm sure some lucky man will be thrilled with him." She smiled over at Levi.

The bell over the door sounded. Emily and Levi turned to see who had entered. William Barns smiled at them. "Hi, Levi. I stopped by to see if you were able to finish the girls' pull ponies."

Levi nodded. "They're in the back. I'll go get them."

Emily Jane wondered where the girls were. "Pull ponies?" she asked instead.

William walked over to her. "Yep, they are little ponies that the girls can pull across the floor."

She frowned, unable to picture what he was talking about.

"You'll see in a moment." He smiled.

Unable to contain the question any longer, Emily Jane blurted out, "Where are the girls?"

"Anna Mae asked if she could take them over to Miss

Marsh's dress shop with her." He shook his head. "She thinks the girls need to be around the ladies."

Emily Jane hid her grin. Anna Mae had mentioned the girls needed new dresses for church. "Maybe I'll go over there, too. I need to be with the ladies more, too."

He frowned.

She laughed.

"Here you go, William." Levi walked over to them and handed William the little wooden horses. One was painted white, the other black. A long light rope had been tied to each of their necks and little wooden balls were attached to their hooves.

He held them out for her to see. "See? Pull ponies."

The door jingled again. Levi turned to help his new customer.

"I see." Emily Jane shook her head. Rose and Ruby were going to be very spoiled little girls if everyone continued to shower them with gifts. Yet Rose and Ruby were sweet girls and motherless.

William studied her face. "Too much?"

"Not at all. They will love them."

"Would you like to get a cup of coffee with me?" William asked.

She hesitated.

"I'll even throw in a piece of pie."

Emily Jane grinned. "Pecan?"

"I'm sure Beth has pecan. Let me pay for these and we'll be on our way."

She picked up a small hand mirror. Butterflies had been painted on the handle. A perfect gift for Anna Mae. As she followed him, Emily Jane asked herself,

What am I doing? She answered her silent question. *Spending time with a friend—that is all.* Still, she worried that they might become more than friends. Would that really be so bad?

Chapter Thirteen

Sunday morning, William plopped the girls into the wagon and hurried toward church. He hadn't asked Emily Jane for her help. He couldn't bring himself to do so, since she already watched them during the week. They'd enjoyed an hour over coffee and pie, but William couldn't see himself imposing on Emily Jane. She'd shared her ideas of coming up with more pie and pastry dishes. Creating recipes and building a recipe book for her bakery seemed to be where all her dreams lay. Taking care of the girls really was an inconvenience to her. Not that she'd say so, but he'd seen the way her eyes had brightened and her voice had sung with dreams of being independent. He sighed.

William looked over his shoulder at Rose and Ruby. They both giggled as he jogged along the path to church. The little ribbons waved as the light breeze pushed their hair out of their faces. They were his responsibility, not Emily Jane's or anyone else's. He loved them and didn't mind taking care of them.

As he hurried to the church, he questioned his sanity in attending the service. How would he keep two little girls quiet? William knelt down beside the wagon and smoothed the black curls on each little head. Rose grabbed his hand and pressed it against her soft cheek. Love wrapped around his heart like a warm blanket. As long as there was breath in his body he would never let anyone hurt them. He would be their protector, their hero. Guiding them, correcting them, loving them would always be his main purpose.

Therein lay the crux of the matter. The most important thing he could teach them would be the salvation story, that Jesus loved them and gave His life for them. And just like he needed help with their physical care, he needed backup with their spiritual care. Therefore, they needed to be in church, and that trumped worrying about how quiet or not they were in the service. As long as their papa was gone, it was his job to make sure they learned whatever they could of church at their age. But, oh, how he wished he'd thought to prepare snacks and a few toys. His determination faltered a few minutes. Then he gritted his teeth, gathered them up into his arms and carried them inside.

Everyone stood with a hymnal in their hands, voices raised in song. William looked about for a place to sit. The little church was packed. Again the desire to return home hit him hard.

Motion caught his eye, and he glanced toward the middle of the pews. Anna Mae signaled for him to join her and Emily Jane. She gave Emily Jane a little shove and whispered something in her ear.

Emily Jane looked his way, and the most beautiful welcoming smile graced her face. With a will of their own, his legs carried him and the girls toward her.

Anna Mae stepped out into the aisle to let him in, and Emily Jane scooted farther into the pew. As soon as he was between them, Anna Mae stepped back into the pew, sandwiching him and the girls in the middle.

Ruby leaned over his arm, stretched toward Anna Mae, and Rose did likewise, reaching for Emily Jane.

Both women took the little girls and offered him more smiles. A hymnbook was thrust into his now-empty hands. Emily Jane's sweet voice rose in song as the congregation sang "In the Sweet By and By." He loved the sound of her dulcet voice lifted in praise.

Rose and Ruby sang out in babyish babble, bringing a smile to his face. His sister would have been proud of her little girls. Their tiny eyes sparkled as they clapped their hands and sang unto the Lord. William exhaled a long sigh of contentment. He'd made the right choice. It felt good.

The final "amen" resounded, and Emily Jane gathered up her purse and Bible. William and the girls had distracted her so much from the service that she couldn't say what the sermon had been about if her life depended on it. If she were truthful, though, with herself, William had been the primary distraction.

Every time she'd inhaled the rich warm fragrance that was the essence of William, her heart had been set aflutter. When he'd arrived, his hair had still been damp.

Now the ends curled around his ears and neck looking as soft as the girls'. Her fingers itched to touch him.

Had she lost her mind? Sniffed too many raw spices? What was wrong with her? Where had those thoughts come from, and in church, too! Emily Jane hoisted Rose up higher on her hip as she walked toward the preacher, who waited by the door to greet them.

"It's nice to see you this morning, Miss Rodgers."

She shook the minister's hand. "Thank you. It's nice to be here."

"I see you have a little visitor with you." He reached out and shook Rose's chubby little hand.

Emily Jane smiled at the shy look on Rose's face. "Yes, this little darling is Rose."

"It's nice to meet you, Rose." He turned to William, who held Ruby. "And you must be the little girls' father."

William answered with a tight smile. "No, sir. I am their uncle, William Barns." The two men shook hands.

"I'm glad you could make it this morning, Mr. Barns. I hope you will return."

William nodded. "I'm looking forward to it. That was a mighty fine message. I enjoyed it."

Emily Jane continued out the door. It was good that he had been able to focus on the sermon even if she hadn't. She saw the little wagon sitting beside the porch and carried Rose to it.

Storm clouds blocked the sun that had shone so beautifully earlier in the morning. She sighed and knelt down beside the wagon. "Rose, it looks like I may not be able to plant my herb garden this afternoon."

Rose pulled herself to the side of the wagon and reached for Emily Jane. "Up," she said.

"Sorry, little one. I have to head home as soon as your uncle William gets out here in case I get the chance to get those seeds in the ground." She pried little hands from the front of her dress and kissed them to soothe the building protest.

"Hello, Emily Jane."

Mrs. Wells and Mrs. Harvey stood beside the wagon looking down on her. She straightened and smoothed out invisible wrinkles in her skirt. "Good morning, ladies. Did you enjoy this morning's sermon?" Where was William? He should have been out already.

"Yes, we did," Mrs. Harvey answered.

"Up," Rose demanded again, latching on to the material of Emily Jane's dress.

"Would you be interested in baking a cake for the women's spring festival this year?" Mrs. Harvey asked.

"Spring festival?"

Mrs. Harvey's eyes grew big. "Oh, that's right. You weren't here last year when we had it. It's the social event of the year."

Mrs. Wells snorted. "Really, Sylvia. That is laying it on a little thick, don't you think?"

"Not at all. As soon as the crops are in the ground, we celebrate with a small fair and a barn dance. It's an all-day event. And the best part is that it's mainly for us women."

Mrs. Wells nodded. "That part is true. The fall festival is for the whole family, but the spring one is for us ladies."

Sylvia Harvey sighed. "Anyway, as I was saying, would you be interested in baking the cake?"

Emily Jane looked from one woman to the other. She wanted to help out but not if it meant hurting someone else's feelings. Violet came to mind. Had she made last year's cake?

"I wouldn't ask but Violet recommended you. She said it's a tedious job that you would enjoy." Mrs. Harvey rushed on. "You see, we ladies want it to be bigger than last year and much prettier."

William chose that moment to walk up. "Good morning, ladies. If you will excuse me, I'll take Rose and be on my way." He hurriedly put Ruby in the wagon with her sister and made his escape.

Disappointment seeped into Emily Jane as she watched him hasten away. Not even a goodbye to her. She sighed. Hadn't she just said she wanted to hurry home and plant her seeds? So why was she feeling as if her best friend had just dismissed her without a backward glance?

William called back over his shoulder to her. "Thanks, Emily Jane, for watching Rose for me. We'll see you tomorrow morning."

"Emily Jane?"

She kept all expression from her voice as she focused once again on Mrs. Harvey. "When would you need the cake?"

"Next Saturday. We'll pay you for it."

Emily Jane forced a smile. "Can I pray about it today and let you know tomorrow?"

Mrs. Wells waved her hands as if to shoo Emily Jane

away. "Oh, sure, sure. Now that that is settled, let's go have lunch. I'm starving."

At first Emily Jane thought they were inviting her to join them, but the two women turned and walked away, leaving her standing, looking after them. Alone and feeling as if she'd just lost her best friend, Emily Jane started home.

Anna Mae was having lunch with one of her students' families. It was one of the small things the community did for Anna Mae. Each week the schoolteacher had lunch with one of her students and helped the family in any way they needed. Anna Mae had been called on to do everything from helping with schoolwork to tending the children while the parents went for a walk in the woods.

Emily Jane normally went home and baked, but today she didn't feel like baking. She had almost made it to her house when the clouds opened and rain began to pelt her. To her astonishment, tears joined the moisture from the sky on her face. What was wrong with her? She enjoyed Sunday afternoons alone. So, why did she feel so left out today?

Thunder boomed, and the force of it shook the house. Rose and Ruby buried their faces in William's shoulder. Rain pounded the tin roof over his head as he rubbed their backs. "It's just thunder and rain." He comforted them in a soft voice.

William remembered his mother telling him a story from the Bible when storms came. He hugged the girls close. "Rose, Ruby, my mother used to tell me a story about a man named Jesus, and how He wasn't afraid of thunder and rain. Would you like to hear the story?"

They snuggled close. With thumbs in their mouths, Rose and Ruby looked up at him expectantly. Fear filled their young eyes, but William thought he could see trust there, too.

"All right." He cleared his throat and began. "Jesus told people stories called parables that taught them lessons. Kind of like the preacher at church did this morning. Then He decided to take a boat ride with His disciples to the other side of the sea. Well, on the way, He grew sleepy." William grinned down at both the little girls. He wasn't sure if they understood the Bible story, but their small faces were less tense from the storm. "Probably from telling stories." Rose wiggled closer to him. "Anyway, Jesus went to sleep on a pillow." William tried to round his eyes and pretend he was scared. "Well, a big storm came. It was so big that the waves from the sea filled the boat up with water. The disciples got so scared, do you know what they did?"

Both girls shook their heads, and Rose fiddled with the buttons on his shirt.

Whether they truly understood him or not was unimportant to William. He continued. "They woke Jesus up." William nodded. "They woke Him up and asked Him if He cared that they were about to die. Do you know what Jesus did next?"

Again the girls shook their little heads.

William hugged them more tightly and continued. "Well, He stood up and scolded the wind, and then He said, 'Peace, be still.' And the wind stopped blowing and the sea calmed down."

Ruby pulled her thumb out of her mouth with a pop. She sat up and looked over at Rose. They exchanged toothless grins.

Like in his Bible story, all was calm about the house. The thunder had stopped, the rain no longer pounded the tin roof, and there was no wind.

The front door burst open, and Emily Jane came running into the house. She stopped long enough to slam the door behind her but screamed, "Get to the hallway!" Without giving him a chance to respond, she grabbed Ruby and ran toward the hall.

William's heart lurched in his chest. He scooped up Rose and followed Emily Jane. "Why are you so upset? The storm has passed."

"No, it hasn't." She thrust Ruby into his free arm and hurried into his bedroom.

What did she mean? Everything was still. Had the woman lost her mind? He focused on the bedroom doorway, while holding his trembling nieces in his arms.

And then he heard it. It sounded much like a locomotive coming down the tracks fast. He remembered the sound. A tornado would soon be bearing down on them, if it wasn't already. Instinctively, William sank to the floor and covered Rose and Ruby with his body.

Emily Jane pulled and tugged the mattress from his bed over them all. "Help me use this to cover us," she ordered, panting from her excursion and fear.

The girls started to cry. William knew they were unaware of the tornado that bore down on them. All they knew was that the adults' faces had turned as white as sheets and that their friend Emily Jane was scared.

William cringed as lumber and tin splintered apart. Nothing had ever prepared him for the horrible sound. Sheer, black fright swept through him. He grabbed the mattress and shoved Emily Jane and the girls under it. He knew there wasn't enough room for him, so he used his body and arms to wrap them safely within the mattress.

Panic twisted icy fingers around his throat. He had difficulty breathing. Would he remain safe till the storm cleared? Would the girls? And what about Emily Jane? He winged a prayer heavenward, even as he tried to keep his body from shaking. *Lord, please save us and Emily Jane. She risked her life to warn me. Please, keep her and the girls safe.*

Chapter Fourteen

In horrified shock, William watched the corner of the roof lift, then slam back down. The force of the wind raised it again and peeled it back a bit farther, then again slammed it back down. Each time it lifted, things in the house flew around, crashing against the walls and floor. Rain and dirt covered his head and shoulders. The wind sucked at him. With his body covering the mattress, he braced his legs and wedged his shoulders against the hall wall. The roar of the angry cyclone sent a chill up his spine. He could no longer hear the girls' cries, and he fought with all his might to hold the mattress over them.

As suddenly as the tornado had hit, it left. Rain flooded through the gaps in the roof. Emily Jane pushed at the mattress, reminding him that he still had her and the girls covered.

He shifted around and, with his arms and feet, pushed the mattress off them. "Are you all right?"

The girls crawled across the floor and Emily Jane's lap

to get to him, their cries tearing at his heart. Their little faces were as white as goose feathers. Fear rounded their eyes. All they wanted was him, and William reached for them, thankful they were alive.

Emily Jane nodded as she helped the girls over her body, sitting up in the process. "You should have come under the mattress," she scolded. "You could have been killed." Tears washed down her beautiful face.

William heaved her and the girls into his embrace. All three of them wept into his shoulders. He looked up into the sky and thanked the Lord for their safety.

After several long moments, Emily Jane pulled out of his hold. Rain mingled with her tears. "I'm sorry. I didn't mean to fall apart like that." She looked around the room, unaware she still clung to his shirt.

He answered as calmly as he could and hoped his words offered reassurance. "That's all right. My shirt was wet already."

The dimple in her cheek wobbled out. "Good. I wouldn't want to ruin your best Sunday shirt." Neither of them missed the shakiness still in her voice.

The girls seemed to realize the immediate danger had passed and finally quieted down. Rose turned to Emily Jane. "Up." She held her arms out, waiting for Emily Jane to do as she requested.

Emily Jane took the baby and held her close. Ruby laid her wet head on William's shoulder. Her sobs were quiet but still flowing.

"How did you know?" he asked Emily Jane as he stood up with Ruby.

She took the hand he offered but proved unsteady

on her feet, so he clasped her close to his side. "I have been here all spring. This is Texas, and you learn real quickly the signs of a tornado."

William nodded. She was right; he should have recognized the signs, but it had been years since he'd been anywhere near a tornado. If she hadn't come, what would have happened to him and the little girls? He shivered at the thought.

"Thank you." With her hand clasped firmly in his, she followed as he led the way back into the sitting room, stepping carefully around broken glass and overturned furniture.

The couch that he and the girls had been on when she'd rushed inside now lay crushed under the chimney. "I think you saved our lives," William said, solemnly.

"It wasn't me, William. It was God." Emily Jane reclaimed her hand and opened the door and looked outside. She gasped. "Oh, dear Lord, no." Her wail scared the girls, and the crying started back up.

He hurried to her side, and what he saw turned his own legs to mush. Her house had been destroyed. Nothing remained standing. Rubble now lay where her house had once been. He asked the question carefully, dreading the answer. "Emily Jane? Was Anna Mae at home when you came over here?" *God, please, don't let her have been home. Please.*

Everything was gone. Emily Jane swallowed the lump in her throat and answered William. "She's supposed to be at one of her students' homes."

"Thank the Lord."

A crash sounded behind them. Emily Jane turned in time to see the back wall of his home fall. They were in danger. The whole house could come tumbling down around them.

William must have had the same thought, because he grabbed her hand and pulled her out the door. Other people were fleeing what used to be their homes, as well. They turned to look at the house that was still standing, even though it had only three walls.

Emily Jane glanced away from the scary sight. Mrs. Matthews stood in the road. She looked as befuddled as Emily Jane felt. Her gray hair had come unpinned on one side, and her dress was torn at the shoulder. Emily Jane hurried to her side. "Are you all right, Mrs. Matthews? You're bleeding. We should get you to the doctor."

The older woman smoothed her hair back with a shaky left hand. "I believe so." Her shoulder hung at an odd angle, and blood slowly seeped through the sleeve of her dress.

Mrs. Green joined them. "It looks like it hit every house in our neighborhood," she cried, holding on to a small picture frame.

A rumbling started, and everyone turned in the direction it came from. Emily Jane gasped as William's house collapsed upon itself. Only minutes before they'd been standing inside; now it was just a pile of rubble like her own house.

His shoulders slumped, and a whoosh of air exited his lungs. "Thank You, Lord, that we weren't inside."

Ruby patted her uncle's cheek. She stuck her thumb

back in her mouth and looked to her sister, Rose. The two little girls seemed as calm as their uncle.

How could he pray so calmly? Like her, he was now homeless. What were they going to do? Where were they going to go? Tears flowed down her face. She couldn't have controlled them if her life had depended on it.

William turned to look at her and Rose. "Houses can be rebuilt." He cupped her face in one large hand and wiped a tear with his thumb. "I'll help you rebuild yours."

"Emily Jane!"

She turned to see Anna Mae running toward her. Panic and fear distorted the other woman's features. Had she seen the house yet?

Her best friend grabbed her and Rose and hugged them close. "Are you all right?"

Emily Jane clung to her. "I'm fine. But I think Mrs. Matthews should see a doctor."

Anna Mae released her and held her at arm's length. Anna Mae ran her eyes over Emily Jane, checking for any sign of harm. Satisfied she was fine, Anna Mae turned her attention to Mrs. Matthews.

"Emily Jane is correct. We need to get you to the doctor."

Mrs. Matthews shook her head. "No, there will be others that need him much more than myself."

Anna Mae nodded. "That may be so, but we'll let him decide who needs treatment first and who can wait." She took the older woman by her left arm and walked away, weaving in and out of the crowd gathered in the street.

Why wasn't she more like Anna Mae? Emily Jane felt helpless at the destruction about them. She turned to look at the space where her house had stood. Crushed like flatbread.

Bread. Her recipe book. Emily Jane thrust Rose into someone's arms and ran to the house. She stumbled over the rubble that had been her sitting room, into what was left of the kitchen area. Even the stove was gone.

Wood and nails tore into her hands as she desperately dug to find her recipe book. Emily Jane ignored the pain. Every recipe she'd ever created was in it. Her great-grandmother's recipes were within the pages of the two-inch-thick volume. Tears streamed down her face in a flash flood. Why hadn't she left it at The Bakery? Her mother had given it to her the day she'd left home.

A strong arm pulled at her. "Emily Jane, you are tearing your hands up. Stop."

"I have to find my recipes!" Emily Jane sounded like a wild woman, an out-of-control woman, but she didn't care. Her life's work was buried somewhere in the wreckage.

"If you won't stop, I'll help you look." He began tossing boards, broken dishes and all other forms of shards to the side.

Everything was broken or torn. Fire burned in her hands. Emily Jane looked down at her fingers and found them bleeding. She'd been unaware of the pain until now. She looked at William, who continued working at her side. What was she doing? Emily Jane placed a hand on his forearm. "Stop. You're going to hurt yourself."

"No more than you. Look at your hands. I know this is all a shock to you, but the book can be replaced."

His compassion and care for her broke through all her defenses. Great sobs tore through her chest. It was gone. Her most prized possession was gone, but she wouldn't allow anyone to hurt themselves over the recipes. "I'll stop, too." She hiccuped.

He pulled her into his embrace. "Cry it out." William rubbed her back as he held her close. Emily Jane didn't care what others thought; she did as he said and wept till the hurt and despair lessened.

An hour later, the rain still came down in a slow shower. People were digging through the rubble of their homes. Some looked lost and forlorn; others seemed to be on a mission to find something personal, just as Emily Jane had been earlier.

She felt Rose wind her small fingers in her hair. "Eat," the little girl demanded, placing her other hand on Emily Jane's cheek and pulling her around to face her. "Eat," she said again.

"I'm afraid you are going to have to wait a little while, sweet girl," Emily Jane answered. She turned to William. "What should we do now?"

He looked about them at the elderly women and a few men who were now homeless. As they waited to hear his reply, the people shuffled toward him. It seemed the tornado had taken out their whole community.

William sighed. "We rebuild."

Mr. Orson stepped up beside him. "Yes, we rebuild. It's what we've done in the past. It's what we will do now. Well said, young man." He pounded William on the back.

Mrs. Orson looked to her husband and huffed. "And while we are rebuilding, where do you expect us to live?"

Emily Jane made a decision and prayed the school council would agree with it. "We can stay at the schoolhouse and maybe the church."

William nodded.

"Are they still standing?" Mrs. Green asked. Her red hat sat sideways on her head and had definitely seen much better days.

"Yes, they are. And you are more than welcome to stay at the church for as long as it takes to rebuild."

Emily Jane looked to the preacher. When had he arrived? It didn't matter; all that mattered was that he'd answered and said the church would house folks.

More and more townspeople joined them. Each person's face reflected the devastation about them. Would they all band together?

Miss Cornwell shook her head. "It takes money to rebuild." A tear ran down her face. "And I don't have it."

Susanna Marsh came to stand beside Emily Jane. She placed an arm around her shoulders. The smell of roses almost overpowered Emily Jane as she leaned close and whispered, "Where is Anna Mae?"

"With Mrs. Matthews. She took her to the doctor," Emily Jane whispered back.

Susanna began wrapping Emily Jane's hands in a soft cloth. The blood had stopped flowing earlier, but Susanna seemed to feel she needed to cover the wounds.

As she worked, the people around them carried on conversations about what they were going to do.

A school council member came forward. "I am making it official. We'll use the school to house folks. With spring planting under way, the school was going to close soon anyway. I'm sure Miss Leland will be happy to help anyone she can."

Susanna asked in a quiet voice, "Will you be staying at the school with Anna Mae?"

Emily Jane nodded. "If there is room."

"You are welcome to stay with me—both of you are."

It blessed Emily Jane's heart that Susanna would open her home to her and Anna Mae. Susanna once saw them as competition for Levi Westland's bride position, but now she was showing that she was a true friend. She hugged Susanna tightly for a moment. "Thank you, but for now, I think we will be needed to help these folks."

Susanna looked about the crowd of elderly faces and nodded. Then she released Emily Jane and walked over to Miss Cornwell. Susanna slipped her arm around the older woman's shoulders and held her tight. Miss Cornwell hugged herself about the waist and cried softly.

Miss Cornwell was the town spinster. She'd never married. No one knew why. They just knew that she hadn't. Had she ever regretted not marrying? Emily Jane thought, someday, she might ask her.

Susanna spoke into the older woman's ear, much as she had into Emily Jane's moments earlier.

"What do you think she's saying to her?" William asked in a low voice.

Emily Jane gave him a watery smile. "Susanna is probably offering her a place to stay."

Miss Cornwell nodded.

Susanna turned to the crowd. "Ladies, please come over to the Sewing Room, when you can. I have dresses that I want to give you all." Then she led Miss Cornwell away from the crowd.

Tears and rain ran down the women's faces. Susanna had a heart of gold, something she was revealing to many who didn't know her and to those who thought they knew her but didn't. Susanna's gift of dresses wasn't a cheap present, and even though she hadn't meant it to, it had bought her many friendships.

"Those who want to stay at the church, please, follow me," the preacher called as he turned and walked toward the church.

The school councilman said almost the same thing, only he turned toward the schoolhouse. Emily Jane stared after each man.

For the second time in the past year, Emily Jane was homeless. She had no family, no spouse and no one to care what became of her. For a moment she thought about wallowing in self-pity but then realized that her thoughts weren't entirely true. Emily Jane had friends, and her friends needed her.

Rose chose that moment to repeat, "Eat."

Ruby's little voice joined Rose's. "Eat."

"Let's head over to the general store. I'm sure I can get Wilson to open it for me." William started walking.

Emily Jane followed. Thankfully, the rain now came

down in a fine mist instead of the earlier downpour. Rose laid her head on Emily Jane's shoulder. "Eat?"

She patted the little girl's back. "In a few minutes."

William banged on the store door. Within a few moments, a light approached the entry. Mr. Moore opened the door.

"William, what are you all doing out in the storm?" He motioned for them to enter.

Emily Jane inhaled the comforting fragrances. Water dripped on the wooden floors, and she inhaled sharply. "Oh, we're getting the floor wet."

"Never mind the floor. What are you doing out in this storm?" Wilson Moore demanded for the second time.

"A tornado hit our street. All the homes are gone."

A gasp sounded behind the counter. Emily Jane turned to find Carolyn Moore standing there bouncing her little boy against her shoulder. "Is everyone all right?" she asked.

William answered. "As far as we know. Mrs. Matthews went to the doctor with a hurt shoulder. She's the only one that I know of that was hurt."

Carolyn looked to Emily Jane.

Emily Jane nodded her agreement.

"That's disturbing news, William. We heard the strong winds, and then the rain came in torrents, but we had no clue it stirred up a tornado. What can we do to help?" Wilson asked, glancing about his store.

"Eat," Ruby said, rising off of William's shoulder and reaching for an apple.

Carolyn hurried around the counter. "Oh, you poor baby." She touched Ruby's damp locks. "Emily Jane, bring the babies upstairs, and we'll get some food in their bellies. Wilson, you give William whatever he needs.".

At his nod, Carolyn led the way to her living quarters. "I've just put away chicken, mashed potatoes and corn bread. We'll get these girls fed in no time. You must be devastated. Is your home repairable?"

Emily Jane hugged the girls close. "No, all the houses were flattened or close to being flattened. Mine and William's are piles of rubble." She felt tears run down her face. Not only for herself but for her friends and neighbors. What was going to happen to them all? How would William care for the girls now?

William watched as Emily Jane followed Mrs. Moore. Did she know what a blessing she was to others? The way she'd hurried to his rescue when the storm had hit, the way she'd rushed to assure the elders in her neighborhood that they had a place to stay until their homes could be rebuilt, and the way she'd taken Rose and Ruby under her wing to protect and provide for them was something Charlotte would never have done.

Charlotte had been beautiful on the outside but not loving and kind. Emily Jane was both beautiful on the inside and the outside. It was too bad she didn't want children or a husband. William mentally shook himself. He wasn't ready to become a husband and decided to keep all thoughts like those at bay. He and Emily Jane were friends, and that was all they would ever be. Besides, even if he were thinking such thoughts, right now he had nothing to offer her.

Once the women were out of the room, Wilson asked, "What can we do to help?"

William took a deep breath. "You might not like what I'm going to suggest."

"Let's hear it, and then I'll let you know if I like it or not." Wilson crossed his arms and waited.

"Do you mind if we sit and talk? I've had kind of a stressful afternoon," he said, prolonging the moment when he'd tell Wilson what he had in mind.

Immediately Wilson nodded and headed to the back of the store. He motioned for William to sit at the table where the older gentlemen enjoyed playing checkers. As soon as William was seated, he sat, too. "Now that I'm sitting down, what did you have in mind?" he asked with a half grin, his expression one of total seriousness.

William ran his hands through his wet hair. "As you know, most of the people who live on my street are elderly and have very little money. Those homes were all most of them had."

Wilson nodded. "Yes, it's very sad."

"They are staying either at the school or the church. There is no food, no clothes and no bedding at either place," William continued, searching Wilson's face.

"I can help with some of that but not all." He motioned about the store. "I'm sure you noticed this is a small store, and recently I've been struggling to keep it stocked."

William nodded. It was just as he'd suspected. "What would you say if I offered to become a business partner?"

Wilson's eyes grew big as he pulled away from the table. "I thought we were talking about helping our community."

"We are." William crossed his arms over his chest. "Those people are the reason I'm bringing it up now instead of later. Let's put our cards on the table. I'll start. I owned a big mercantile in Denver. But when my sister—Rose and Ruby's mother—died, I couldn't stand living there any longer. So I sold my business and came here. I'd planned on starting a new business as soon as my money arrived from the Denver bank to this bank. Now with the people needing help and you needing help, I thought I'd ask."

Wilson sputtered and started to protest.

William held up his hand to silence the rant that was sure to come. "You just said yourself that you're having trouble keeping the shelves stocked."

Defeated, Wilson looked down at the table. He traced a splintered edge with his callused finger. "That's true, but I didn't plan on selling."

"And I'm not planning on buying."

That caught Wilson's attention, and he looked up. "Then what exactly are you proposing?"

William dropped his arms and leaned forward. "I'm proposing a partnership. A silent partnership."

"Why silent?"

He studied Wilson's face. Now was the moment of truth. "Does it really matter why?" William asked.

Wilson nodded. "It does to me. If you are doing something illegal or underhanded, I won't be a part of it. Even if it means losing this store."

William nodded. "I'm a single man, trying to raise my nieces. I don't want the town to know my financial business. There are fathers with daughters who would do anything to marry a wealthy man. I want a woman to marry me for me, not for how much money I have." He didn't bother telling Wilson he had no intentions of marrying; that was business he hadn't shared with anyone other than Emily Jane.

"That's understandable. So, tell me, how would this partnership work?"

William spent the next hour working out a deal with Wilson that left them both satisfied with the arrangement. Once finished, he walked the few aisles of the store, gathering supplies from each shelf, things the now-homeless people would need in the coming days. As he thought carefully about the items required, the loss the people had suffered overwhelmed his mind and made him choose more carefully. God had blessed him abundantly, and it pleased him to no end to be able to help others. The scriptures were correct when they said, *"It is more blessed to give than to receive."*

He had just finished boxing and loading the supplies when Emily Jane returned with Rose and Ruby. Both little girls wore dry dresses and had the satisfied look of two babies with full tummies. Emily Jane, also, appeared drier than when she'd left.

Carolyn arrived right on her heels with a small wicker basket. "I hope you're hungry. I've made you and Emily Jane several ham-and-cheese sandwiches for later and added a couple of bottles of milk for the girls."

"Thank you. That is very kind." William took a drowsy Ruby from Emily Jane. He nuzzled his cheek against hers, and she cuddled closer into his shoulder. Had they been at home in the rocking chair, she would have been asleep in a few minutes.

Carolyn handed him the basket. "Nonsense. It's the

least I can do, considering." Her flushed cheeks indicated that he'd embarrassed her.

He offered her a smile and then turned to Emily Jane. "Have you decided where you will be staying?"

"The school, I guess. I believe that's where Anna Mae will be, and I plan to help her as much as possible."

William nodded. "I hate to ask, but do you mind keeping the girls with you a little bit longer while I distribute these supplies to the church?" He indicated the wagon full of food and blankets.

Emily Jane hugged Rose closer and reached for Ruby. "I'll be happy to take them with me." But Ruby was having none of it. She strained against Emily Jane's arms, reaching for William.

Ruby whined in a tired little voice. "Me go," she demanded.

He grinned and caved. "I tell you what—I'll take Ruby, and you hang on to Rose." William held his arms out, and Ruby all but jumped into them. His heart soared with love and thankfulness that they were okay. He held her tight against his heart.

Emily Jane nodded and turned to Carolyn once more. "Thank you again, for everything."

Carolyn hugged her. "If you need anything else, please, come see me. I'll help with the girls, too, while you two figure out what the future holds for you."

Her words stayed with William long after he'd left the Moores. What did the future hold for them? How could he help his new hometown? Would Emily Jane continue caring for the girls? So many unanswered questions plagued him as he made his way to the church.

Chapter Fifteen

The townspeople of Granite, Texas, came together in a phenomenal way to help the tornado victims. Last night they'd supplied blankets, pillows, and the women had brought in food for their evening meal. A fresh supply of drinking water and a roof over their heads had felt pretty good by the time they settled down for the night. Emily Jane prayed they didn't get sick from being in the constant drizzle the day before, but there had been no help for it. Everyone had tried to locate their personal belongings, which meant digging through the rubble of what remained.

The sun had yet to show itself when Emily Jane awoke. Her back muscles ached from sleeping on the floor with Rose cuddled up next to her all night. She eased her arm out from under the sleeping toddler, carefully stood and stretched the kinks from her body.

She looked down at her dress and found it wrinkled and soiled in places. As much as she hated to do it, Emily Jane knew she'd have to take Susanna up on her offer of a new dress. But, for now, the one she wore would have to do since she hadn't found any of her clothing in the rubble the night before. It was as if the twister had sucked up all that was valuable and left a pile of matches as payment.

Yesterday, in the final fading light with a soft drizzle drenching her dress and hair, Emily Jane had found her fox pups. Thankfully, they had survived. They were wet and cold, but huddled in their wooden box several feet away from the house. It was as if something or someone had simply picked them up and set them away from the damage. She'd wept, tears mingling with the rain, thankful the Lord had seen fit to allow them to live. Then she'd moved them to the lean-to, the only building on the block that hadn't been struck. William's mare had greeted her with a nervous whinny.

Emily Jane's tears hadn't been just for the pups but for everyone that the twister had touched. Sorrow for their loss but praise that God had spared their lives warred with each other in her heart. They may have lost their homes, but they all had their lives, and that was a blessing in itself.

Now in the gray light of dawn, sadness threatened to overwhelm her as she looked about the room. *Lord, these people are too old to start all over again. Please, be with them in the upcoming days as they realize what all they have lost.*

Thankfully, Anna Mae had agreed to watch over Rose while she worked. The baby slept peacefully as Emily Jane eased her over onto Anna Mae's blankets. Anna

Mae looked up sleepily, then pulled Rose to her side before shutting her eyes once more.

Emily Jane stepped over the ladies who slept closest to her and quietly shut the schoolhouse door behind her. Thankfully, she had a job to go to and some money in the bank. Still, she couldn't help but long for her recipe book.

She hurried down the hill and toward the ruins that once were her home. Though she no longer had a house to care for, she did have animals that would be hungry this morning.

The debris that filled the small dirt street spoke volumes of the destruction that had taken place the day before. Struggling to keep the tears at bay, she focused on the Lord and the fact that He had kept them all alive and most of them safe.

Mrs. Matthews's shoulder had been dislocated when she was slung against her house walls, but other than that, mostly she'd suffered only cuts and bruises. The doctor had popped the shoulder back into place and put her arm in a sling. He'd also stitched up the cut on her arm and given her orders to take it easy for a few days.

A washtub sat in the middle of the road. Bits of clothing were strung across the wood and tin that used to be someone's house. After work, Emily Jane intended to look again for her dresses, since surely they hadn't all been blown away. When she got to where her house had been, she hurried to the lean-to. Scooping up what hay was left, she fed the horse and then checked on the fox pups.

In just the few days she'd had them, they had grown,

and their coats were starting to turn the rich red colors that marked them as a fox. They began to whimper when they saw her. Emily Jane knew they were hungry but had nothing to give them. She picked them up and gave each a cuddle before setting them at her feet.

They followed her to the well, where she dropped the water bucket inside. She heard it splash and then drew it up. Water sloshed over the edges as she hoisted it over the rock ledge. Emily Jane cupped the water into her hands and held it down for the fox pups to lap up.

As the sweet babies drank, she wondered how long it would be before the men in town realized she was keeping fox cubs. That didn't really matter, since it was about time to release them into the wild. She'd ask William for help when she saw him next.

The sun crept up over the hill, casting red, pink and orange rays across the morning skies. After the continued rain all night, the sunshine was a welcome blessing. She tossed the remainder of the water from her hands and dried her wet palms on her apron. Emily Jane untied the bucket from the rope and then scooped the fox pups up in one arm.

Carrying them back to their box, she cooed, "I know you are hungry, and I promise to bring you something to eat in a few hours." She placed them gently into the box. "Until then, you two behave yourselves." Emily Jane filled the horse's bucket with water.

A few minutes later, she entered The Bakery through the back door. Violet Atwood turned with a frown. "What are you doing here, Emily Jane?"

"I work here." She pulled off the dirty white apron

she'd been wearing and grabbed a nice clean one off the hook beside the door.

Violet made a tsking noise. "Yes, but with you losing your house yesterday, I didn't expect you to come in today."

Emily Jane walked to the washbasin and grabbed the bar of soap. She scrubbed her hands and arms until it felt as if her flesh might wash off. The cuts from the day before screamed out as the soap cleansed them.

"Where else would I be? Sitting in the schoolhouse? I don't want to just sit idle." Emily Jane wiped her hands dry. What she didn't say was that she didn't want to dwell on her future. What kind of future was it anyway? She had no place to live, and the money she'd saved up for her bakery would now have to be used to move into a new home. Her recipe book was probably long lost; even if she found it, the rain had probably ruined it. A single tear escaped and ran down her cheek. She swiped at it angrily. What was the matter with her? She was alive. Yet she wanted to be a baby and cry over a lost recipe book. *Shame on you, Emily Jane,* she scolded herself.

The house she and Anna Mae lived in didn't belong to them. So, for Anna Mae and herself it wasn't a matter of rebuilding; they would just have to find another home. Anna Mae could travel between her students' homes. Emily Jane didn't have that luxury. Not that staying with other families was much of a treat.

Emily Jane turned to face Violet. "Please, just let me work."

Violet came over and hugged her. "Of course. You are always welcome here. I just thought…"

"I know and I appreciate your thoughtfulness, but I need to work." Emily Jane began to gather ingredients to make a large batch of cinnamon buns. They were her specialty and her comfort.

"I'm glad you're here." Violet put the coffee on and began working alongside her. "I don't suppose you were able to save your recipe book."

She groaned aloud, unable to squash her grief a moment longer. The tears that she'd fought earlier rolled in huge rivulets down her cheeks. "Not yet. After work I intend to go through the rubble of the house and see what can be salvaged. I'm praying I'll find it undamaged, but with the rain and the wind, I'm not holding my breath."

"Oh, Emily Jane. I'm so terribly sorry. I know how much your grandmother's recipe book meant to you." Violet slipped an arm around Emily Jane's shoulders and squeezed her tightly for a moment. "I feel so helpless. I wish there was something I could do."

"Letting me work helps me get my mind off of things, so I appreciate it. You're helping me more than you know." For a moment they both became lost in their own thoughts.

Emily Jane knew that, like everything else, the book could be replaced. It would take time, but she could do it. Time? What would time bring for her?

As she kneaded the dough, Emily Jane thought about her future. What was she going to do? As they always did, her thoughts went to William and the girls. She knew her feelings for them were more than friendship, but she refused to call it love. She wasn't ready to give up her independence. Falling in love with William would lead to her wanting to be with him and giving up her dream of being independent and owning her own bakery. No, she was not in love with William. Maybe it was time to move to another town before she did start thinking in terms of love. Could she leave them? Her heart broke at the thought.

A week after the tornado, William left the bank feeling better than he had earlier that morning. The banker had accepted his plan and stipulations. His money had arrived several days before, and he, now with the aid of the banker, could help the elders of Granite, Texas, start rebuilding.

Over the past week, everyone had worked nonstop cleaning up the wreckage the tornado had left behind. It had soon become apparent that even though most of them owned their lots, none of them had the funds to rebuild. William knew he did, and he'd thought up a way to help everyone so that they could care for each other and have a roof over their heads while doing so. This afternoon, the plan would be revealed to the homeless citizens of Granite.

As they often did, his thoughts moved to Emily Jane. After the first night, she and Anna Mae had moved into Beth's Boardinghouse. They pooled their funds and rented a room together. But each evening the two ladies returned to the school to help with the evening meals. William found himself impressed with each young lady. They could have remained at the boardinghouse each evening, reading, quilting, sewing or just relaxing, but chose instead to help those less fortunate. That took character, Christian character, and he knew the Lord would bless them for their efforts.

Emily Jane offered to take the girls again, but with so many of the elder ladies wanting something to do with their time and offering to watch the girls while he worked, he'd assured her they were well taken care of. William hadn't realized that having the ladies care for the twins would limit his time spent with Emily Jane. Oh, how he missed her. He had made a huge mistake but had no plans to right the situation.

He told himself it was for the best. On the day of the tornado, William had wanted nothing more than to take her hurts away. A part of his heart had melted, and he found himself in deep waters. Totally new territory for him. The emotions created an uneasiness in him, making him feel insecure. He simply couldn't have that. He needed a clear head. In the first place, the odds were stacked against them. Emily Jane didn't want children and he did. Secondly, he hadn't heard a word from his brother-in-law. William feared Josiah was dead. Why else would he leave the girls for so long? So, that meant whoever William married would start off with a ready-made family. Not many young ladies were up for that.

He worked his way up the street toward the church. Thanks to the banker, who had agreed to make the announcement, William's plan would be revealed. However, the town would only hear that an unnamed beneficiary had offered a substantial sum of money to build a large building. Sixteen rooms to be exact, for those who couldn't afford to rebuild and didn't mind living in one home with other people. It would be much like a boardinghouse, but they wouldn't have to pay rent.

William was no builder, but he'd drawn out the house plan. Each person or couple would have two rooms to call their own. He expected most to have a bedroom and a sitting room, but that was entirely up to them. A large kitchen would be situated at the back of the house, and a great room would be in the center for dining and visitors.

When he entered the church, William slipped into one of the back pews. Mrs. Green and Mrs. Harvey held his sleeping nieces a few benches in front of him. Mr. and Mrs. Orson occupied the same pew as he did.

Mr. Orson leaned over. "Cutting it close, aren't you, young man?" he asked, with a twinkle in his eye.

"Had to work," William replied. It was the truth. He'd put in his hours at the store with the Moores. He'd stocked shelves with the merchandise that they'd ordered a few days before. It felt good to help others. He liked working. Nothing made a man feel better than a good, hard day's work.

"I think our friendly banker has been studying his books again and found another way to make a profit. Why else would he call this meeting?"

Before William could answer, Mrs. Orson hissed, "You two quiet down. Here he comes."

Everyone craned their necks to see what the banker would have to say. William watched as Amos and another young man walked up to the platform. Each young boy held a corner of William's drawing between them.

"Thank you all for coming," the banker said loudly.

"I'm sure you're all wondering why I called this meeting."

Mrs. Orson huffed. "Why else would we be here?" she whispered loudly.

"Well, a few days ago I had a gentleman come into my office who was very concerned about your well-being." He paused as the crowd began to murmur.

"Who is this man?" Mrs. Wells demanded.

The banker raised his hand. "He's asked me to keep his identity a secret."

Again the small congregation began to mutter among themselves. William wondered if Mr. Anderson was ever going to tell the people why they were here. He stood up and walked toward the platform.

Once he stood by the banker, the crowd quieted down. "Ladies and gentlemen, give Mr. Anderson a chance to finish. I, for one, want to know what this is about." William searched the small sea of faces until he found Emily Jane.

She sat with Anna Mae, Susanna Marsh and Miss Cornwell. Her sad eyes held his for several moments. He made eye contact with each person.

"I believe you can continue now, Mr. Anderson." William sat down in the front pew.

"As I was saying, the bank has been given a large amount of money to help you rebuild your homes." The room remained silent, so the banker continued. "Your benefactor has a suggestion on how to use the money but wants you to know that it is only a suggestion. If you do not want to build according to his plan, you each will be allotted equal amounts of the money."

Whispers broke out about the church once more.

"I know this is a bit of a shock, but if you will look this way—" He pointed to the drawing the two boys held on the platform. "This is a plan for a rather large house. In it are sixteen rooms." Mr. Anderson indicated eight rooms on each side of a big box. "Those are the rooms. Now, what he thought was that the six people and Mr. and Mrs. Orson who lost their homes could live in two rooms each."

"All together?" Miss Cornwell asked.

He nodded. "Yes, but, please, let me finish before you ask questions or make any rash decisions."

She nodded. "Please, continue."

"This room—" he pointed to the box at the back of the house "—is the kitchen. And this room—" he pointed to the room in the front "—is the great room. It could be used as a dining room and a sitting room."

William waited. He couldn't see their faces. What were they thinking? That he was insane. The silence continued. Were they in shock?

He stood once more and faced them. "What do you think?"

They all began talking at once. William held up his hand. "Please, one at a time."

Mrs. Orson raised her hand and shook it in the air. Her lips were thinner than normal. Whatever she had to say might as well be said first. "Mrs. Orson, do you have a question?" William asked.

"Yes, I do. Will you be living in this big house?" She pointed at the drawing.

"No, ma'am. As much as I like this idea, I'm afraid

the girls would be too noisy to live in a community home like this one." He offered her a smile.

"Then where will you live?" There was genuine concern in her voice.

"I plan on rebuilding my grandmother's house," he answered, wondering where she was going with this line of questioning.

She nodded. "So those precious children will be close by, so that we can still watch them for you while you work?"

He couldn't contain the big grin that split his lips. A couple of weeks ago this woman and her friends had complained about his nieces. Now she wanted them close by so that she could take care of them. God had a way of working things out. "Yes, ma'am."

Miss Cornwell raised her hand. "Where will the house be?"

"Well, since you all own your lots, we were thinking of putting the house right in the middle of your land," the banker answered. "This house will be very large. Each room in this house has been designed to be very spacious. It will take up most of the street."

Mrs. Green raised her hand. "Who will own the house?"

"Your secret benefactor. But he can never make you move out because it will be on your land," Mr. Anderson answered. "I'll see to it that this is done legally, and you will never have to worry about losing your home by the hands of the bank or any man."

The questions continued for the next hour. William

was thankful that Mr. Anderson had anticipated all their concerns.

He was surprised when Emily Jane raised her hand. The banker responded. "Yes, Miss Rodgers."

"Mr. Anderson, who are the eight people who will receive this house?" Her voice sounded small and lost to William's ears. He hadn't spent a lot of time with her since the tornado had blown both their homes away. Looking at her now, he saw the dark circles under her eyes and the fatigue in the droop of her shoulders.

Mr. Anderson pulled a paper from his front pocket and began to read the list of names. "Mrs. Lois Green, Miss Gertie Cornwell, Mrs. Mary Wells, Mrs. Sylvia Harvey, Miss Emily Jane Rodgers, Miss Anna Mae Leland and Mr. and Mrs. Orson."

Mr. Orson spoke up. "That is only seven. You said there are eight rooms."

"That is correct. Your benefactor had also anticipated Mr. Barns moving in, but as you've just heard, he has no intentions of doing so. The eighth set of rooms is for your families when they come to visit," Mr. Anderson explained, and he folded the paper with the names on it and put it into his pocket. "This is an all-or-none deal, folks."

The room began to hum again.

William stood once more. "Since this is a decision that only the eight people on Mr. Anderson's list have to make, I suggest that the rest of us return to our own business and allow them the chance to decide in private what they want to do." He started walking toward the door. As he passed Emily Jane's pew, he looked into her troubled eyes.

What would her decision be? Would she be willing to live in the same house with seven other people? If truth be told, he'd done this for her. Had this eased her mind any? Or would she continue to fret about her future?

Chapter Sixteen

Almost two hours later, Emily Jane left the church with the realization that she would have a real home soon. The eight people had agreed to let their benefactor build them a house. There had been a discussion as to who in the community could afford to be so generous. It was decided that the benefactor was probably none other than Levi Westland.

His family owned the largest cattle ranch in the area, and Levi himself owned at least three of the town businesses. He was known for helping the orphans and the widows. Once that conclusion had been made, the elders had agreed that they were safe in allowing the house to be built on their lands.

She'd seen hope in their eyes for the first time in days. Mr. Anderson had assured them that building supplies would be ordered from the sawmill that evening and that their new homes should be completed by the end of summer, if they could get the locals to help with the building.

"Emily Jane!"

She stopped and looked behind her. Mrs. Harvey hurried toward her.

"The ladies and I were talking this morning and we wondered if you would still consider baking the cake for the spring festival. Only this year it's going to be the summer festival." She held her sides and panted as she waited for Emily Jane to answer.

"I'd have to ask Mr. Westland if I can use The Bakery kitchen to make it. But if he says yes, I'll be happy to make the cake." It was nice that the women still wanted to have the celebration.

Mrs. Harvey smiled. "No need to ask him. You can bake it in our big kitchen that the men will be building for us."

Emily Jane shook her head. "I'm not sure the house will be completed in time. Didn't Mr. Anderson say it would probably be the end of the summer before it would be complete?"

"Well, yes, but I really think the men can get it up faster. We women could help during the weekdays, and they could work on it on Saturdays." Mrs. Harvey seemed confident, and Emily Jane didn't want to discourage her, so she kept her thoughts to herself.

With a house that size, it would take more than a few months to build. For one thing, the men would not be able to work on it every weekend. They had businesses and farms to run. And, even with the best of intentions, the women were up in age, and after a few days they would have aches and pains in places they'd forgotten they possessed. No, she wouldn't share all of that with Mrs. Harvey. Emily Jane doubted a house that size could be completed by the end of summer, but only time would tell.

"I'll be happy to make the cake, Mrs. Harvey."

Those were the words the woman really wanted to hear. Emily Jane was rewarded with a huge smile. "Thank you." Mrs. Harvey turned away. "I need to go, but I'll talk to you soon."

Emily Jane didn't want to go back to the boarding-house just yet. The Nelsons, the owners of the house she and Anna Mae had shared, had decided to sell the lot and lean-to, so it was time to do something with the fox pups. They were now about eight weeks old, and it was obvious that they weren't just puppies. They no longer stayed in the box, so she'd shut them up in the lean-to; but now they'd have to be released.

She pulled the door open, expecting to be welcomed by wiggly fox pups. Instead, the giggles of little girls tilted up the corners of her own mouth. For sure there hadn't been much lately to laugh about. What a lovely sound. Emily Jane stepped inside and allowed her eyes to adjust to the darker interior of the building.

"Emily, would you hold the door open for me?"

The way William said only her first name made the blood course through her veins like an awakened river. It didn't come out harsh-sounding as her name often did when people used both Emily and Jane. Her hand fluttered against the door's jagged edge. "Sure." She stepped back as he passed with his mare in tow.

The fox pups raced out after him, and Rose and Ruby crawled rapidly behind the foxes. The little girls squealed with joy as the pups bounded to them, licking their faces and knocking them over.

William's warm laughter drew her focus back to him. "I think the girls have found lifelong friends to play with."

"That would be nice, but Mrs. Nelson told me this morning that they're selling the lot and lean-to, so it looks like I will have to take them to the woods and release them." Sorrow touched her heart. Coming each morning to take care of the fox pups had added meaning to her days. Now, well, like everything else, she was about to lose them. Tears pricked the backs of her eyes, Emily Jane refused to release them.

"Mr. Nelson gave me the same news. I'm moving Bess to the livery. She should have been there all along anyway." William stroked the mare's nose while watching the little girls play with the foxes. "Would you like us to go with you to release them?"

Emily Jane shook her head. "No, I'll do it." She didn't want to do it alone but also didn't want William and the girls to see her cry. Which she was sure would happen when she had to let them go.

"Do you have to do it right now?" He looked into her green eyes as if searching for the answer to his question there. "Would it hurt to wait a few days?"

Her breath caught in her throat at the intensity of his gaze. "I suppose not. Why?"

"Well, while I was visiting with Mr. Nelson this morning, he told me about a small farm on the north end of town that recently went on sale. Saturday, if you have the time, I'd like for you to go with me to look at it."

Emily Jane watched the girls cuddle the fox pups close to them. What would a few more nights in the lean-to hurt?

"The girls will be coming, too. We could make a day of it." His deep blue eyes beseeched her to say yes.

It would be nice to get out of town. "What time did you plan on going?" she asked.

"I thought we could go as soon as you finish work."

She grinned at him. "I'll go under two conditions."

"And what would those conditions be?" Playful suspicion filled his voice.

Emily Jane deliberately stalled. She looked at the little girls, who crawled after the fox pups in what used to be the backyard of her home. They were cute together. If only they had a place to keep them.

He cleared his throat.

She couldn't contain the teasing grin that tore at her face. He'd suffered long enough. "One, that you allow me to pack a picnic, and two, that when it comes time to let the fox pups go, you won't laugh if I cry."

William dropped the mare's lead rope and walked over to her. He slipped his arm around her shoulders and gently pulled her to his side. "I promise to eat all your picnic lunch, and I never laugh when a woman cries."

It felt good standing in the shelter of his arm. Emily Jane enjoyed the sensation for a few more moments before pulling away from him. It wouldn't be proper for anyone to see them standing so close. She scooped up a running pup and then collected the other one. "Let me put the foxes away, and then I'll help you take the mare to the livery." For some reason she didn't fully understand, Emily Jane wasn't ready to leave his presence just yet.

As she entered the small shed, Ruby's and Rose's cries filled her ears. They were another reason the fox pups had to go back into the wild. The little girls were becoming attached, but like her, right now, they were homeless and had no place for wild pets.

As she set the fox pups into the last stall and shut the door, Emily had a horrible thought. With William thinking about buying a farm out in the country, how often would he and the girls be in town? Once a week? Sundays only? Or maybe Saturdays to get supplies? She would see them only once a week. Suddenly all pleasure left her. How had her life become such a battle? Sadness and loss were her daily companions. And now she might have another huge loss to adjust to. Emily Jane didn't want to admit that she would miss William as much as the girls, but her heart whispered, *"You know you will."*

William immediately missed not having Emily Jane pressed next to his side. What had possessed him to hug her close like that anyway? Was it the sadness in her eyes? Or was it something else?

He picked up a sobbing Rose and put her in the wagon and then did the same with Ruby while Emily Jane put the fox pups back into the lean-to. "You can play with them again tomorrow." William pulled the girls back to the little mare and picked up her lead rope. He looked back at them to see that they had discovered their stuffed animals and were now happily playing.

Emily Jane walked toward him. Her shoulders were

slumped. So many changes had happened in her life the past couple of weeks. When she came even with him he asked, "What was the final decision up at the church?"

Her dimple flashed as she looked up at him. "They are going to build one big house."

How did she do that? Go from being sad to smiling with the beauty of a child? She had to be hurting over the fox pups, but Emily Jane hid it well. She took the handle of the wagon from him. "I'll pull them."

William walked beside her. As they walked to the livery, the girls chattered away behind them, not making one lick of sense.

"I'm glad you were able to save the wagon," Emily Jane said.

"Yes, I lost the high chairs, but Levi has offered to make me another set at the cost of the lumber. Did you know the sawmill was one of the first businesses in Granite?"

She nodded. "Yes, and we are glad to have it. Not only does it help Levi's business, but it also helps other people make sheds and lean-tos behind their houses."

They walked in silence for a few moments. Then she asked, "Do you think the big house will be finished by the end of summer?"

William didn't want to hurt her, but he had to be truthful. "I don't see how. It will take a lot of men to work on it, and most of them don't have time, especially at this time of year."

"That's what I thought, too. I really wish Mr. Anderson hadn't built everyone's hopes up so high."

It was William's turn to nod. "I'm sure he meant

well." Still, he had to ask himself why the banker would make such an empty promise.

"Tell me about this farm we are going to look at Saturday," Emily Jane said, changing the subject.

"There's not much to tell. All Mr. Nelson said was that it belongs to an older couple who are thinking about moving back East. It has a house, a barn and a nice garden spot." He looked back, checking on the girls. "It would provide a roof over the girls' heads."

Sadness filled her eyes once more. Had his comment reminded her that for now she was homeless? William hated that he'd possibly hurt her in some way. "Emily, is there anything I can do to help you?" William reached out and took her free hand in his as they walked. It wasn't much comfort, but for the time being it was all he could offer.

She didn't pull her hand from his, but she heaved a big sigh. "Thank you, but I'll be all right. Once I replace a few personal belongings, I can start saving money for my bakery again." Her voice rang with determination, but he watched the play of emotions cross her features. Fear of the unknown, sadness and uncertainty flickered a moment. Then she gave him a half smile and released his hand. "Well, you are here, and everyone is in one piece, so I think I'll head back to the boardinghouse."

"Thank you for walking with us. I'm looking forward to Saturday," William said, not ready to let her go just yet.

"Me, too. I'll see you then."

With a heavy heart, William watched her walk away. How he wished he could get the house built faster, but to do so he'd need a lot of help. There were plenty of men in Austin who would love to work on the house, but hiring them would cost lots of money. Even with his inheritance, William knew he couldn't hire all that were needed.

Levi Westland stood within the livery doors. "Nice to see you again, William," he said, patting a big white stallion.

"Afternoon, Levi."

Levi knelt beside the girls' wagon. "I'll keep an eye on these two while you take care of your business with Mr. Hart."

Rose pulled herself up to the side of the wagon and gave Levi a big grin. It always amazed William how quickly Rose took to others, and Ruby, on the other hand, had to warm up to them. "Thank you. I won't be but a second."

Levi lifted the girls out of the wagon and sat down beside the door with them. He pulled out one of their toys and began to play with them. Assured they would be all right with Levi, William went in search of Mr. Hart.

It didn't take long to settle on a boarding price for his mare, and then William hurried back to Levi and the girls. The girls were curled up in his lap sucking their thumbs as he told them a story. Rose and Ruby loved hearing stories, and Levi was telling them about Jonah and the whale.

William waited until the story was complete and then took Ruby from Levi's arms. "Who knew you were such a good storyteller?" he teased.

Levi grinned. "It's easy to tell a story that you've read many times from the Bible." He pushed himself off the ground, bringing Rose with him. She yawned and snuggled more deeply into his shoulder. "Then again, judging from that big yawn, I might have bored them." A deep chuckle shook his shoulders.

Ruby grinned up at William. "Eat?" she asked.

"Sure, sweetie. Let's go see what they are serving tonight at the schoolhouse."

"Mind if I walk with you?"

"Not at all." William picked up the wagon handle and looked inquisitively at Levi. "Is there something you want to talk to me about? Or were you headed that way anyway?"

Levi fell into step with him. "Both."

"Talk away. I'm all ears."

"It seems someone donated the money to build the new big house, and I've been given credit for doing so." Levi shifted Rose on his hip.

Was Levi asking him if he'd donated the money? Or was he simply sharing information? William decided to wait him out and see what he'd say next. "That's very interesting."

"I thought it might interest you."

William ignored the other man's searching eyes. He didn't want anyone but the banker to know that he was the benefactor. "Why is that?"

Levi rubbed his chin. "You may not know this, but I grew up on a ranch not far from this town. I know every person that lives here and can't think of a one that can afford to pay for such a large home. Now, you, on the other hand, are new here, and I don't know what your financial situation is, and really it's none of my business. But I do know that my family isn't responsible for this blessing."

William smiled. "Well, if you are looking for me to say I did supply the blessing, it isn't going to happen. I guess we will just have to let sleeping dogs lie, as they say."

Levi slapped him on the back. "Agreed. That's what I'm saying, too. When asked, I'll just continue to say that the benefactor wanted it to be secret."

At that moment, William recognized a new friend in Levi. Levi knew that he was the benefactor but also planned to keep his secret. How many others would guess that it was him who had donated the money? Did it really matter? The scripture came to mind: *but when thou doest alms, let not thy left hand know what thy right hand doeth.* William would keep the secret and let them continue guessing.

"You know, it's going to take a lot of men to build a house that big." Levi glanced at him again. "I'm thinking another secret benefactor might be needed. Do you suppose the one who supplied the house will mind if someone else supplies the manpower to get it built?"

William chuckled. "I'm sure he wouldn't."

Levi slapped him on the back again. "That's exactly what the banker said, too."

William silently thanked the Lord above for the good people of Granite. Now Emily Jane would have a home sooner than they'd both expected. He felt a warmth enter his heart. He knew his feelings for Emily Jane were growing, but he also knew she was dead set on having her bakery without a husband and kids. And that was a huge obstacle to get around.

Chapter Seventeen

Saturday morning, Emily Jane's tummy wouldn't stop fluttering. Was she coming down with a stomach ailment? Or was it the simple excitement of doing something different with her day? She added another deviled ham sandwich to the picnic basket, then a small bag of sugar cookies; lastly, she put a bowl of the deviled ham in the basket and added a spoon so that she could feed it to the girls.

Walking to the foyer, where she'd decided to meet William and the girls, she tried to decide if there was anything she'd forgotten. She placed the basket on the small settee and sat down beside it.

Beth came down the stairs. She looked as pretty as a picture. Not a wrinkle in her dress or a hair out of place. "Good morning, Emily Jane. Where are you off to?" Beth set a box on the floor beside the couch.

She didn't want to answer Beth but didn't see a way out. "Mr. Barns has asked me to accompany him and the girls into the country." Emily Jane thought about adding that she would be watching the girls and releasing her fox cubs back into the wild but realized less information might be better than too much.

"Would you like to borrow one of my hats? That sun is going to darken your freckles." Beth sat down beside her on the settee. "I have a big floppy one that would match the blue in your dress."

"Thank you for the offer, Beth, but I've never worn a hat." Emily Jane looked at Beth's white skin. There were no flaws on her face.

Shock filled Beth's voice as she asked. "Why ever not?"

Only prideful women wear hats—Emily Jane's father's voice filled her thoughts. "My parents didn't approve of them."

A mischievous look crossed the other young woman's face. "Your parents aren't here now, are they?"

"Well, no."

"I'll be right back. The hat will save your skin, and no harm will be done. Your parents will never know. Besides, you are a grown woman." Beth hurried up the stairs.

Emily Jane shook her head with a smile. Beth had been kind to her since she'd moved in and only meant well. So, if wearing a hat would put a new smile on her face, Emily Jane would wear it.

Beth arrived with a pretty floppy hat in her hand. "See? It matches your dress perfectly."

"So it does." Emily Jane took the offered hat and placed it on her head. She stood up and walked to the looking glass that hung beside the door. It really was a pretty hat.

Today Emily Jane wore one of the two dresses that Susanna had insisted she take. It was a pretty blue with white buttons that ran down the front. The light blue hat had a white ribbon around the rim. If people didn't look too closely, they would think she was pretty.

"Thank you, Beth. It is very beautiful."

The other woman beamed. "I knew it would look wonderful on you."

Emily Jane sat back down. "What are you doing today?"

Beth picked up the box she'd set down earlier. "I'm going to take this dress to Martha, a friend of mine who has been sick. Unfortunately, she's lost a lot of weight, so I'm hoping this dress will fit her." A sadness entered Beth's eyes. "She's so young."

"If it's all right with you, I'd like to pray for her. God is the great physician, and I know He can heal her." Emily Jane smiled. She truly believed what she'd just told Beth.

"Thank you. I'd like that, and I know Martha will appreciate the added prayers."

The two women joined hands; Emily Jane bowed her head and began to pray. "Thank You, Lord, for loving us and watching over us. Beth and I both love You very much, and as Your children we come before You. You said if any of my children need anything all they have to do is ask. Well, Father, we are asking You to reach down and touch Beth's friend Martha. She has been sick a long time, Lord, and we know You can heal her. We ask for her healing in Jesus's name. Amen."

Emily Jane released her hands. "If there is anything I can do to help you or Martha, please, tell me."

A soft smile touched Beth's face. "You already have. Your praying with me has made me feel better. Thank you." She picked up her box, then opened the door.

"You're welcome," Emily Jane answered, happy that she'd been able to pray with her friend.

Beth walked out just as William pulled his horse and wagon in front of the house.

Emily Jane picked up her picnic basket and followed Beth outside. The warm morning breeze lifted the hat. She grabbed at it with her free hand.

William jumped down from the wagon. Beth waved at him as she passed. He nodded at her.

Emily Jane walked to the wagon. The tummy butterflies returned in full force. Rose and Ruby sat in their little box in the back of the wagon. They squealed and reached for Emily Jane.

"I hope I haven't kept you waiting," William said, taking the basket and giving her a hand up onto the wagon.

"Not at all. I needed to visit a little while with Beth anyway." She sat down and arranged her skirts. Then Emily Jane turned and kissed each twin.

They giggled and tried to get her hat.

William pulled himself up beside her. As he took the reins, he asked, "New hat?"

"Beth loaned it to me."

He smiled over at her. "It's very pretty on you."

A compliment? She felt a little uneasy. His sapphire eyes looked straight ahead as he gently slapped the reins over Bess's back.

A soft laugh drifted from his side of the wagon seat. "We're friends, Emily Jane. No need to get all nervous about a compliment."

How had he known? She cut her eyes under the hat to look at his profile. Was it possible that over the past few weeks they'd grown so close that they knew what each other was thinking? If so, that was dangerous. Maybe after today, she should put some distance between herself and William. People who could read each other's minds and expressions, from her experience, seemed to be in love. She wasn't ready for love. Yes, distance after today would be the best solution for them both.

William stopped at the lean-to that housed the fox pups and helped Emily Jane down.

"I'll be right back." She disappeared quickly into the small building.

He hated that she had to give up her fox pups. But it was for the best. So far the men hadn't been aware of them. If they had found out, William was sure they would have demanded she kill them. He thought about getting her a puppy to replace the fox pups. Would she want a replacement?

Emily Jane returned with the wooden box that had housed the fox pups when she'd first gotten them. They'd grown and were even now peeking over the top. Red tongues licked at her fingers and hands as she carried them to the wagon.

"Why don't we put one in with the girls and you hold the other one?" William asked, taking the box and helping her back into the wagon.

"We can try. I'm not sure if it's safe for the fox pup or the girls." She took the box back from him and set it on the wagon floor.

Rose and Ruby kicked their legs and squealed when they saw their furry friends.

"You play nice with the baby," Emily Jane said as she put the fox pup in the box with them. At least it was tall enough that even if the fox could get away from the girls, it couldn't get out of the box. She cuddled the second one to her as she watched the girls and pup.

The wagon shifted under William's weight as he pulled himself back up. He studied the girls trying to pet the fox and laughed as they attempted to avoid its quick tongue. "See? I think they will be all right. It's not that far out to the Guthrie place."

"You're probably right. But I think I'll keep a close eye on them, just the same." Emily Jane stroked the little fox's head that she held in her hands.

To distract her, he asked, "What do we have in that basket?" He glanced over his shoulder at the girls once more before flicking the reins and setting the wagon into motion.

"Just sandwiches, pickles and applesauce for the girls."

Disappointment filled his voice. "No cookies?"

As he hoped, she laughed. "Of course there are cookies."

"Sugar?"

"Your favorite?" Emily Jane asked, already knowing that he favored the sugar above all the rest.

"And the girls'," he agreed, nodding.

Once more she laughed. He loved the sound of her merriment. Emily Jane was unlike any woman he'd ever met. She was joy and sunshine, even when she was sad. Over the past few days, he'd come to realize just how much he liked her. William told himself he wasn't falling in love with the little redhead, but he was having a hard time convincing himself it wasn't true.

They were on the edge of town when a group of men in wagons of all sizes came rumbling down the road toward them. The wheels dug deep into the dirt, causing big ruts in the otherwise smooth road. William pulled to the side to let them pass. Emily Jane noticed all kinds of carpentry tools in the wagons as well as tents. One wagon was loaded down with bricks; the two big oxen that pulled it brayed as they slowly passed.

"What are they doing here?" He could hear the hopeful wonder in her voice.

William shook his head. "Maybe they are passing through."

Her voice sounded doubtful. "Perhaps."

Did Emily Jane sense that he knew more than he was saying? William decided not to look at her but to focus on the group of men as they passed.

A woman driving a covered wagon stopped next to them. "Where can I find the general store?" She was a heavy woman with a thick accent.

"Just continue on Main Street, and it's on your left,"

William answered. Then he asked a question of his own. "Where are you all headed?"

She laughed heartily. "Granite. We've all been hired to do a big job here. I'm the cook for this outfit and need supplies."

"What kind of big job?" Emily Jane asked. William knew instinctively what she was thinking.

"We're building the Elm Street house. It's a biggun, too. Something like sixteen bedrooms." She slapped the reins across the horses' backs and started them moving again. "Thank you for the information, folks. Be seeing you around."

As soon as the wagons had all passed, William pulled back onto the road. "It looks like the house might be finished by the end of the summer after all." He grinned across at Emily Jane. He felt as if a weight had been lifted from his shoulders.

"I'm glad. I have been concerned that the hopes of the others would all be crushed if we had to go into winter and they were still living in the school and church." Emily Jane looked back at the girls, who were all smiles.

William looked to his right. Mr. Nelson had said a small road to the right would take him straight to the Guthrie farm.

Emily Jane turned on the seat and played with the girls and fox pups. He'd picked up a few wooden blocks from Levi, and Emily Jane was showing them how to stack them up and knock them over. "There were a lot of men in those wagons." Her voice sounded concerned.

"Yes, there were. It means the house will get built much faster." He saw the small road and turned.

"Where do you think they will all sleep? And what about food supplies?" She handed Ruby a block, then turned to look at him with those clear green eyes.

"Well, they seemed to have lots of tents, so I imagine they will use those and the wagon beds. As for food, the cook was on her way to the general store for supplies, and if I don't miss my guess, they will also do some hunting to supply their meat." It was sweet that Emily Jane was concerned for the builders' well-being. Every day his respect and feelings for her grew, whether he wanted to admit it or not. He shook his head. If he didn't miss his guess, he was a doomed man.

Chapter Eighteen

William pulled up in front of the small farm that seemed to appear out of nowhere. He set the brake on the wagon and then hopped down.

Rose clung to the side of the box. "Up," she said, reaching for William.

He pulled the little girl out of the wagon and into his arms, then turned to help Emily Jane down.

Emily Jane scooped up Ruby. The little girl reached out and touched the rim of Emily Jane's hat. "Pittie."

"Thank you. I think you look very pretty today, too." Emily Jane hugged the little girl close before handing her down to William. She climbed out of the wagon and then took Ruby back.

A man came out of the barn, followed by a woman about his age. "Good morning," the man called.

William stepped in front of Emily Jane and Ruby. He offered the couple a smile and tipped his hat to them. "Good morning. Is this the Guthrie farm?"

The older gentleman nodded.

His wife walked around him with a big grin on her face. "James, this must be the Barns family. Mr. Nelson told you they might be coming out to look the place over, remember?"

The man rolled his eyes. "Of course I remember, Esther. How could I forget? You've been talking about it all morning."

"So I have." She walked up to William and Rose. "I'm Esther and this is James."

William smiled. They were an interesting couple. Mrs. Guthrie looked as if she wanted him to hand Rose over but was too polite to ask. "I'm William, this is Rose, and Emily Jane is holding Ruby." He realized that they thought Emily Jane and the girls were his family. Since he didn't know the Guthries, William decided not to correct them. He would before they left but not yet.

"It's nice to meet you all. If you will excuse me, I need to go check on my bread. James, bring them up to the house when you're finished. I'd like to visit for a spell."

Mr. Guthrie nodded at his wife. Then he said, "The farm's not big. If you will follow me, I'll show you around." He reached under his big floppy brown hat and scratched his head.

William did as he asked. Their first stop was the barn. It was average size, held hay on one side and had three horse stalls on the other. Out the side door was a small fenced-in area for the horses to walk around in. A swayed-back horse stood in the yard, drinking from a watering trough.

"That's Spot. She's getting on in years, like Esther and me," he said by way of introduction to the horse.

William nodded, unsure what to add to that bit of information. He looked over his shoulder and saw Emily Jane looking at the little mare with pity in her eyes. It was obvious she thought the old gal should be turned out to pasture.

James Guthrie led them out a side gate made of oak branches and wire. "Behind the barn is the woodpile. I'm sure you could move it closer to the house, if you are so inclined. Personally, I use it as an escape from being cooped up all winter." He practically whispered the last part so that Emily Jane wouldn't overhear.

William watched her bury her face in Ruby's shoulder. If she was trying to hide her smile, she'd failed miserably. Her dancing eyes gave her away. "I'll keep that in mind," he said, turning back to the old man.

"We have a small orchard over this way." He started down a grassy hill that led to a cluster of fruit trees.

"What kind of fruit do you raise?" Emily Jane asked, sounding interested.

James looked over his shoulder. "We have fig and apple. Folks said the apples wouldn't do very well, but the missus and I have beautiful fruit every summer." Pride filled his voice.

"Oh, William, just think of the hot apple pies in the winter." Emily Jane's eyes were large and awe filled.

The old man laughed. "My Esther has a fig pie that brings folks to eat from miles around. I'll bet she'll share the recipe with you, Mrs. Barns."

Emily Jane opened her mouth, and William assumed she was going to object to being called Mrs. Barns. He shook his head at her, silently asking her not to say anything. It worked, because she closed her mouth and then smiled at the older gentleman. "That would be very nice of her. I'll be sure and ask when we get back to the house."

When James continued down the small incline, Emily Jane looked at him with a frown. He mouthed, "Please, trust me on this."

She nodded and followed behind him.

As he listened to the man describe every inch of the farm, William's mind flew with other thoughts. Mr. Guthrie had assumed they were married. It would be nice to have Emily Jane as a part of his family. She was kind, loving and honest. Why not ask her to marry him? If he was to buy the farm, the girls would need a constant caregiver, not just a part-time one. Emily Jane cared about the girls; it was evident in the way she spoke to them, touched them and even disciplined them. It would be convenient to have her with them all the time.

He wasn't doing it for love; no, his heart couldn't take being broken, and that was what happened when you loved someone. A person lost all objectivity. Even lost their own identity and became wrapped up in the other's life. No, it was all for the girls that they should marry. Supply a stable home. Who knew if their father would ever return? It certainly wasn't looking as if that would happen.

What was he thinking? Emily Jane followed the older gentleman to the orchard. She could see the unripened fruit hanging from the limbs and inhaled, hoping to catch a hint of their sweet fragrance. The Guthries didn't seem like a dangerous couple, and yet, she had the feeling William didn't trust them. Or was it that he hoped for a lower price on the farm, if the older couple thought they were married?

"Eat!" Ruby called, smelling the sweet fruit.

The old man laughed. "Makes me hungry, too, little one."

"We'll eat in a little while," Emily Jane told her.

"Eat!" Rose called from behind her.

"Later," William answered her.

The two girls began to pout and fuss. Emily Jane set Ruby down and held her hand while she walked her around. Distracted, Ruby quit fussing but not Rose.

William set her on his shoulders and held her hands while he walked among the trees, admiring the fruit that hung heavily from the branches. "You have a nice crop this year."

"We've had this amount for the past two years. Last year, the missus sold several baskets of both apples and figs to Mr. Moore at the general store." He crossed his arms and beamed with pride. "Come harvest time, someone's gonna be busy for sure."

After visiting the orchard, they all headed back to the house. Mr. Guthrie showed them the well beside the house and Mrs. Guthrie's vegetable-and-herb garden. A small chicken coop sat behind the house, and a cow bawled for their attention in a lean-to beside the outhouse.

Emily Jane was tired of being out in the sun and wanted to see the inside of the house. Not that it would ever be hers, but she'd come this far; now she was simply curious. She looked to the house several times, trying to get William to take the hint and ask to see inside.

She'd about given up when Mr. Guthrie said, "I believe your missus would like a gander at the house."

William looked at Emily Jane, and she felt her cheeks grow hot at having been caught by the old man. He grinned and then said, "Lead the way, Mr. Guthrie."

He didn't have to ask twice. "Be honest with ya. I'd like a cold glass of milk myself." Mr. Guthrie opened the door and waited for Emily Jane to pass.

She stepped into a small mudroom and grinned. This house reminded her a lot of home. Her parents' house had a mudroom, and if she wasn't mistaken, the door before her led into the kitchen.

The older woman stuck her graying head through the entry. "Come on inside. I have hot bread and butter waiting for you and those sweet girls."

"Oh, Mrs. Guthrie, you shouldn't have. I packed us a nice picnic lunch."

"Now, don't you go fretting none, Mrs. Barns. I promise it won't spoil their lunches."

Emily Jane followed her into a nice airy kitchen. She didn't feel right, letting the couple believe that she and William were married. "Please, call me Emily Jane." The table had been set with a platter of bread and a saucer of butter. Four plates sat about each side of the square table.

"Are you sure I can't offer you and the mister some lunch, Emily Jane? It really is no bother."

William answered before Emily Jane could. "No,

ma'am. As nice as that sounds, we have another errand to run before it gets too late."

"I sure could use a nice cup of cold milk," Mr. Guthrie hinted to his wife.

She ignored him and asked, "Mr. Barns, I'd like to hold that little one, if you don't mind." Her eyes beseeched both Emily Jane and William for permission.

He smiled. "Rose is the friendly twin. I'm sure she won't mind." William handed the baby over.

"Well, looks like if a man wants cold milk, he has to get it himself," James gruffed. "Come on, Mr. Barns. I'll show you how to have some of the coldest milk this side of Austin." He turned and stomped back out of the kitchen.

William glanced at Emily, shrugged and then followed. The amused look on his face said he liked the Guthries. She just hoped he told them the truth about their relationship.

"What did he mean she's the friendliest? Aren't they the same?"

Emily turned her attention back to Mrs. Guthrie. "No, Rose is never shy around strangers, but Ruby here takes a while to warm up to folks." She hugged Ruby to her.

"Well, I've never been around twins, so had no idea."

Rose reached up and touched Mrs. Guthrie's wrinkled cheek. She smiled and then gave her an open-mouthed kiss on that same cheek.

Mrs. Guthrie laughed. "Kids always did like me. We had six of them. But two of them died, and the rest moved away." Sadness filled her eyes. She stared out the window.

After several long moments, Rose hugged the old woman, bringing her back to the present.

She looked at Emily Jane and gasped. "Where are my manners? Please, sit down and give these babies some bread and butter."

"Thank you." Emily Jane sat. The girls were getting heavier. They'd soon be walking on their own, but for now carrying them left her arms tired.

"You have lovely children. How old are they? One?"

Emily Jane hated not telling her the complete truth. "Yes, they are one."

"When are their birthdays?" She buttered a slice of bread, then tore off a piece of it and handed it to Rose, who had already started trying to get her hands on it.

"I don't know."

"Oh?" Curiosity sounded in the older woman's voice.

"William had the girls when we met." Well, that was the truth.

"Oh, newlyweds." She nodded as if that was what she thought. "You know, being young, in love and starting a new life together is some of the best years of your life. And this farm is just what you need to raise these pretty girls." She tickled Rose's belly.

"Mrs. Guthrie?"

"Please, call me Esther. All my friends do." She seemed unaware that Emily Jane was feeling more and more uncomfortable with their deception.

Mr. Guthrie's voice stopped Emily Jane from telling Esther the truth. "Well, looks like we got ourselves a buyer, Esther." He walked to the table, set a jug of milk on it and then laid his hand on his wife's shoulder.

William walked to the table and stopped next to Emily Jane's chair. "Hold on a minute, James."

The older man's face crumpled. Esther sighed.

Emily Jane looked up at William. He stared down into her face. Then he said, "Before we agree that we're buying this place, we need to be honest with you."

James stood up straighter. "What do you mean?"

William stood a little taller. He should have told them sooner. "I can't buy your farm until I tell you that Emily Jane and I are not married."

"I see." A stern expression came across the older man's features. "And why did you let us assume you were?" he asked.

William looked down at Emily Jane. "Well, sir. It wasn't until after we arrived that I realized I should have come out here on my own. I let you believe we were married because I was trying to protect Emily Jane's reputation."

Emily Jane gasped. He looked at her and knew she hadn't considered how it would appear to others, coming together to look at the farm with no intentions of marrying.

"But to lie about it is even worse. So, I'd still like to buy your farm but will understand if you don't want to sell it to a single man."

For the first time Esther spoke. "Who do these beautiful little girls belong to?"

"They are my nieces. My sister was killed a few months ago, and I'm taking care of them until my brother-in-law comes to claim them." William put his hand on Emily

Jane's shoulder. "Emily Jane has been helping me with the girls."

"And did the tornado truly take your home in town?" Mr. Guthrie asked.

Emily Jane stared at the tablecloth. "Yes, sir. It took both our homes." She answered without looking up. "I have to ask your forgiveness also."

Mr. Guthrie sighed. "Little lady, there is nothing to ask forgiveness for. If I had been in your young man's shoes, to save my Esther's reputation, I would have done the same." He looked to William. "Thank you for coming forward with honesty. I'll sell this place to an honest man, single or married."

Esther nodded her head in agreement.

William wasn't sure if they simply wanted to sell the farm or if they truly liked him and Emily Jane. Did it really matter? He didn't think so. Mr. Guthrie said he understood and was still willing to sell him the farm. "Thank you. I'll talk to the bank first thing Monday morning."

The two men shook hands, and Mrs. Guthrie grinned ear to ear. "I'm glad you and the girls will be living here, Mr. Barns. This farm was a nice place to raise our family. I'm sure you will enjoy it, too."

He nodded. Mr. Guthrie had said the same thing as he'd drawn the jug of cold milk out of the well. And William had to agree, the farm really would be a nice, quiet place to raise a family.

William glanced at Emily Jane, who was busy helping the girls with their snack. What would it be like to live here with her? Raise a farmyard full of kids, work the orchard and come home every night to a hot meal and a smiling Emily.

Get those thoughts out of your mind, William Barns. One, Emily didn't want a farmyard full of children, and two, until Josiah came for the girls, Rose and Ruby were the only children he should be thinking about.

Still, it wouldn't hurt to ask Emily Jane to marry him and help him take care of the girls. If he did, what would she say? There was only one way to find out.

Chapter Nineteen

An hour later, William helped Emily Jane back into the wagon. Mr. and Mrs. Guthrie passed the little girls up to them. "Thank you again," William said as he sat down.

Emily Jane checked on the fox pups. They stuck their little noses out of the box. The little girls squealed at the sight.

"What have you got there?" Mr. Guthrie asked, coming around to look into the box.

She straightened her spine, afraid the old man would want to kill them. "Two baby foxes."

He reached in and patted their heads. "What are you going to do with them?" His even tone told Emily Jane that the man was refraining from saying what he really thought. Her father often got that tone when he disapproved of something.

William answered, "We're going to take them up the road a bit and turn them loose."

Mrs. Guthrie stood off to the side, wringing her hands in her apron, a worried expression on her face.

"That's not a good idea." Mr. Guthrie looked up at Emily Jane.

"Why's that?" William asked.

Emily Jane knew what his answer would be. He'd say they would just be a nuisance to the farmers in the area. But she was surprised when the old man said, "They won't make it."

Emily Jane's stance of defiance changed to concern. "Why not?" Her voice quivered.

Mr. Guthrie looked at his wife. "The missus adopted a set of baby foxes a few years back, and they were just too friendly with folks. Ended up getting shot by the neighbor."

William patted Emily Jane's back. "We'll take them deep into the woods."

She knew he was trying to comfort her, but her mind raced at the horrible things that could happen to the babies. Her babies. She didn't want to desert them in the woods. Emily Jane stooped down and put Rose into the big box and then picked up one of the fox pups. Rose immediately grabbed the other one.

Sadness filled Mrs. Guthrie's voice. "They'll just follow you back. We tried that, too."

Panic filled Emily Jane. "Oh, William. If they follow us back, the men will kill them." How could she have been so stupid? She'd doomed the poor fox pups to certain death by keeping them.

"I know, but we don't have any place to keep them," William reminded her.

"You could leave them with me," Mrs. Guthrie said, quickly.

"Now, Esther. We are selling this place, remember? And we can't take them with us." Mr. Guthrie dropped an arm around his wife's shoulders.

Emily looked to William. If he bought the farm, would he be able to keep the fox pups? Her eyes searched his. She didn't want to come right out and ask him to keep the pups, but she didn't want to leave them in the woods where they would die.

"Mr. Guthrie, would it be too big of an inconvenience for your wife to keep an eye on them for a few days?" William continued to look deeply into Emily Jane's eyes.

He was going to do this for her. Her papa would never have bowed to such a simple request, and yet this man seemed to care about her and the fox pups. With difficulty, Emily Jane pulled her gaze from his. She feared he could see to her very soul. If he did, then he'd know that, with every kind action he showed her, her heart melted just a little more toward him.

The older woman clapped her hands. "I thought you'd never ask. Of course I'll take care of these darling babies."

Emily Jane quickly grabbed up the box she'd brought the fox pups in and handed it to her. "Oh, thank you." With one last stroke of its reddening fur, she handed the pup she held to Mr. Guthrie to place into the box. Then she proceeded to ease the other one out of Rose's grasp.

Rose fussed and tried to get the pup back. When Emily Jane passed it down to Mr. Guthrie, Rose let out a scream that caused the birds in a nearby tree to take flight.

Emily Jane picked up the little girl. "Rose, we have

to leave the foxes here. Mrs. Guthrie will take good care of them, and in a few days you can come back and see them."

As if she understood, the little girl rested her head on Emily Jane's shoulder. She stuck her thumb in her mouth and watched as Mr. Guthrie put the fox pup in the box with her sister. Not for the first time, Emily Jane realized that the fox pups were twin girls, like Rose and Ruby.

"Thank you, Mr. and Mrs. Guthrie. We appreciate all that you are doing, and I'm looking forward to seeing you, Mr. Guthrie, at the bank on Monday."

The old man looked up with a smile. "I'll be there when the doors open."

William's handsome face broke into a wide grin. He looked about the farmyard with a satisfied expression. His gaze turned to the farmhouse. Emily Jane thought she knew his thoughts. He was thinking about the large kitchen with the table in it for eating. And the fact that it had three bedrooms would give him and the girls lots of room. He looked down at her and grinned. "I'm glad Mr. Nelson told me about this place. It's perfect."

Something in his eyes made her want to stay here with him, make a home for the girls and just be content to spend her days baking and cooking for a family. Emily Jane thought about her parents in that moment. Her mother had probably thought the same way when they'd first married, but look at her now. No, what William's eyes offered was a fantasy.

Her gaze moved to the Guthries. They stood side by side. His arm was around Esther's shoulders, and he looked down at his wife. Love radiated from his face.

He only had eyes for Esther. Had he even absorbed what William had said? Or was his heart too full of love for his wife to hear anything?

What would it be like to have a man so devoted to you that he only had eyes for you? Seeing the older couple together made her question her earlier thoughts about her parents. Were they still in love like that? Was her father simply burdened with raising such a large family?

If so, Emily Jane didn't want a large family. She glanced back at William, who had taken his seat at the reins and had reached for the wagon brake. He was a handsome man who seemed to have a big heart.

Lord, I don't want to fight Your will for my life. My heart is set on owning and running my own bakery. Not on marriage and having children. Please, help me to be able to put distance between William and the girls. I know I can't have both, and right now I'm not ready for love and a family.

William glanced over at Emily Jane. They'd been riding for about ten minutes from the Guthrie farm, and she'd already gotten the girls to lie down and take a nap. She faced forward as the wagon rambled on, but she remained silent. What was she thinking?

"I can hear the river from here. Would you like to stop there and have our lunch?" he asked to break the silence.

Emily Jane nodded. "The Guthries turned out to be really nice people, didn't they?"

"They sure did. I'm glad we came out here today."

He'd seen the way she'd studied them right before they left and hoped she'd voice some of those thoughts now.

"Me, too." Emily Jane glanced back at the sleeping girls and smiled. "I think Rose and Ruby liked them, too."

He turned the wagon onto a rutted path. The little mare picked up the pace at the smell of water. "Those little girls like everyone."

Emily Jane chuckled. "True." She glanced his way, and his heart skipped a beat. The hat on her head seemed out of place, and yet it gave her a more grown-up look. He loved it when they felt the same about things. He wasn't very experienced in matters of the heart, but when they agreed, it bonded them a little bit more each time. He had to admit that something in her manner soothed him.

A grove of trees came into view. William turned the little mare toward it. They would be close enough to the river to enjoy the sound and sweetness of its waters but far enough away that the little ones wouldn't fall in when they woke up and started exploring.

"Should we wake the girls?" Emily Jane asked when he set the brake.

William looked back at their sweet faces. "No, let's let them nap."

She nodded and leaned over the seat to grab the picnic basket. William jumped out of the wagon and turned to help her down.

Emily Jane handed him the basket. She glanced once more at the little girls, then placed her small hand in his. William felt a small jolt of electricity pass between them. They both pulled back and then laughed. "That was some shock," she said, replacing her hand in his so that he could help her down.

Once on the ground, William released her and walked to the tree he thought would offer them plenty of shade for their meal. "How does this look?"

Emily Jane joined him. "Perfect." She looked up into the tree branches and grinned.

"This big oak would make a great tree for a swing," William said, his gaze following hers.

"In Kansas we lived on the plains. I have to admit I like these trees much better than no trees." Emily Jane turned her pure green gaze upon him. "We never had trees like this when I was a kid. And definitely no swing."

He opened the basket and found a lightweight blanket on top of the food. As he spread it out, he said, "I miss the aspen trees in Colorado, but these oaks are really nice, too."

She waited until he was finished spreading out the blanket and then sat down. "Even if we had had trees, I wouldn't have had time to swing in a tree."

William studied her serious face. "Too many brothers and sisters to watch?" he guessed.

Emily Jane nodded. "And too many chores to do." Sadness filled her voice and face.

Wanting to cheer her up, William nodded. "I'll be right back. There's something in the wagon I've been meaning to give you." He felt Emily Jane's curiosity peak as her gaze followed him back to the wagon.

Careful to keep it concealed, he carried his surprise

back to her under a small towel. William hoped it would bring a smile to her face. He held the towel-wrapped gift out to her.

"You shouldn't be buying me gifts," she said, warily eyeing the package as if it might bite her.

He smiled. "I didn't buy it." William pushed it toward her again.

Emily Jane tentatively took it. "A book?" She looked up at him in confusion.

He laughed. "Unwrap it and find out." William held his breath as she slowly began to remove the towel.

A squeal tore from her throat as the last layer of fabric came off. "My recipe book! However did you find it?" She hugged it to her chest in delight, then lovingly caressed the front cover.

William sank down onto the blanket beside her. "I think it was a God thing. I was going through the rubble of your house and saw a bucket that didn't look damaged. Thinking I could salvage it, I picked it up and your book was resting underneath."

She opened it up and saw the water marks around the edges of the pages. "I never thought I'd see it again."

"I'm sorry about the water damage, but I think most of the recipes are still good." He lay back and then turned on his side, propping his head up and watching her as she examined each page.

"Oh, William, you have no idea how much this means to me." Her green eyes glistened with unshed tears.

"I'm glad you like it."

"I love it."

"Enough to marry me?"

Chapter Twenty

Emily Jane looked over at him with a smile. Surely he joked? But he wasn't smiling. William had to be teasing. He hadn't just seriously asked her to marry him. Had he? Emily Jane studied his handsome features. His eyes searched her face.

"No, stop kidding around," she answered, now feeling very uncomfortable.

"I'm not kidding. I've been thinking about it all day. If I move out here in the country, I'll need someone to watch the girls, and I don't expect you to drive out here every day."

She sat up straighter. "Do you hear yourself?"

"Yes, I do. Think about it. I'll make sure that you are taken care of. You'll make sure the girls are taken care of and you will be able to cook up those recipes to your heart's content." He motioned at the book within her lap.

Emily Jane pushed up from the blanket. "No, I will not marry you."

William looked as if he'd been slapped. "Why not?"

"I've told you, I want my own bakery. I want the freedom of running it."

Confusion laced his handsome face. "I didn't say you couldn't have your own bakery. Maybe we can work something out."

How? How could she have her bakery and live out of town, take care of a husband and two children?

One of the twins woke up and began to cry. Even now, they couldn't discuss her reasons for not wanting to get married because the children needed tending.

The two little girls pulled themselves up and looked over the wagon bed at them. Emily Jane walked to them. "I'm ready to return to town, William. We can eat on the way."

"Very well." He sighed heavily.

She put her recipe book on the bench and then pulled herself up. When he arrived at the wagon, William handed her the picnic basket. Confusion continued to fill his features. How could he not understand her reaction?

They rode to town in silence. She fed the girls small bites of the deviled ham she'd prepared earlier, and William ate his sandwiches.

"Emily, can't we please talk about this?"

It was her turn to sigh. She glanced in his direction. How did she explain to him that she cared about him and the girls without building his hopes of marriage?

"Look, I know you are angry, but I meant no harm to you. We could be a family without…" His face reddened, and the words were stuck in his throat.

"I'm not angry, William. I understand what you are

offering, but you don't understand. I have dreams of my own. I've told you, I want to buy my own bakery. I care about you and the girls." She paused to take a deep breath. "More than I should, but that doesn't mean I want to marry you. I still want to be a part of yours and the girls' lives but not through marriage and not because I'm in love with you."

"Are you?"

She looked at him in confusion. "Am I what?"

"In love with me?" Was that hope in his voice?

Emily Jane shook off the question. "No, I care about you but, like we agreed on before, only as a friend."

He turned his attention to the narrow road. "I'm buying the farm, Emily. I can't bring the girls in to you every day, and I don't expect you to come out there." His voice held a hint of sorrow that she couldn't ignore.

"I don't know what the answer is, William." Emily Jane thought of him marrying someone besides her. And the thought of him offering anyone the same marriage of convenience as he'd just offered her sent sharp pains into her heart, almost bringing her to tears. She didn't want to lose William and the girls, but she couldn't have it both ways.

The sun was beginning to fade as they pulled up in front of Beth's Boardinghouse. A horse and wagon stood in front of the walkway. Emily Jane felt the dull sense of foreboding. Only one person owned a rig like that pulled by that certain gelding. Her father had arrived.

William mentally beat himself up. He'd gone about asking Emily to marry him the wrong way. He hadn't wanted to spook her with words of love or caring. Love might have been a little too strong for the emotions that he felt for her anyway. But, still, he'd made it sound like a business arrangement, and now that he looked back on their conversation, he realized he was the only one who would have benefited from his proposal. She must think him the most conceited person she'd ever met.

"Oh no, oh no, oh no." Her whispered cry carried to him as he pulled up in front of Beth's Boardinghouse.

He set the brake and then turned to see what distressed her so. She seemed to be focused on a gelding and wagon in front of them. "What's wrong?"

"My father is here."

Fear laced her voice. Her face had gone white, and the freckles on her nose seemed bolder. Protective feelings mounted up in William. "Can I help?" he asked, not sure what her answer would be.

She shook her head hard, and then as if she remembered she was wearing the hat, Emily Jane gasped and ripped it from her head. "Why is he here?" she whispered, covering her mouth with her free hand.

"Maybe we should go find out." William had never seen anyone react to their parent the way Emily Jane reacted to hers. "What are you afraid of?" he asked.

Emily Jane's green eyes swam in tears. "He's going to make me go home. I'm not married like I'm supposed to be." For a second she seemed lost in her own tormenting thoughts. Her eyes grew wide, and a lone tear slipped out one corner. "Oh, William, I can't go back there. I can't."

He took her by the shoulders and turned her to face

him. "Emily, you don't have to. You are a grown woman, and you've been on your own for a while now."

She shook her head back and forth. "No, I'll have to go back. I can't defy my papa. I can't."

William's heart went out to her. "He wants you to get married?"

The tear made a slow trek down her cheek. "Then we can tell him that I asked you to marry me. It's the truth." With his thumb he caressed the tear away.

She went very still. "You did, didn't you?" She spaced the words evenly as if testing them for authenticity.

He nodded and offered what he hoped was an encouraging smile. "I did. And if we need to say we're engaged, we can always call off the wedding after he goes home." William paused.

Emily Jane wiped the moisture from her face. She took a deep breath.

"You going to be all right?" He watched as she understood that he really did care about her.

The realization seemed to help her to regain control of her fearful emotions. She straightened her shoulders. "Yes, thank you."

William climbed down from the wagon and then helped her down. He handed Emily Jane her recipe book and then reached for Rose. The little girl giggled and hugged Emily Jane's neck as he passed her over.

Ruby held out her arms. "Up," she said, reaching for him.

He pulled the girl from the wagon bed and hugged her close. William brushed a gentle kiss across her forehead. The twins may not be his children by birth, but they brought overwhelming joy to his life. He could not imagine ever hurting them or causing them fear. How could any man do that to his daughter? Emily Jane should be thrilled to see her papa, not fearful. His lips pressed shut, so no sound would burst out, but he had no intention of letting her father browbeat her into doing something she didn't want to do. William wasn't looking forward to meeting her father but purposed in his heart right then to stand firm beside her for as long as she needed him.

A few moments later, they entered the foyer. Beth Winters hurried to meet them. "Emily Jane, I am so sorry. Your father is here, and I thought he knew that you hadn't married Levi, and I'm afraid I told him." She stopped and nervously dusted her hands over her apron. "And I'm afraid he's angry."

Emily Jane stood taller. "It's all right, Beth. Papa is always angry about something. Where is he now?"

Beth pointed toward the dining room. "I seated him as far away from the door as possible. I wanted you to have time to compose yourself before having to see him." She reached out and gave Emily Jane a hug about the shoulders. "I really am sorry."

William was proud of Emily. He knew how scared she was, but she didn't show it now. His eyes locked on to hers. For a brief moment she allowed him to see her insecurity. Just as quickly she concealed it and smiled at Beth.

"Thank you for letting me know he is here, Beth. I'll go see him now." Emily Jane handed her recipe book to Beth. "Would you mind putting this in my room for me?"

"Not at all." Beth took the book.

William watched in appreciation as Emily Jane swallowed hard, lifted her chin and walked with unhurried purpose to the dining room. Unsure if he should follow or not, William hung back.

Beth whispered, "Don't leave her alone with that man, William. He's mean."

"He's her father, Beth. At some point I'll have to leave her alone with him," he whispered back.

She gave his shoulder a shove. "Well, now isn't that moment. Get in there."

William followed Emily Jane. She still held Rose, so if her father wondered why he was there, he could always say he had to claim his niece. Her skirts swayed slightly as she walked casually toward her father's table.

Emily Jane stopped beside his chair. "Hello, Papa. What brings you to Granite?" Her voice sounded calm, but her hand shook against Rose's back.

"Can't a father come visit his married daughter?" He wiped his mouth with a linen cloth off the table.

She nodded. "He could, but as you already know, I'm not married."

"Yes, I found that out from a stranger. Why didn't you write your mother and me and tell us you are still unwed?" His gaze connected with William's, who now stood behind Emily Jane. He picked up his coffee and returned his look to his daughter.

William stepped up beside Emily Jane. He hoped his presence would give her the assurance that she wasn't alone.

Emily Jane looked at him. "Well, Papa, I really didn't

think you cared one way or the other. Several months ago you sent me off to marry a complete stranger."

He sat forward in his chair. "Girl, you're sassing me."

She shook her head. "No, sir. I'm telling the truth."

William's heart went out to Emily Jane. He could tell that for the first time in her life she was facing her past hurts. He prayed that her father would see her for the woman she'd become during his absence, instead of the young girl he'd sent away.

She was pushing her father's temper with her answer, and Emily Jane knew it. But she was an adult now, and though she still respected him, it wasn't in the same way she had as a child. He looked older than he had when she'd last seen him.

Her father studied her. "We'll talk about your behavior later. Who is this young man that seems to be hovering around you like a buzzard?"

It would be better for all involved not to take offense to his reference to William. "Papa, this is William Barns and these sweet little girls are Rose and Ruby. Mr. Barns's nieces." She forced a smile as she made the introductions.

William reached across the table and shook her father's hand. "It's nice to meet you, Mr. Rodgers."

"Emily Jane, I'm sure this young man would like to be on his way. Why don't you give him back that baby and have a seat?" He cut the meat on his plate with decisive force.

Before she could answer, William pulled out a chair and sat down. "I appreciate your concern, sir, but if you don't mind I'd like to get to know my future father-in-law better." He put Ruby on his knee and pulled out the chair beside him for Emily Jane to sit in.

Her father leaned back in his chair and crossed his arms. "Well, that is something I hadn't heard about, yet."

"That's because he just asked me this afternoon." Emily Jane took her seat and immediately had to move a water glass out of Rose's grasp.

"So when is the big date?"

Emily Jane looked to William. "We haven't set one yet, Papa. He's just asked me." She prayed her father would be happy with their engagement and go back to the Kansas farm he'd left. With it being planting season, she was surprised to see him here. What was so important that he'd come?

He nodded. "I see. Well, I'll just stick around until the knot is tied. Can't have you losing another husband."

More shaken at his words than she dared to admit, Emily Jane protested. "But, Papa, it will be months from now. And don't you have a farm to plant?"

The older gentleman dropped his napkin to the table and stood. "Nonsense, girl. All you need is a preacher and witnesses. The boys and your mama can take care of the farm for a few more days."

Once more her gaze moved to William. He sat observing them closely. What must he be thinking? Perhaps this was what he'd wanted all along. A flicker of apprehension coursed through her. Was she jumping out of the frying pan into the fire? Her mind worked overtime, torn by conflicting emotions. What did she want? Was she brave enough to stand up to her father? Could she tell him she'd changed her mind? Or the truth that she'd already refused William's offer of marriage?

"Well, since you don't seem to have any further objections, I suggest you get busy making arrangements. I'll be leaving soon." He threw the cloth napkin on the table and stood to leave.

Emily Jane called out, "Papa."

A smug look came across his face. She'd seen it many times when he'd caught one of her brothers in a lie. He enjoyed taking them to the woodshed and helping them to remember why they should never lie to him. "Yes, daughter?"

"Where are you staying?"

The grin left his face. "Got the last room at the hotel this afternoon. Can't really afford it, but since you don't have a home for me to stay in, I'll have to make do." He started to leave, then turned to face them again. "I'll see you in the morning. We have much to discuss."

Emily Jane nodded. She didn't like the way he said "we have much to discuss." Those words usually meant bad news for her. He'd said them the night he and Mother had told her she was answering Levi Westland's mail-order-bride advertisement. She couldn't bear to look at William, so she traced Rose's little hand. It didn't escape her notice for one moment that her fingers shook uncontrollably.

Beth hurried to their table. "Can I get you all dinner?" she asked.

William nodded. "Yes, Emily and I have a lot to

talk about, so we might as well feed the girls at the same time."

Emily Jane wasn't sure she liked William telling Beth or anyone else they had things to talk about. She wasn't sure what her father had in mind but knew that whatever it was, it meant bad news for her. She sighed. Could this day get much worse?

Chapter Twenty-One

Emily Jane admired Beth Winters. Beth ran Beth's Boardinghouse and had once confided in Emily Jane that doing so had always been her dream. She had also said that she was saving her money to buy the boardinghouse from Levi Westland. Beth's future and that of her son's would soon be even more secure.

Beth and Amelia Blackwater carried over two high chairs for the girls. Amelia was new in town and had been looking for employment. Two days ago, Beth had rented Amelia the last available room in the boardinghouse.

Emily Jane realized that Amelia was wearing a kitchen apron. Had Beth hired her? The smile Amelia gave her confirmed that the girl was pleased with herself.

Things seemed to be falling into place for everyone but her. If only her father hadn't shown up. Emily Jane didn't know what to do. Her dream of owning a bakery was evaporating before her like early morning mist on the river's waters.

"Levi thought our customers might enjoy having these," Beth said as she set them up next to the table. "They are sure coming in handy today."

She took Rose from Emily Jane and put her into one of the chairs. Amelia did the same with Ruby and then returned to the kitchen.

Emily Jane listened as William ordered the girls mashed potatoes, peas and creamed chicken. How far would she go to avoid going home with her father? Would she marry William?

Rose and Ruby looked at each other; their sweet grins touched her heart. What if their father never came back? If she married William, even in name only, and their father didn't come back, that would make her their adopted mother.

William reached across and laid his hand over hers. "What do you want to do now?" he asked in a soft voice.

She wanted to cry but now wasn't the time. "I don't know. I never thought he'd want to stay for the wedding."

"I know you don't really want to get married. Do you want to tell him we had a fight and the wedding is off?"

If they did that, her father would insist she go back to Kansas. Back to taking care of her brothers and sisters. Back to cooking plain meals. And there was no way she'd ever get her own bakery. If she married William, she'd be moving out to the farm, raising two little girls, instead of eleven, and she'd never own her own bakery. A pounding began in Emily Jane's head. "Not yet. Maybe if I pray and sleep on it, I'll come up with something."

Amelia arrived with William's and the little girls' food. She set a plate of meat loaf, mashed potatoes and peas in front of Emily Jane. "I didn't order this." Even if she had, she couldn't eat a bite. Her stomach rolled at the thought.

"I ordered it for you," William said, pulling Rose's and Ruby's plates out of their reach. "Girls, you know we pray first."

Emily Jane bowed her head and listened to the short prayer William offered up for their meals. All the time, her mind raced. What was she going to do? No matter what she chose to do, her dream of owning a bakery was long gone.

While he prayed for their meals, William silently tacked on prayers for Emily Jane. His heart ached for her. She really was between a rock and a hard place.

As soon as he said, "Amen," Emily Jane pushed her plate back and picked up the glass of water. "Thank you for ordering for me, William, but I'm really not hungry." She set the glass back down without taking a drink then reached over and fed Ruby a bite of her mashed potatoes.

William spooned potatoes into Rose's mouth and then took a bite himself. He didn't want to push Emily Jane either way. But he didn't want to lose her, either.

"Papa is going to expect us to talk to the preacher tomorrow," she said in a soft, sad voice.

"Is your father a churchgoing man?" William continued to help Rose get her food into her mouth.

"Yes, back home he makes sure that our family fills

up the first two pews. You'll see tomorrow. Papa will be on the front row waiting for me to join him." She offered Ruby a drink.

"Since you are marrying me, shouldn't you be sitting with me and the girls?" Had he overstepped his bounds? William held his breath while he waited for her answer.

He was pleased to see a smile creep across her lips. "Yes, I should."

William shared the grin with her. "Well, I never get there early because of the girls. I don't know why tomorrow should be any different. I'll pick you up, and you can ride in the wagon with us."

Emily Jane's brow furrowed. "I don't know. Papa is a stranger here. Maybe I should get up early, go to the hotel and then sit with him during the service. He said we had more to discuss."

William nodded. He wasn't going to try to talk her out of sitting beside her parent. Emily Jane knew what was best for herself. He just hoped she wouldn't change her mind and leave him. William didn't want to go so far as to say he'd fallen in love with Emily Jane, but he would miss her if she left town. Something tugged in his heart. He refused to even consider that he had deeper feelings for Emily Jane than just friendship.

They continued the meal in silence, each of them deep within their own thoughts. Rose and Ruby laughed, played and smacked their lips as they ate.

Once the girls were finished, Amelia arrived at their table with a damp cloth to clean the potatoes from the girls' faces. Emily took it and washed first Rose's face and then Ruby's.

Was Emily Jane aware that she'd taken over the care of the girls even when he was present and could have washed their faces? Tenderness covered her expression as she talked softly to the girls and brushed food from their dresses. She kissed them each on the cheek and giggled when they returned her affections.

William stood. "Are you ready to head back to the school?" he asked, picking Rose up.

The little girls both kicked their legs. Emily Jane lifted Ruby and carried her out to William's wagon while he paid for their dinner. He'd never dreamed this morning that he'd be engaged this evening, but he was. What would tomorrow bring?

It was all William could do to get the girls dressed and himself to the church before the service actually started. They'd always been close to late before, but today he had to get there early. There was no way he would let Emily Jane down.

Out of respect, she'd decided to sit with her father. And William had promised to be beside her. If they were engaged, it was expected.

He'd prayed most of the night about what he and Emily Jane were doing. Deep in his heart, William felt peace. She might not be aware of it or want to admit it, but they were going to be married. So, telling her father they were was the truth.

William stopped just inside the church door. It took only a moment to locate Emily Jane and her father sitting in the front row. As he made his way down the aisle, William marveled that Emily Jane's father was a churchgoing man but seemed so hard on his daughter. He still couldn't understand what kind of man would send his daughter off to marry a complete stranger.

Emily Jane's relieved eyes rose to meet him. She held her hands out to Rose, who immediately reached for her. "Good morning."

Her smile touched that soft spot in his heart. "Good morning." Their hands brushed as he handed Rose to her. Her eyes widened, and she quickly looked away. William grinned, knowing she'd felt that spark between them, too.

He took his seat. Her father leaned forward and nodded, then leaned back in his seat. There was no time for further interaction with anyone else. The preacher started the service.

When the final "amen" was said, Mr. Rodgers stood. "You have a good man of God here," he said, picking up his hat and slapping it against his blue-jean-clad leg. "I think he'll perform a good wedding ceremony."

Emily Jane nodded and also stood. "William and I intend to talk to him about our wedding as soon as everyone heads home."

William continued to hold Ruby in his lap. He nodded his agreement with Emily Jane. Not sure what to say, he decided to let father and daughter visit. The rest of the congregation made their way to the back of the church.

"Since we didn't have enough time to visit this morning, I think I'll just wait here with you," her father said, sitting back down. "We can catch up until the preacher gets done, and then you two can carry on with your business."

Emily Jane sat down. "How is Mama?" She sounded like a little girl.

His features softened, and he touched her shoulder. "She is well. Been worried about you."

"I'm sorry about that, Papa." Emily Jane hugged Rose to her. "I couldn't come home."

He put his head in his hands. "I know. We thought we were doing the right thing."

Emily Jane touched the top of her father's head. "Papa, I've got a good life here. I'm fine. Tell Mama I'm doing well."

Her father raised his head. "How can you say you have a good life here and are doing well? You are homeless and work in a bakery. From what I can see, you haven't any money, and other than saying you are getting married to this man, I see no change in you. None."

"I love my job and have friends here," Emily Jane answered, lowering her head. "How did you want me to change?" she asked, hurt easing through her voice.

He sighed. "I wanted to see you in a nice home, pretty clothes and at least one baby on the way by now. Instead I found you like this." His voice sounded bitter.

William couldn't be quiet any longer. "Mr. Rodgers, your daughter is one of the sweetest women I've ever met. She had a home before the tornado came. She's respected in this community. I'm blessed that she's agreed to marry me."

Her father stood once more. "Well, then perhaps after your wedding I can go home and tell her mother that her eldest daughter has turned into a woman she can be proud of."

William stood, too. "Emily Jane is already a daughter to be proud of."

Mr. Rodgers smiled. "Glad to hear you feel that way, son." He glanced over his shoulder. "Well, here comes the preacher. I'm heading back to the hotel for some lunch. Feel free to join me, when you get done."

William watched him shake the preacher's hand and then continue out of the church. One moment Emily Jane's father seemed to be a caring, loving father and then, within a blink of the eye, a man who seemed to enjoy making her feel small. He reached over and took her hand. "Are you feeling all right?"

Emily Jane looked up at him. "Yes. Papa means well."

He wasn't so sure of that, but William was wise enough to keep his opinion to himself. "Good. Are you sure you want to go through with this?"

She nodded. "When I told Papa that I have a good life here, that I love my job and that I have friends here, that was the truth. I'll be a good wife to you, and for as long as they need me, I'll take care of the girls."

"And I promise, I'll never ask more from you than what you are willing to give." William smiled at her. If they lived to be a hundred years old, he intended to make Emily Jane happy and never make her feel insignificant.

"I'm sorry to keep you two waiting. It seems everyone wanted to talk today." The preacher sat down on the platform. "What can I do for you today?"

Emily Jane looked to William to answer.

He rubbed the back of her hand with his thumb, enjoying the softness. "We would like to get married," William blurted out.

"Today?"

Emily Jane pulled her hand from his and massaged it with her other one. "No, not today but within the week."

"I see. May I ask why you are in such a hurry?" he asked, looking from one face to the other.

Again Emily Jane answered. "My father is in town for a few days, and I'd like him to be at my wedding."

"Did you have a day in mind?" the preacher asked.

William waited. When Emily Jane didn't answer, he turned to her. "Would Wednesday afternoon be a good time?"

She nodded.

The preacher tapped the top of his Bible. "Are you both sure this is what you want? Marriage is a lifelong commitment, not something to be taken lightly."

William answered, "I'm ready." His confidence spiraled upward. For once in his life, he felt sure of himself and his rightful place in the universe.

"Me, too." Her clear green eyes locked on to his. To his interested amazement, a spark of some indefinable emotion glowed with tenderness, and, could it be love? Powerful relief filled him. Then it was like watching a veil cover her face as her lids lowered and hid her thoughts from him. But not before he saw the expression of reproach and defeat cross her features. She sighed and then gave a resigned shrug.

Emily Jane looked defeated. She had given up. Surrendered. What did it all mean? A warning voice whispered in his head. Charlotte hadn't cared about him, either. Would time prove the same with Emily Jane? Was it too much to expect love and admiration from the woman he married?

Chapter Twenty-Two

Emily Jane couldn't believe it was her wedding day. So many people had graciously come forward with gifts for both her and William. There was one, though, that she had exclaimed over with intense pleasure. Susanna Marsh definitely knew how to make a bride happy.

Susanna had worked night and day to finish her gift for Emily Jane. A wedding dress cut and sewn from her own special design. It had taken Emily Jane's breath away. And now Emily Jane stood in front of the mirror draped in the many folds of material. The shimmering light green fabric twirled about her, making her feel like a princess from one of Anna Mae's storybooks.

"Here is a sixpence to put in your left shoe," Anna Mae said, holding out the coin.

Emily Jane frowned but took the money. "And why am I putting this in my shoe?"

"It represents wealth and financial security." Susanna giggled as she straightened out the hem of Emily Jane's dress.

"What about the rest of the poem? Did you get something old, something new, something borrowed and something blue?" Millie Westland asked.

Millie was a newlywed herself. She'd married Levi back in the fall. They were expecting their first child in a couple of months.

"No. I didn't know I was supposed to have all that stuff," Emily Jane answered, wishing the hummingbirds in her tummy would settle down.

"You can't get married without them," Anna Mae said, agreeing with Millie.

"Well, I think I can take care of the something borrowed," Millie said, taking a pretty comb from her own hair and handing it to Emily Jane. The little diamond studs reflected the light.

Were those real diamonds? "I can't accept this, Millie. It looks expensive." Emily Jane tried to hand it back to her.

Millie laughed, and her big tummy jiggled. "You are only borrowing it, Emily Jane." She tucked her hands over her belly. "I won't take it back until after the ceremony."

Emily Jane turned it over and over in her hand. It really was beautiful.

"Your wedding dress can be the something new." Susanna stepped back and looked at her. "You look beautiful."

Emily Jane felt her cheeks grow hot. "Thank you."

"She still needs something old and something blue," Millie said, easing down into a chair.

Anna Mae sat Emily Jane down on a stool in front

of a mirror. "Here, let me put the comb in for you." She began combing Emily Jane's hair. "Your hair is so pretty. I wish mine was red instead of this mousy brown."

Before Emily Jane could answer, Amelia breezed through the door, her cheeks red, her breath coming in soft gasps. "Whew, I thought I wouldn't make it in time. I ran all the way from the restaurant." Her mouth formed a perfect O. "Emily Jane, you are so beautiful."

"What's that you've got, Amelia?" Susanna reached out to touch the flowers Amelia carried.

"I made this bouquet for you, Emily Jane. If you don't want to carry it, I will not be offended at all." She colored fiercely and scuffed the toe of her shoe against the floor. Emily Jane could not believe a woman as lovely as Amelia lacked confidence. She rushed to assure Amelia how touched she was by the gesture.

"They're beautiful, Amelia. I love them. I hadn't even thought of a bouquet." Bluebonnets mingled with baby's breath and green ivy. A white-and-green ribbon formed a delicate bow, and amazingly the green ribbon drew the green shimmers out of her dress. She reached for them, but Amelia held them out of her reach.

"Umm, there's something else. I took the liberty of going into your room. I hope you don't mind." She offered them a small, shy smile. She turned the bouquet over, and the base of the arrangement was Emily Jane's cookbook.

Emily Jane bit her lip to stifle her cry of joy. The exclamations of her friends echoed her feelings exactly. She flung her arms around Amelia, happiness bubbling in her heart. "Thank you, thank you. It's perfect."

"Stop that right now." The smile on her face belied the threat in Susanna's voice. "You'll put wrinkles in your dress before you ever walk down the aisle."

"Well," Anna Mae said matter-of-factly, "that takes care of the something old, the book, and something blue, the flowers."

"Now that I have everything from the poem, what is the point of having them?" Emily Jane asked, looking at the faces of her friends. "I mean what's the purpose?"

Susanna smiled. "They are supposed to bring you luck."

Luck. Emily Jane didn't think she needed luck.

Over the past three days, she'd begged God to get her out of this mess, but He'd remained silent. She cared about William but still resented the idea of giving up her dream for marriage and children. Since the Lord had not intervened, Emily Jane resigned herself to the fact that having a bakery must not be the will of God and that she would make William the best wife that she could be.

She hadn't seen much of him. On Monday he'd gone to the bank and bought the farm. The Guthries had come to town with a single wagonload of the things they wanted to take with them back East and left town almost immediately after the sale was completed.

William and her father had stayed away while Emily Jane and her friends planned the wedding and the reception. Beth Winters had insisted on baking the wedding cake. Carolyn Moore decorated the church pews with streamers and flowers. Millie Westland had hired a group of musicians to play during the reception. It was going to be a wedding party that would be talked about for months to come. At least, that was what Millie had said. The kindness of her friends and the local townspeople filled her heart with joy. She exhaled a long sigh of contentment.

"Ladies, it's time to go," Levi Westland called through the door.

Millie giggled. "Come on, ladies." She opened the door to her husband.

Levi nodded his head at the women as they came out of Emily Jane's room. "There are two wagons out front to take everyone to the church," he said, smiling down at his pretty little wife.

Emily Jane's hand shook as she closed the door to her room. Her heart hammered as she walked down the boardinghouse stairs. Her knees trembled. The girls chattered all the way to the church, but Emily Jane remained silent, fingering the ribbons on the bouquet. She took deep breaths until she was strong enough to raise her head.

Was William as nervous as she? Was he having second thoughts? Did he feel as ill equipped as she did at undertaking the task before them today? One thing was for certain. They both walked into it with their eyes wide-open.

The church looked like something from a fairy-tale book. Green ribbons hung along the bench edges. Tiny blue-and-white flowers were interwoven within the ribbons. The church smelled of pine and honeysuckle. But none of this compared to Emily Jane.

She seemed to glide down the center aisle on her father's arm. The green gown she wore brought out the color in her beautiful eyes. Her red hair had been piled on top of her head, and ringlets framed her face. A comb pulled back one side, giving her a glamorous look. How had he missed how beautiful she truly was? Carried away by his own response, he failed at first to notice the heartrending tenderness of her gaze. Everything took on a clean brightness, and his pulse quickened in giddy happiness. And then she stood in front of him.

He stepped forward, and Mr. Rodgers placed her small hand within his. Her mere touch made him want to vow eternal love for her. He held her hand throughout the ceremony, gently caressing the back of it with his thumb. William repeated his vows, unaware of them because his true focus was on the lady at his side.

At the preacher's instruction, he slipped a simple gold band onto her left ring finger. It wasn't enough. She deserved so much more. A knot tightened his throat as she repeated her vows with a gentle softness in her voice.

He could barely stand still as Emily Jane studied his face unhurriedly, feature by feature, as if analyzing his reaction to every nuance of the ceremony. William felt as if they were the only two people in the world, wrapped in a silken cocoon of closeness. He'd had no idea that getting married would feel this way.

"You may kiss the bride," the preacher said in a loud voice.

William released her hands and gently cupped her face. Their first kiss. Her long lashes closed over her eyes.

Lowering his mouth, he took his first taste of her sweet lips. Raising his mouth from hers, he stared into her eyes. Why had he waited so long to kiss her? She tasted so much better than his beloved sugar cookies.

To his surprise, Emily Jane had returned his kiss. Her mouth moved shyly under his before she pulled away. He squeezed her hand, encouraging her, letting her know he loved her participation. A pink flush covered her cheeks, bringing out the freckles.

Without reservation, William ran his thumb over her mouth and then leaned his forehead on hers. They were husband and wife. Emily Jane had stolen his heart at their first meeting. Why hadn't he been aware of it all this time?

The minister patted him on the shoulder, then whispered close to his ear. "Face the congregation so that I can present you."

William reluctantly did as asked but used the occasion to wrap her briefly in his arms.

"I present you with Mr. and Mrs. William Barns."

The wagon bumped along the road to the farm. His gaze slid across the bench to where his wife sat. She'd changed into a light blue day dress, but her hair still remained up off her neck and shoulders, revealing freckles there, as well. Why that pleased him he couldn't tell, but his smile broadened in approval.

She'd been quiet for the past fifteen minutes. Was she as overwhelmed as he felt? Emily Jane shyly glanced his way, and once more that charming, soft pink flush filled her cheeks.

"I still can't believe we're married," he said to break the silence.

"Me, either." She fiddled with the fabric in her lap. "I hope you don't regret marrying me."

He reached out, touching her elbow. "Why would I?"

She wiggled around on the seat so that she faced him. "You might meet a woman that you fall in love with."

William grinned. "I might have already found that woman."

She exploded. "Then why in the world did you marry me?" Tears spilled from her eyes. "You should have told me."

He guided the mare to the side of the road and set the brake. There were those tears again. William tried to take her hands in his, but she pulled them away. Her eyes accused him of wrongdoings. "I did tell you."

Emily Jane shook her head. The curls about her face caressed her cheeks. "No, you didn't. I would never have married you if I had known."

"That's what I was afraid of," William confessed. He had never liked to see a woman cry, but in this case it sealed in his mind a certainty that Emily Jane had feelings for him. Why else would the thought of him loving another cause such a reaction? He felt his confidence grow.

She sniffled. "I don't understand. Why marry me when you could marry someone you loved?" The freckles across her forehead bunched up in a frown.

William sighed. He ought to own up sooner rather than later, or matters could get completely out of hand in a hurry. However, this wasn't how he'd planned on telling her. He'd wanted to do so over dinner, but here they sat. He gentled his voice and said with quiet emphasis, "Emily Jane, I did marry the person I love."

Confusion and understanding warred together in her beautiful expressions. "You love me?" she whispered.

William brushed back the hair at her temple. Just touching her sent a surge of joy through him. She was his. They'd gotten married, and he'd just told her he loved her. He nodded. "I do. I think I have since the moment I met you but was too stubborn to allow my head to hear what my heart was already saying."

More tears filled her eyes. "Oh, William. I love you, too. But…"

He rested a finger across her lips. "All I need to hear is that you love me. I know how you feel about having children, and I've decided I'm happy raising Rose and Ruby. And when Josiah comes for them, we can still be happy without children."

She removed his finger from her lips and offered him a small smile. "What if I change my mind and want to have children?"

"Then we will have children." Was she trying to tell him that if he wanted children she'd change her mind and have them? Or was she simply letting him know that she wasn't dead set against having children? It didn't matter. He loved her no matter what.

"William Barns!" The shout startled them both.

Emily Jane looked over her shoulder to see who had called his name. A big man riding a roan-colored horse barreled down on them. His shoulder-length brown hair flew behind him like a waving flag under his dark black hat.

"Who is that man?" She turned to find that William had jumped down from the wagon and seemed to be taking a fighting stance.

The big man jumped from the horse, not giving it time to stop. He raced to William and grabbed him in a bear hug. The horse spun around and pranced back.

Emily Jane looked about the wagon for a weapon. She searched under the seat and found the shotgun. Just as her hand clasped the barrel, she realized they were laughing and slapping each other on the back.

"Josiah, I didn't recognize you with that long hair and beard. I think you took twenty years off my life just now. But, boy, am I glad to see you! I thought you might be dead!" William said excitedly.

Emily Jane sank to the wagon seat. Her legs shook like cold jelly. She placed a hand over her heart and watched the two men. Her brothers acted that way when they hadn't seen each other in a few days.

William looked up at her with a huge grin. "Emily, I'd like you to meet Josiah, Rose and Ruby's father. Josiah, this is Emily Jane Barns, my wife."

If she hadn't still been shaken up, Emily Jane might have laughed at the shocked expression on Josiah's face. He looked from her to William and back again.

In a gravelly voice, Josiah said, "Nice to meet you, Mrs. Barns."

"Please, we're family. Call me Emily Jane." She smiled down at him. Now that she knew who he was, she could see Rose and Ruby in his features. Mainly his cheekbones. Josiah had the same high cheekbones as the twins. Their black curls must have come from their mother, William's sister.

"Speaking of family, where are my girls?" He turned to William.

William slapped him on the back. "They are in town with Anna Mae Leland. The town schoolteacher. Why don't you come out to the house with us, and I'll catch you up?" William climbed back up into the wagon with Emily Jane.

Josiah nodded and swung back up into the saddle. He moved so fast, Emily Jane wasn't sure when his feet left the ground. She listened as he and William called back and forth to each other, neither seemingly able to wait for the overdue conversation till they got to the house.

"I'm sure glad to see you. Like I said earlier, I thought you were dead." William looked up at Josiah, riding as close to the wagon as he could get.

"I'm sorry about that. It took longer than I'd anticipated to catch my prisoners." Josiah's gaze moved to Emily Jane.

She smiled at him but didn't comment. It was obvious he wondered how much she knew about him and his reason for being separated from the girls.

"How are my girls doing?" he asked, patting the roan.

William shrugged. "I think they are good. I'm sure they've missed you."

"They are such babies, William. I'm not sure they know how to miss anyone." His sad eyes looked down on them. It was clear that Josiah missed his wife.

With a shake of his head, William answered, "I think you will be surprised."

They arrived at the farm. Emily Jane waited for William to help her down. She wasn't sure if they were going to have a houseguest or not.

"I'll put the horse and wagon away and be right in," William said, giving her a kiss on the cheek.

She felt a blush splash across her face and nodded. Emily Jane took the bag he handed her and hurried to the house. Once inside she looked about. This was her new home.

Standing in the sitting room doorway, she looked to the left where the Guthries had left their dining table and chairs. She knew from her last visit that the kitchen was through the next door to her left of the dining room. A stairway led to the two bedrooms on the second floor.

Taking a deep breath, Emily Jane climbed the stairs. The room on the right was obviously William's. A large bed, armoire and dresser filled the space. She crossed to the window and looked down into the front yard.

William and Josiah stood beside the barn. He'd released the little mare into the corral, and the two men rested their arms on the top fence rail, visiting. William turned and looked at the house. His head came up, and he gazed straight at the bedroom window. Could he see her? Or had he just sensed her watching them?

Emily Jane backed away from the window. Now that Josiah had returned, how much would things change? Would he need someone to watch the girls for him and ask her? Or would he take the girls and return to Denver? Her heart ached at the thought of the girls leaving.

She walked over to the bed and sank into the mattress. Did this mean that she could stay in town and work at the bakery? Would she be content to live on the farm and work in town? Her mind raced a mile a minute with questions and uncertainties that only her husband could answer for her. Her husband. My, but she did like the sound of that.

Chapter Twenty-Three

William stood in the bedroom doorway watching his new wife sleep. Her red hair spread out over the pillow, and sooty black lashes rested against her freckled skin. He'd never seen a more beautiful woman.

He'd spent the night talking to Josiah and learning that his brother-in-law had pursued the bank robbers all the way to Mexico. They had given Josiah a merry chase, and he'd felt obliged to share all the obstacles the chase had entailed. After he'd caught them, it had taken another two months to get a trial date for the men. Then another to locate William and the girls.

Josiah had fallen asleep downstairs on the settee. William now stood watching Emily Jane sleep.

He tiptoed to the window and pulled the rocker beside it. The sun peeked over the horizon in the east. William watched as shades of pinks, oranges and fiery reds filled the morning sky. His gaze moved back to the bed.

Emily Jane smiled in her sleep. Did that mean she

was happy? Or was she dreaming of the bakery that she no longer thought was within her grasp?

He sat down and waited for her to wake up. Until she knew just how much he loved her, William intended to keep his promise of a marriage of convenience. A yawn expanded his chest, and his eyes began to drift shut. He'd rest a few minutes and then wake her; William couldn't wait to give Emily her wedding present.

The hot sun and a cramped neck woke him. The bed was empty. Emily Jane had spread the quilt back over it and was nowhere to be seen.

William pushed out of the chair with a groan. He moved to his wardrobe and pulled out a fresh shirt. A glance at his feet reminded him he'd slept with his boots on.

Her sweet laughter drifted up the stairs. William followed the sound and found his lovely wife sharing a cup of coffee and eggs with his brother-in-law. An unfamiliar twinge ripped across his chest.

When she saw him enter the room, Emily stood and came to his side. She tiptoed to give him a kiss on the cheek and whispered, "Thanks for letting me sleep."

He couldn't resist and turned his face quickly and captured her lips with his. Her lips were warm and moist. His mood turned suddenly buoyant.

A hearty laugh surrounded them.

Emily Jane jerked away from him. "I'll get your coffee and eggs."

William released her and glared at his brother-in-law, who had spoiled the kiss. "Thank you."

"I thought you were going to sleep the day away." Josiah leaned back in his chair and sipped at his coffee.

He walked to the table and sat down. Emily Jane handed him a steaming cup. William smiled his thanks to her, then turned his attention back to Josiah. "Well, someone kept me up all night."

Emily Jane gasped.

He continued: "With tales of chasing bank robbers and the woes of finding a good judge." William grinned at his brother-in-law, who seemed not to have noticed Emily's gasp.

Josiah dropped his chair to the floor. "Guilty as charged." He set the cup on the table and stood. "Now that you are up, I'd like to head back to town and get my girls."

William took the plate of eggs from Emily. "And go where with them?"

Emily Jane put a hand on his shoulder. She tilted her head and waited for Josiah to answer.

"I'm not sure. I can always go back to Denver." Even as he said it, William knew that wasn't his plan. Like him, Josiah would always associate the city as the place where Mary had died.

"You and the girls are welcome to stay out here with us," Emily Jane offered. She squeezed William's shoulder, and he looked up at her.

She had to be the most generous person he'd ever met. He reached up and laid his hand over hers.

"Thank you, Emily Jane. But are you sure you want two little girls underfoot night and day?"

William held his breath as he waited to hear what she

would say. She'd offered their home, but had she really thought about what she'd said? And once he'd given her his wedding present, would she regret her offer?

This was just the opportunity she'd been waiting for. The little girls needed a woman in their lives. And truth be told, Emily Jane loved them.

She'd worried about Rose and Ruby while the men had slept. What was Josiah going to do with them? He was a single man who probably hadn't taken care of them a full day of their lives.

Emily Jane smiled at Josiah. He'd confided in her that he wasn't sure what he was going to do now that he'd caught the bank robbers that had killed his wife. He'd resigned as sheriff when he'd returned to Denver and come in search of his girls.

"I'm sure. Besides, you two will be here to help with them."

She picked up Josiah's plate and carried it to the washbasin. While William and Josiah had slept, she'd familiarized herself with her new kitchen. Mrs. Guthrie had left almost all the dishes, pots and pans and utensils that she would need to cook and bake.

Now that she knew the girls would be living with her, Emily Jane almost felt like this was home. The night before she'd confided in William that she loved him. She'd realized while they were talking about children that having her own child would be nothing like raising siblings. A small smile touched her lips at the thought.

"She seems pretty sure to me," William said.

Emily Jane felt his gaze upon her. She nodded at him.

"Well, if you are both sure. I promise to try not to overstay our welcome." He picked up his black hat and placed it on his head. "I'll go take care of the horses while you finish up your breakfast. Then I'm heading to town to get my girls."

William swallowed a big bite of scrambled eggs. "Give us a few minutes and we'll ride in with you."

Josiah chuckled. "I was hoping you'd say that. I've no idea where this Mrs. Leland lives."

"Miss Leland," Emily Jane corrected him absently. Why were she and William returning to town? Maybe he felt they needed supplies.

Whatever the reason, she was glad. Papa had said he'd be leaving right after lunch, and Emily Jane wanted to say goodbye to him. He was a hard man at times, but she knew he only wanted what was best for her and she loved him.

The door closed behind Josiah, and Emily Jane turned to her new husband. "Yesterday, I didn't have a chance to give you my wedding present. Would it be all right with you if I give it to you now?"

"You didn't have to get me a present." William smiled, pleased.

She offered him a returning grin. "Maybe not, but I wanted to." Emily Jane hurried to the bedroom and pulled out the package she'd stashed under the bed. Then she walked back to him, praying he'd like her gift. It had cost almost all the money she'd saved for her bakery, but now that she was no longer going to pursue that dream, Emily Jane had bought the gift for William.

"That is a big package," William said, standing to take it from her.

Emily Jane slipped into the closest kitchen chair and watched as he pulled the pretty blue, green and white ribbons from the butcher paper that held her gift. She watched his face and was happy to see the joy that leaped into his eyes as he pulled the present out.

William turned the picture of the elk in his hands. "How did you know?" he asked in wonder. Pleased, he touched the smooth wood and admired the many colors that accented the piece.

She giggled. "I asked Levi if there was something in his store you might like."

The smile slipped from his face. "Emily Jane, this is too much." He laid the elk on the table.

"No, it isn't." Tears filled her eyes as she thought of the love he'd proclaimed, and just knowing that he'd been willing to let her continue to work at the bakery was more than enough reason for her to use the money to buy the gift for him.

"Honey, that was the money you were saving for your bakery. Why would you spend it on a piece of painted wood?" His eyes questioned hers.

Emily Jane saw the emotions warring within their depths. Was he happy or sad? She couldn't be sure. She realized that now that Josiah had returned, she and William could try to make her dream of owning a bakery come true. But even though she really wanted to have the bakery, now that William was in her life, that dream didn't seem as important as it had before. He now gave her life meaning, and she wanted to enjoy every moment of their time together.

Emily Jane realized she'd been silent for too long. Doubt now filled his face. She stood and walked to him. "I love you, William, so very much it hurts in here." She clasped both hands over her heart. "I wanted to give you something that I knew you loved. The bakery was a dream but you are real, and I want to spend my days being with you."

Tears filled his eyes. William pulled her to him, and she relaxed against him as his arms tightened about her small body. She could feel his breath against her cheek and hear his heart beat in her ears. How good the Lord had been to her to give her this man. She smiled. This was where she truly belonged.

"Oh, excuse me." Josiah began to back out of the door he'd just barged into.

Emily Jane pulled out of her husband's arms. "We're ready," she called to Josiah. She looked up into her handsome husband's face. They had their whole lives before them.

He slid his hand down her arm and clasped her hands in his. "Yes, we are." William held her hand as they followed Josiah to the wagon.

He lifted her up and then said, "Thank you for my gift. I'll cherish it always."

Emily Jane sat on the seat beside her new husband as they rode toward town. Her life had changed over the past few months. She had changed. Emily Jane tossed her head back and enjoyed the warm sun on her face and the feeling of being loved.

It didn't take them long to reenter Granite. Their first stop was the boardinghouse, so that Josiah could get the girls. Anna Mae was in the dining room feeding them lunch when they arrived.

Rose and Ruby saw their father at the same time. Both girls began chanting. "Da! Da!" They tried to fling themselves from their high chairs to get to him.

Emily Jane watched, her heart in her throat as he pulled them from their chairs and buried his face in their little necks. The girls grabbed his head and gave him openmouthed kisses on his cheeks, his ears and all other places where they could reach.

They refused to let him go, so great was their joy at seeing their papa. Josiah's tear-smothered voice whispered their names over and over as he examined their fingers, their little heads and legs. He seemed to be committing them to memory. Emily Jane swallowed hard and bit back tears.

When Josiah gained control of his emotions again, she introduced him to Anna Mae, who appeared tongue-tied. What in the world? One thing Anna Mae had never been without was words. She could talk the rings off a rattler. She watched with interest as the schoolteacher excused herself to get the girls' things from her room. "I'd like to go say goodbye to Papa," Emily Jane said to William.

He nodded. "Josiah, do you want to wait here for us to come back?"

Josiah looked confused. "I figured I'd just take the girls back out to your place."

William smiled. "Yes, but you'll need our wagon

to get them there. I'm not sure even you could hold on to two squirming girls and keep that roan of yours in check at the same time."

A cloud of red raced up his neck and into his face. "I suppose you're right. I'm out of practice and didn't think that through," Josiah admitted. He continued to hold on to his girls; they stroked his hair and face with their tiny hands. "We'll be fine waiting here."

"We'll be back shortly." William took Emily Jane's arm and turned her toward the door. "I've also got a wedding gift I want to give you before we head home."

Home. It had been a long time since Emily had a home. She smiled at him. "I am so happy, I don't need a present."

"And your happiness is all I need," William answered. "But you will like this present or I'll eat my hat."

Emily Jane chuckled as they stepped out into the sunlight. He continued to hold her arm as they ambled down the walkway. Tiny currents of electricity seemed to pulsate where his fingers connected with her arm. He steered her past their horse and wagon.

"I thought we'd walk, if that's all right." William slid his hand down her arm and then clasped her fingers in his.

How could she refuse? Emily Jane's heart pounded in her chest as they approached the hotel where her father stayed. Thanks to his arrival, she'd married William and realized that he was nothing like her father.

Mr. Rodgers was just coming out of the hotel when they arrived. Emily Jane released William's hand and hurried to hug her father. "Papa, I just wanted you to know that I'm so glad you came."

"I am, too." He held her away from him. "I know you think your mother and I were being cruel when we set you from our home, but, daughter, you must know that it broke our hearts to do so."

Emily Jane started to say she understood, even though she really didn't, when he raised his hand and stopped her from speaking.

"We wanted you to have a better life than what we could supply. I'm sorry if we hurt you." His green eyes glistened in the noonday sun.

Were those tears in his eyes? She rushed back into his embrace. "I love you, Papa."

He wrapped his strong arms around her. "I love you, too, EJ."

Emily Jane pressed her head against his chest and listened to his strong heartbeat. He hadn't called her EJ in a very long time. She remembered sitting on his lap as a little girl and listening to his heartbeat. Back then, he'd called her EJ. Then more children had been born, and Emily Jane and her father had grown apart. She thanked the Lord for giving her this time with him again.

She stepped out of his embrace. "You and Mama will come see us again, won't you?"

"Lord willing." He picked up his ragged bag and walked to his wagon and horse.

Emily Jane hadn't thought about it before now but wondered if her father would have left without saying goodbye if she hadn't shown up when she had.

As if to answer her question he said, "I planned on

stopping by your place on my way out. I guess you saved me a trip." He put his bag in the bed of the wagon and then looked to William. "Take care of my little girl."

William stepped up and shook her father's hand. "I will do my best, sir."

"See that you do." He pulled himself up on the wagon.

The wagon held supplies and a bedroll. Emily Jane said a silent prayer for her father's safety on the way home. It was a long trip, and he wasn't getting any younger. She wished now that he'd brought one or two of her brothers with him to keep him company on the return trip.

Her papa reached down one more time and took Emily's hands in his. "Your mother and I love you very much and are proud of you, EJ." He released her hands and smiled. "We'll see you soon."

"'Bye, Papa. I love you." Emily Jane felt tears run down her face as he drove away.

William pulled her against his side. "We can go visit them whenever you want." He kissed the top of her head.

Emily Jane accepted his comfort until her father turned the corner and drove out of sight. Then she wiped her face free of moisture. "Thank you." She sniffed and forced a smile on her face. "Now, did you mention a wedding present?"

"Indeed I did. Come with me." William grabbed her hand and walked to The Bakery. He used a key, opened the door and then pulled her inside with a smile.

Why on earth would William give her a cookie or cake as a wedding gift? He knew she could make her own.

Bringing her here was confusing. She'd quit her job

to move out on the farm with him. What was he thinking? When he continued to grin but not say anything, Emily Jane confessed, "I don't understand."

"What do you want more than anything?" he asked.

Emily Jane still didn't comprehend. She had no desire to hurt his feelings, but the truth came out before she could think of a way to soften it. "Not a cookie," she said.

He laughed. "I don't know. The owner of this place makes the best sugar cookies I've ever tasted. You sure you don't want a sugar cookie?"

Thankfully, the place was empty of customers at the time, or like her, they would probably think the man had lost his mind. She tilted her head and looked up at him. "You do know that I was the one who made the sugar cookies when I worked here, right?"

He nodded. "And as the new owner, you can still make them." The grin on his face grew even larger.

"New owner?"

William grabbed her around the waist and swung her about like a small child. "This is my gift to you, The Bakery." He laughed as he looked up into her face. "It's all yours. You are the proud owner of your own bakery."

Emily Jane merely stared at him, tongue-tied. Through the roaring din in her ears, she breathed one word. "Mine?" William had bought her The Bakery. She took a quick breath of utter astonishment.

He pulled her over to one of the tables and sat her down. His face had gone from excited and happy to concern. "Emily Jane, I thought you'd be happy."

Emily Jane found her voice. A cry broke from her

lips. "Happy! 'Happy' doesn't begin to describe what I feel right now." She jumped up and walked to the counter. "When did you do this? Why did you do this?" She ran her hand lovingly over the smooth, cool surface. Her heart sang with delight.

"On Monday, when I bought the farm for Josiah and the girls."

She halted. Shocked. "What did you say? For Josiah and the girls? I thought you wanted the farm."

William laughed. "I'm no farmer. At first I'd thought the farm would be a good place for us to take care of the girls, but the truth of the matter is I'm a businessman."

Emily Jane knew he'd owned a store in Denver, so she nodded her agreement. She hadn't been able to picture him farming but hadn't had the heart to say so.

He took her hands in his and led her to the nearest table, where he pulled out a chair for her to sit down in. Once seated he said, "A few weeks ago, I became a silent partner of the general store. Levi and I have been discussing a couple of other businesses that I might like to invest in later. I probably should have told you earlier, but I wanted you to love me for me and not for my wealth."

Emily Jane didn't say anything; it was apparent William needed to talk.

"I realize now that that was wrong thinking. You are nothing like Charlotte. You have shown me nothing but love and kindness. You helped me realize that I can freely give my heart to you and never fear you will crush it." He knelt down in front of her. "I hope you don't mind that I gave the ranch to Josiah." There was a question in his statement.

"Of course I don't mind, but where are we going to live?" she asked, still feeling at odds with the world and everything in it. Her life felt topsy-turvy. If that was such a thing.

"Here."

"Here?"

He shook his head and chuckled. "You really are confused, aren't you?"

"It would seem so." She stood and walked to the large window that overlooked the street. How many times had she wished for a bakery like this one?

"Have you ever been upstairs?" William asked, taking her hand in his.

She shook her head no. Emily Jane had always assumed that Violet lived up there but had never visited her.

"Come on." He pulled her through the kitchen and up the back stairs. Another key unlocked the door.

"I thought Violet lived up here." Emily Jane entered the living space. It was wide-open. A couch with a small table in front of it sat on the left-hand side of the room; farther back was an open doorway where she could see a bed and dresser. To her right was an open kitchen area. She realized that it was directly over the kitchen in the bakery below.

"No, she moved out about a month ago. Levi said that she's moved into a small house a couple of streets over."

Emily Jane looked at him. Was it true? This was all hers? The Bakery? The living area above it? Everything? She had to know. "So we really can live here?"

He took her hands in his. "This is your Bakery. This is your home."

Emily Jane closed her eyes. Her arms circled her husband in a close embrace. God had brought a man into her life who loved her and was willing to help her live her dreams.

"Thank you for the bakery and believing in my dreams. I was so afraid you would be like my father and try to control me. Instead you have proved once again that you support my dreams and that you care enough about me to give me the freedom I need."

His heartbeat filled her ears, and she smiled. William Barns loved her. His heart beat for her. She couldn't believe how blessed she was.

She leaned back and looked up into his face. Brilliant blue eyes stared into hers. Emily Jane reached up and cupped his face in her hands. "Thank you so much. I love you more than words can ever express." Then she pulled his lips down to hers.

She gloried in the plan God had designed for her life. With certainty she knew that this man who held her tightly would love her for the rest of her life.

Epilogue

Emily Jane Barns couldn't wipe the grin from her face. The cake she'd baked for the summer festival was spectacular. She'd been working on the design for over a month. She stood back and admired her handiwork. It was four tiers tall and as round as a wagon wheel. The icing was done in red, white and blue. Stars decorated the top.

As was common nowadays, her thoughts turned to her husband. They'd been married three months now, and her husband had been busy building the town. William had recently opened a small restaurant and had also hired their first newspaperman, Mr. Sweeney, who now produced a weekly newspaper in Granite, Texas. He'd also given Amos his first real job as an assistant to Mr. Sweeney.

Emily Jane couldn't stop the smile from spreading across her face. Her husband was well respected by everyone, and Emily Jane couldn't be prouder of him.

She'd been busy herself. Taking care of the girls and running the bakery had taken most of her time and energy. But she'd loved every moment. She touched her stomach and grinned.

"That is a beautiful cake," Susanna said, coming to stand beside her. "When do we get to sample it?"

Emily Jane laughed at her friend. "Not for a couple more hours. According to Mrs. Harvey, the cutting of the cake takes place shortly after our picnic lunches."

Susanna frowned. "Who made her boss?"

"No idea, but I wouldn't cross her if I were you." She grinned at the dressmaker. "Isn't she one of your best customers?"

In defiance, Susanna dipped her finger in the icing at the bottom of the cake and licked the sweetness off. "No, but her best friend, Mrs. Anderson, is."

Emily Jane grinned. Mrs. Anderson was the bank president's wife and the richest woman in town, if you didn't count the Westland women.

"Where is that handsome husband of yours?" Susanna asked, changing the subject.

Emily Jane knew William was somewhere on the fairgrounds but where exactly, she wasn't sure. She looked about. "He's here somewhere."

"Have you told him about the baby yet?" Susanna whispered.

Emily Jane felt her jaw drop. "How did you know?" she hissed.

Susanna laughed. "I'm the one that does your dress measurements, remember? I couldn't help but notice your waist is a little thicker."

Emily Jane looked down. Was she showing already?

Susanna hugged her about the shoulders. "Don't worry. It barely shows."

Was she going to be like her mother and blossom with child immediately? Emily Jane wondered what her mother would think when she told her she would soon be a grandmother. She smiled.

Next month, they would be going to Kansas. Just her and William. Violet would continue running the bakery, and William was lining up helpers even now to make sure the restaurant continued running smoothly in his absence.

"I can't wait until the other ladies find out. Can you imagine all the baby quilts and clothes you'll be getting?"

"Shhhh, I haven't told William yet, and I don't want him to find out from you." Emily Jane shook her finger in her friend's face. "Hear me?"

"Yep, but it's gonna cost you one banana nut bread loaf to keep me quiet," she teased.

"I'll give you two not to tell anyone, not even Anna Mae. I want to be the one to tell him." Emily Jane smoothed the fabric over her tummy and grinned.

"Deal. Isn't that him over by our new sheriff?"

Emily Jane's gaze followed Susanna's pointing finger. William was standing beside Josiah. Josiah had proved he wasn't much of a farmer either and had recently taken the job of sheriff. They were on the edge of the woods where a horseshoe game was in progress not too far from them. Rose and Ruby played on a colorful blanket at their feet.

"Yes, it is. If you will excuse me, I have some important news to tell my husband."

Susanna's laugh followed her across the field. Emily Jane saw several of her old neighbors and smiled. Their home had been built, and now they lived as one family. She was happy for them and Anna Mae, who lived with them. Emily Jane saw her friend and waved to her.

As if he sensed her approach, William turned and smiled at her. His beautiful eyes held hers, and she prayed that their baby would have his wavy black hair and sparkling blue eyes.

She started to walk toward him when another bout of morning sickness assaulted her. Why now? Why so late in the morning? She didn't want to be sick now, but there was no stopping the nausea that engulfed her.

Emily Jane clutched her queasy stomach. Sweat broke out on her face, and she doubled over, sure that the contents of her stomach would soon be on the ground.

Susanna hurried to her side. "Are you all right?" she asked, motioning for William to come over.

She nodded. "I'm just sick to my stomach."

William hurried to her side. "Emily?" His eyes searched hers.

"I'm all right. Just feeling sick to my stomach." She tried to stand upright, but again a wave of queasiness enveloped her like a black cloak.

"Maybe we should take you to see the doctor." William's voice shook with concern.

Susanna thrust a glass of water into her hand and a piece of dry bread. "She probably just needs to sit down. The excitement of the day or this heat could be the problem."

"Thank you, Susanna." Emily nibbled at the bread.

William's jaw set. "I still think you need to go to the doctor."

A small crowd had gathered. Expressions of concern

had Emily Jane feeling embarrassed. This wasn't how she wanted to tell her husband they were going to have a baby.

Susanna smiled at them all and announced, "She'll be all right. It's just the heat. Let's give them some room."

Emily Jane offered her friend another weak smile as the crowd dispersed. Susanna shooed people away from her and William.

Once they were alone, Emily Jane smiled at her husband. "I've already been to the doctor, William." The bread was doing its job. Emily Jane stood slowly. She still felt a little ill but not enough to throw up.

He cupped her face in his hands. "Why didn't you tell me you are sick?" His eyes searched hers. Did he think he could see what was ailing her by looking into her eyes?

She smiled. "Because I'm not really sick." Emily Jane enjoyed the confused look on his face. How many times had he shocked her with something wonderful? Now it was her turn to surprise him. "I'm going to have our baby."

His eyes widened. He merely stared at her, tongue-tied. The tenderness in his expression touched her from the tips of her toes to the top of her head. She laid her hand against his chest. He cleared his throat, but his voice still sounded hoarse. "Are you sure?"

Emily Jane nodded. "The doctor says I'm only a couple of months along, but, yes, I'm sure." Her hand moved to her stomach.

"A baby." He whispered the words. His hand covered hers, and a grin split his face. "My baby," William whispered in awe.

She chuckled. "Well, mine, too."

His blue eyes searched her face. "Are you happy about the baby?"

Emily Jane understood his concern. How many times had she said she didn't want to have children? Complained about having to take care of her siblings? It was no wonder he was worried now.

She led him to a hay bale and sat down. Emily Jane took his hands in hers, like he'd done to her so many times, and explained. "Yes, I am very happy. Before I met you I thought children were things to stop you from achieving your dreams, but I was wrong. When God places a dream on your heart, He makes sure you accomplish that dream. Having children is a blessing from God, and I'm thrilled He's allowing me to pursue my dream and have children with you."

William looked deeply into her eyes once more. "Emily Barns, I love you more than you will ever know."

She was breathless at the love reflected in his gaze. Emily Jane saw the truth of his words in the planes of his handsome face.

He stroked the side of her face. "Are you sure you are all right?"

Emily Jane nodded. "I've never been happier."

When he pulled her close and kissed her softly, she felt the deepness of his love. Emily Jane relaxed into his embrace and sent up a prayer of thanksgiving for a man who had made all her dreams come true.

* * * * *

Dear Reader,

Thank you so much for reading *The Texan's Twin Blessings*. Emily Jane spoke to my heart the moment she stepped onto the pages of *Groom by Arrangement*. She wanted to be a woman who could do as she pleased but still craved the love of a good man; thankfully, William stepped onto the page and made her dreams come true. Emily Jane also has a love for wild animals. Dear reader, please do not pick up baby foxes like Emily Jane did in this story.

I hope you will watch for Anna Mae's story coming soon. She is a woman who trusts the Lord but doesn't trust men. Twice burned, she has no intention of falling in love; teaching school is now her only love. Or so she thinks.

Again, thank you for reading. I would love to hear your thoughts on the book. Feel free to email me at rhondagibson65@hotmail.com or write to me at PO Box 835, Kirtland, NM 87417.

Warmly,
Rhonda Gibson

REQUEST YOUR FREE BOOKS!

2 FREE INSPIRATIONAL NOVELS
PLUS 2 *FREE* MYSTERY GIFTS

Love Inspired® HISTORICAL

*When a young woman works for the most handsome
hotel owner in Denver, can true love be far behind?*

Read on for a sneak preview of
THE MARRIAGE AGREEMENT.

Jonathon's eyes roamed Fanny's face, then her gown.
Appreciation filled his gaze. "You're wearing my favorite
color."

"I…know. I chose this dress specifically with you in
mind."

Too late, she realized how her admission sounded, as
if her sole purpose was to please him. She had not meant
to reveal so much of herself.

He took a step forward. "I'm flattered."

He took another step.

Fanny held steady, unmoving, anxious to see just how
close he would come to her.

He stopped his approach. For the span of three heart-
beats they stared into each other's eyes.

She sighed.

"Relax, Fanny. You've checked and rechecked every
item on your lists at least three times, probably more. Go
and spend a moment with your—"

"How do you know I checked and rechecked my lists
that often?"

"Because—" his expression softened "—I know you."

There was a look of such tenderness about him that

for a moment, a mere heartbeat, she ached for what they might have accomplished together, were they two different people. What they could have been to one another if past circumstances weren't entered into the equation.

"We're ready for tonight's ball, Fanny. *You're* ready."

She drew in a slow, slightly uneven breath. "I suppose you're right."

He took one more step. He stood so close now she could smell his scent, a pleasant mix of bergamot, masculine spice and…him.

Something unspoken hovered in the air between them, communicated in a language she should know, but couldn't quite comprehend.

"Go. Spend a few moments with your mother and father before the guests begin to arrive. I'll come get you, once I've changed my clothes."

"I'd like that." She'd very much enjoy the chance to show him off to her parents.

He leaned in closer. But then the sound of determined footsteps in the hallway caught their attention.

"That will be Mrs. Singletary," she said with a rush of air. The widow's purposeful gait was easy enough to decipher.

"No doubt you are correct." Jonathon's gaze locked on her, and that was *not* business in his eyes.

Something far more personal stared back at her. She had but one thought in response.

Oh, my.

Don't miss
THE MARRIAGE AGREEMENT by Renee Ryan,
available July 2015 wherever
Love Inspired® books and ebooks are sold.

Love the Love Inspired book you just read?

Your opinion matters.

Review this book on your favorite book site, review site, blog or your own social media properties and share your opinion with other readers!

HLIREVIEWSR